RIPE FOR VENGEANCE

A GREENHOUSE MYSTERY

RIPE FOR VENGEANCE

WENDY TYSON

WHEELER PUBLISHING
A part of Gale, a Cengage Company

Copyright © 2019 by Wendy Tyson.
Wheeler Publishing, a part of Gale, a Cengage Company.

Wheeler Publishing Large Print Cozy Mystery.
The text of this Large Print edition is unabridged.
Other aspects of the book may vary from the original edition.
Set in 16 pt. Plantin.

**LIBRARY OF CONGRESS CIP DATA ON FILE.
CATALOGUING IN PUBLICATION FOR THIS BOOK
IS AVAILABLE FROM THE LIBRARY OF CONGRESS**

ISBN-13: 978-1-4328-7890-0 (softcover alk. paper)

Published in 2020 by arrangement with Henery Press, LLC

Printed in Mexico
Print Number: 01   Print Year: 2020

For Sue.

ACKNOWLEDGMENTS

As always, I'm grateful for my family, for Frances Black of Literary Counsel, and for everyone at Henery Press. Special thanks to Stephanie Wollman, my dial-a-nurse-practitioner, for her endless patience with my endless medical questions.

ONE

June in Winsome held the promise of the seasons. Lawns were green, not yet flecked with the brown that would invade during late summer, when too little rain and too much heat plagued the area. Perennial gardens were starting to bloom, their foliage vibrant and full, and vegetable gardens were alive with waving fronds of garlic scapes and neat rainbow rows of lettuces, cabbages, kale, and tiny green tomatoes. If hope were a season, it would be spring, and to Megan Sawyer, lawyer-turned-organic-farmer, nothing embodied spring like early June on Washington Acres farm.

But as Megan dunked fragile heads of butter lettuce in ice cold water, it was dread she felt, not hope. Megan and Dr. "Denver" Finn, Winsome's handsome veterinarian and Megan's boyfriend, had arranged to meet for lunch, but he got hung up on a mysterious emergency. Denver had been

9

unusually cryptic on the phone the first time he called, and to make matters worse, Megan heard sirens in the background. Her mind wandered to barn fires and other tragedies. Unwilling to let her imagination get too far afield, she focused on the tender green leaves before her.

Megan surveyed the farm. From her perch outside the barn, she could see Clay Hand, her farm manager, weeding down by the tomato beds, his long, lean back stretched over the maturing plants. Brian "Brick" Porter, her farm hand, was mending the back side of the largest greenhouse, a white t-shirt tied around his head to ward off the sun's rays and soak up sweat. And although she couldn't see them, she heard the hammers and drills of the construction team she'd hired to start renovations on the old Marshall place, the historic but derelict house next door that would eventually become an inn and workshop.

All was right with the world. Except deep down, Megan knew it wasn't.

When Denver finally called at 2:12, she jumped at the sound of the phone. "Hi," she said warily.

"Well, Megs, I think I need ye. I'll explain when you get here. Will you please bring the truck — with the cap on it?" Denver had been born in Scotland, and although he'd lived in the United States for his adult life, his brogue became more pronounced when he was tired or upset.

"Is anyone hurt?"

"No, not exactly. Look, I have Bobby next to me and he needs help. Just come. We can discuss it when you get here."

Bobby was Bobby King, Winsome's young Chief of Police. Bobby showed up wherever there was trouble. This meant there was trouble, which didn't do much to calm Megan's agitated nerves. "Where's here, Denver?"

"Mimi's Warehouse and Storage."

Megan dragged the cooler of water into the barn and closed the door so that she could hear Denver better against the backdrop of the construction next door. "The self-storage place?"

"Right. Mimi's, on the right about a mile from Canal Street. And bring some cool water too. A nice big jug of it. And some old blankets. And maybe some apple slices."

The truck? Water? Blankets? "Did you find a dog?"

"No, Megs. We found a pig."

"I've named her Camilla, after my great-aunt, who was a pig farmer back in Scot-

11

land." Denver's eyes crinkled in amusement. "She's a sassy one, but sweet. Just take it slow."

Megan peered into the storage unit, which had been blocked by a tall gate, the kind you'd use to corral a busy toddler. Inside the five-by-five space were bales of hay and a small, young pig. The pig's skin was pink with splotches of dark gray that shown through a light coat of bristly white hair. The piglet lay on her side, eyes closed, snoring lightly. She appeared to be in good health.

"There's no food or water in here."

Denver nodded. "Aye, which is part of my concern. The unit is pretty clean, and Camilla seems as healthy as a . . . well, pig. Still, if she'd stayed here long under these conditions, things would be grim."

"Camilla. I like it." Megan turned toward Denver. "It's a climate-controlled unit?"

"It is. Still a little warm."

Megan stared at the pig, who was still sleeping despite the audience. Megan shook her head. "Why would a pig be in a storage unit?"

"Exactly what we want to know." It was Bobby who answered. He leaned his tall, heavy-set frame against a wall. "This is illegal *and* against the rules of the unit.

12

Management called animal control and the police. I called Denver here."

"Because you're a softy." Megan smiled.

"Because I'm practical. No use wasting animal control's time on a pet pig when Denver was just passing through this side of town."

Denver looked at him quizzically, about to protest, but Bobby held up a hand. "We all know what animal control would do."

Megan nodded. Maybe a shelter, if one would take a pig. Or she'd be given to a farm or sanctuary farm — maybe. Or put to sleep. Megan watched Winsome's young police chief with renewed affection. His girlfriend, Megan's shop clerk and friend, Clover Hand, had recently become a vegan, and Megan figured her pro-animal stance may have had something to do with this compassionate act.

"Can she stay with you?" Denver's eyes were soft and blue and full of empathy, and Megan knew there was no way she could refuse.

"Of course. We already have two dogs, a dozen chickens, and two goats, so we definitely need a foster pig named Camilla to round things out." Megan watched the pig sleep. "Who rented the unit?"

King glanced behind him at a man so tall

13

and lean and quiet he blended into the shadows. The man stepped forward and Megan noticed a pressed green shirt with the storage business name emblazoned on the pocket, a set of lock cutters in one hand. He was young, mid-twenties, tops, and wore the earnest expression of someone trying hard to do a good job despite the ridiculousness of what he's been faced with.

The man reached his hand out and Megan shook it. "Assistant Manager, second shift. Happy to meet you. I'm the one who found the pig."

"Followed the crumbs," King said approvingly.

The manager nodded. "In a way. Saw dried corn kernels in the elevator. No food of any kind allowed in here. Attracts rodents and bugs, both no-nos. Figured someone was keeping grain, some kind of animal feed business. Checked around, saw a larger pile of corn near this unit. When I pressed my ear against the wall, I heard squealing. Called the person listed on the unit's lease, and when I didn't get an answer, I cut the lock." The man looked very proud of himself. He turned toward King. "Still can't reach the lessor. Tried six times. Whoever it is has no voicemail set up."

"Who's leasing the unit?" Megan asked

14

King. "Someone we know?"

"Man named Saul Bones."

Megan raised her eyebrows, her glance bouncing between King and Denver. "Saul Bones. As in —"

"Saw bones." Denver's mouth set in a grim line. "Right."

A sick joke or a real name? Megan wondered. Before she could ask the questions that had queued up in her mind, King said, "Looking him up back at the station. He hasn't really done anything that warrants serious concern, but this is odd." King shrugged. "Figured we'd check him out."

Camilla had awakened. After standing on her hind legs to get a good look at these strangers, the little pig started running top speed around her cell, butting her head against the gate, squealing madly.

"She's hungry," Denver said. "Shall I load her into the truck? I'll follow you over and we can get her settled in the barn."

Megan agreed. She chewed on her bottom lip, considering the animal's situation. Who rents a unit and puts a well-cared for pot-bellied pig inside? Was she someone's pet? Was she staying there temporarily before being sold to someone else?

And that name: Saul Bones. A sense of humor — or something more ominous?

Bibi, Megan's grandmother, also known as Bonnie Birch to the rest of the world, fell instantly in love with Camilla. She'd never admit it, of course, but after Clay created a pen for the pig inside the old section of the massive stone barn, Bibi took to feeding her personally. She collected kitchen scraps and watched contentedly as Camilla snorted and gulped her way through salad greens, root vegetables, and apples, a treat Bibi used to feed the pigs she and her husband raised years ago.

"She'll be just fine," Bibi said, scratching the course skin behind Camilla's ears. Camilla leaned into the touch, her eyes half-mast. "Good girl," Bibi crooned. To Megan, Bibi said, "She's not an eating pig."

Megan said, "Looks like she's eating just fine."

Bibi scowled. "You know what I mean. Camilla here isn't livestock."

"I know, Bibi. We wouldn't do that even if she were."

"Well, she's not. She's like no pig I've ever seen."

Megan smiled. Beyond the barn, Megan could hear the whirl and pounding of the construction crew next door. Megan spoke louder over the din. "She's a Vietnamese potbellied pig. I only know that because Denver told me."

Bibi leaned down to look into Camilla's eyes. The day was quickly warming, but the interior of the old barn was cool and slightly damp. The pig seemed to like the feel of the floor, cold dampness and all. She sprawled on her side, gazing up at Bibi with what looked to Megan like adoration.

"Whoever had her took good care." Bibi squatted down and rubbed Camilla's neck. Bibi wore a white "Winter in Winsome" t-shirt, and the pig lifted her head and rubbed it against Bibi's side, smearing dirt along the edge of the pristine cotton. Bibi didn't seem to notice. "She's a fine pig," Bibi said softly.

Megan, trying to hide her growing amusement, watched her grandmother. Bibi wasn't one for outward shows of affection, and this was as close as she came to doting on an animal. Megan had to admit: even with her underbite and noisy table manners, Camilla *was* pretty adorable.

"Don't you need to be somewhere?" Bibi asked. "I don't think you have time to stand around laughing at me and this pig."

Megan's grin widened. "I'm not laughing at you."

Bibi stood. With a final glance at Camilla, she turned toward Megan. "They're all God's creatures. I'm just tending to an animal in need." She broke out into a smile, and it took years off her eighty-five-year-old face. "She is really cute."

"That she is." As though on cue, Camilla looked up at them, let out a snort, and, with a flop and the pig version of a sigh, extended her body out on the cool dirt. Laughing, Megan glanced at her watch. "I need to meet Denver at the restaurant in forty-five minutes." She looked down at her jeans and sneakers. "I can't exactly go like this."

"This is the dinner with his college friends?"

Megan nodded. "Fraternity brothers from Colorado State. Jatin, Xavier, and Chase. The guys and two women are in the area for a charity event."

Bibi shot Megan a questioning look. "What kind of charity?"

"There's a local school for kids with behavioral and emotional issues. Denver said these guys all work for the same company, and the company is sponsoring a mentoring camping trip." Megan shrugged. "Because they were in town, they called

18

Denver and asked to get together. He invited me. I'm just not in the mood."

"Get in the mood." Bibi motioned toward the door. "Go get fixed up and have a good time. You deserve a social life."

Megan kissed her grandmother on the cheek. "I guess it will be fun to see another side of Denver. I've never met anyone from his past other than his aunt."

"You can tell a lot about a person by the company they keep." Bibi squeezed Megan's arm. "Go. Have fun. I want to hear all about it tomorrow."

TWO

Basil was an Italian restaurant tucked into a strip mall on Route 611, not far from Doylestown. Its interior was awash in beige: beige plaster walls, beige tablecloths, beige linens, beige-stained maple floors. But despite the bland location and décor, the food was excellent, which was why Denver had chosen it as the reunion spot.

Megan arrived a few minutes late. A young hostess led her toward the back of the restaurant, to a semi-private room from which laughter was erupting. The hostess turned toward Megan to indicate that she'd arrived at her dinner party, but she couldn't hide her eyeroll when another bray of laughter rang out. Megan interpreted this to mean Denver's friends were an outgoing crowd, maybe a little too loud for this establishment.

"Enjoy," the hostess said.

Megan thanked her. Social gatherings

20

were never easy, and meeting a group of college friends was no exception. Despite working with the public at the café and farmers markets, and years of practicing law before that, she wasn't particularly extroverted, and walking into a party that was already underway lived between root canal and scrubbing toilets on her favorites list. Despite her angst, Megan pulled her shoulders back, took a fortifying breath, and searched the long table for Denver's face. When he saw Megan, his face lit up. He stood and squeezed his way around the table toward her.

A hush fell over the table except for the source of the loudest laughter. The man on the other side of where Denver had been sitting was talking to the slender brunette next to him. A shock of dark, straight hair hung in his face. He had a chiseled chin, and hawkish brown eyes that stayed affixed to the brunette with a hungry, almost leering stare. At first glance, he seemed handsome in a Hollywood sort of way, but as Megan watched him carry on, his features became more vulgar, his mannerisms seemed aggressive. He paused, and the brunette glanced at Megan. She smiled.

"Friends, I would like to introduce my special friend," Denver smiled at Megan, "or, if I may be so bold, girlfriend, Megan Sawyer. Megan is a farmer and a business-woman. She's quite good with an ax and a shovel, so I would be careful to remain on her good side."

Laughter from around the table. The dark-haired man kept talking.

"Chase, you're quickly earning yourself a place at the head of her hit list." Denver kept his voice light, but Megan heard the underlying steely tone.

The brunette shot out a bony elbow, and the dark-haired man stopped talking.

Denver continued. "The rude man across the table is Dr. Charles 'Chase' Mars. Pharmacologist and now VP of Strategic Interface for BOLD Pharmaceuticals, with 'bold' obnoxiously spelled in all caps." Chase nodded. "The woman next to him is Dr. Barbara Little, Chase's boss and our former favorite party crasher."

Denver turned toward the other end of the table. An elegant dark-skinned man in a red Polo shirt sat staring at Megan with a mix of curiosity and practiced nonchalance. Denver said, "Jatin Patel. Former fraternity brother and now VIP at BOLD." Jatin smiled and nodded. He had warm, cocoa-brown eyes, and they seemed to study Megan with an intelligent detachment she found unsettling.

Jatin said quietly, "Unfortunately, our friend Xavier Jones couldn't be here. He wasn't feeling well."

Megan said, "Nice to meet all of you. I'm sorry he couldn't make it."

Next to Jatin sat a woman Denver didn't introduce. Seeming to recognize his oversight, Denver cleared his throat. "And of course, Martine Pringle. PR Director for BOLD."

"Wonderful to meet you," Martine said. She was fine-boned, and tight-lipped with high cheekbones accentuated by a severe bun. Her dark eyebrows clashed with ashblonde hair. "And nice to see you again, Denver."

Denver nodded. More silence, this one awkward. Denver pulled out a seat for Megan before reclaiming his own spot next to her. He waved to the waiter, who brought Megan an iced tea, a menu, and a small plate of herbed focaccia.

"Does everyone from the fraternity work at BOLD?" Megan asked to no one in particular.

It was Barbara who responded. "Sure feels that way. Chase and I were some of the company's first employees. We brought Xavier and Jatin on. We tried to entice

Denver to join us, but his love of animals was too strong."

Megan swallowed a piece of bread and said, "Are you all in the same department?"

Barbara shook her head. "No, no. Chase and I are on the development side — the science end of things. Xavier is investor relations, and Jatin is finance."

Megan noticed that once again Martine was left out. "And you," Megan said, trying to pull the quiet woman into the conversation. "I guess as the public relations person, you're in a different group?"

Martine shook her head. "Corporate." With a sideways glance at Denver, she said, "I'm here to capture the weekend on film. It's good press."

Chase said, without a hint of irony, "What good is a charity event if you can't capitalize on it?"

Another elbow from Barbara. "The trip was my boss's idea. Pioneer Village School helped Harriet's daughter. She thought we could give back by coordinating a mentoring event. Hook up troubled kids with members of the corporate world. Give them the chance to learn, ask questions. Maybe even consider a career in STEM."

"Science, technology, engineering, math," Jatin said to Megan.

24

Megan caught Denver's smirk behind his beer stein.

Megan said, "Thank you. I know what STEM means."

"Yes, well. The big boss charged Barbie here with rounding up volunteers." Chase pushed back from the table. "Guess who got stuck with the job?" He fluttered the fingers on his large hands. "People who owed her."

"You mean my *friends*?" Barbara's laugh sounded brittle. "Anyway, we're each paired with a student at the school. We'll do a hike-in-and-camp at Lyle Lake State Park along with a few staff from the school, and hopefully we can keep in touch with our charges after the long weekend is over. We're planning future trips — career fairs, internships. Harriet even created a scholarship fund to help student alumnus who complete this program and have no funds to go to college. She's serious about this. Especially about attracting more girls to STEM vocations."

"And these kids are special," Jatin said quietly. "They have emotional and behavioral issues that don't allow them to fit in easily, so the exposure will be good for them."

Megan was impressed. Giving kids a

chance to better their lives? A pretty generous endeavor for a corporation — if there was proper planning and follow-through. She looked around this table. She had her doubts. This group didn't seem like the altruistic sorts, but to be fair, she'd only just met them.

When the waiter showed up to take their orders, Megan whispered to Denver, "Pioneer Village School. Isn't that where your aunt's foster son goes?"

"Dillon? Yes. In fact, he's going on the trip." Denver shot Megan the amused half-smile she loved: blue eyes crinkled, mouth slightly upturned. Knowingly amused. "Wondering which of these delightful beauties he'll get as his mentor?"

"Kind of."

The waiter returned with appetizers. He placed a beautiful mezze plate, a platter of beef carpaccio, and fried calamari on the center of the table before walking away again.

Reaching for the beef dish, Chase said, "So, a farmer, huh? As in overalls and cows?"

"As in organic vegetables and cut flowers."

"Organic? Sounds like a shitty way to make a living." He laughed at his own pun.

No one else did. Scraping half the appetizer onto his own plate, he said, "Seriously, how do you make ends meet? I've heard farming these days is a losing proposition. You can't make money on vegetables. Animal production is where it's at. Large scale." He stuffed a forkful of raw steak into his mouth and looked around the table for confirmation. "What do they call it? Factory farming."

Everyone was looking down at their plate. Everyone except Martine, whose stare was firmly on Denver. Megan turned toward her boyfriend. His focus was on Chase, who he was watching with a mixture of amusement and disgust, seemingly unaware of Martine's attention.

Megan leaned forward, baiting Chase. Casually, she said, "Have you done any reading about the impact of industrial agriculture — on the workers, the environment, or the animals?"

He shoveled in another forkful. "Is eating research? If so, I've done plenty of research." He grinned. An elbow shot out and tapped Barbara's side. She ignored him. "Lighten up. I'm just messing with you."

"Chase has a long history of messing with people," Barbara said. "He wasn't always the serious scientist."

"In fact, he should write a book." Martine's voice rang out in the silence that ensued. "About his time with The Rolling Stones."

"The Rolling Stones?" Megan said. "Really."

"Really. You don't believe it?" Chase eyed her sideways."

"I'm not so sure I believe it." Megan spooned calamari on her plate, working hard to maintain a poker face. She'd never been good at poker — and there was a reason.

"Chase was quite the musician in his day," Martine continued. Her voice had taken on a low, gravely tone. "Played the guitar for the Stones."

This time Chase had the decency to blush. "I was back-up to back-up. For two nights."

"In Los Angeles," Martine said, as though that made it more significant.

Megan glanced at the blonde. Was she PR for the company — or for Chase?

"That's great," Megan said. "I had no idea."

"Clearly you haven't been working with him," Barbara joked. She softened the comment with a smile, but the knowing expression on Jatin's face said she wasn't kidding.

"Enough about us." Jatin clapped his hands together. "Denver, we're happy to see

you so happy. After what happened with —"
His voice trailed off.

"Oh, just say it. Lilian. His ex-wife. No one liked her much anyway." Chase slammed back his beer, wiped his mouth with the black linen napkin, and turned his frown to Martine. "Someone missed their shot at the university's most eligible bachelor."

Another awkward silence before the waiter rescued them with heaping plates of pasta and seafood. Denver rarely mentioned his ex-wife, who'd cheated on him years before.

"I'm sorry," Denver whispered in Megan's ear.

Megan squeezed his thigh under the table. She raised her glass. With a broad smile and a gusto she didn't feel, she said loudly, "Cheers! To old friends and new adventures."

"I'm sorry," Denver said again later. They were back at Washington Acres. Megan had sat on an old wooden bench and was watching Denver examine Camilla. "They weren't quite that bloody awful in college."

"They were fine. You have nothing to apologize for."

Denver looked up from the pig. "Ta, but they were horrible tonight. The whole lot of them. Those poor laddies and lassies tomorrow. They don't quite know what they're in for."

Megan's smile was full of empathy. "They'll be earning their scholarships, that's for sure. Tell me — who is Martine?"

"The PR person for the group."

"No, she's more than that. I caught the bit about your ex-wife. And she spent half the evening watching you."

"Aye, I was hoping ye wouldn't notice."

"Well, I did. What's the deal?"

Tired of Denver's ministrations, Camilla gave a snort and backed away. She shook her head, then ran around the pen, making squealy noises as she went.

"Here now," Denver said. His voice was gentle. "You're a wee thing. Settle."

Camilla stopped and considered Denver before racing in his direction. Megan thought the little pig was going to bowl him over. Denver stayed seated and said her name again, more sternly this time, along with a string of Gaelic words Megan couldn't quite make out. When Camilla stopped short of plowing into him, he gave her a pat and scratched behind her ears.

"There, there. You've been through a lot. Settle now." Camilla looked about to argue, but instead she flopped down on her side, her head against Denver's leg, leaning into the caress.

"Pigs are smart. Before long she'll be hanging with your canine crew. Watch, though. They're natural predators, dogs. They can get testy when they smell dinner. And to them, Camilla here may smell like dinner."

Megan nodded. She'd watched earlier as Sadie and Gunther, her two dogs, examined the newcomer through the makeshift barrier. They seemed accepting — but she knew there'd be a grace period before they could all be alone together.

"Martine?" Megan said again.

"Aye. Martine."

"Another long-time friend?"

"No, Megs."

"Clearly this wasn't the first time you met."

"No, it wasn't."

Megan stood, stretched. "You're being annoyingly coy."

Denver's eyes narrowed. "Why the interrogation?"

"Is that what I'm doing?"

Camilla raised her head and placed it in Denver's lap. He responded with a smile that tugged at Megan's insides. With his tousled auburn hair, dimples, and blue eyes,

he could charm her out of a bad mood —
most days. Maybe she was pushing . . . but
she felt him pulling away and didn't understand why.

Denver sighed. "No, it's a fair question.
Just not something I much want to discuss.
I met Martine during some dark days. My
then-wife Lilian and I were having problems, and I went to New York to get away.
To think. I ran into Chase. He was there on
BOLD business. He introduced me to
Martine." Denver shrugged. "We went out
once. Just for drinks, nothing happened. I
was still married, and although I guess I
could have justified a one-nighter, my vows
meant something to me."

"That was it?"

"Martine tried to keep in touch, but I was
going through the divorce." He closed his
eyes. "Dark days. I had no idea she was
coming this weekend."

"Chase didn't warn you?"

A twisted smile. "Does that surprise you?"

Megan shook her head. Chase hardly
seemed sensitive enough to care — even if
Denver's discomfort would have occurred
to him. The thought of him dealing with
troubled teens . . . maybe she was misjudg-
ing him. He'd been in the music industry;
maybe there was more substance than

seemed apparent.

Megan crawled over the temporary barrier and sat next to Denver. She took his hand. Camilla eyed her with contented curiosity.

"They're an interesting bunch," Megan said.

One eyebrow shot up. "Again, you're being kind."

They both laughed.

"Tell me about them. From before, when you were in college. Chase was a guitar player? I'm guessing he was a little more laid back as a younger man?"

Denver nodded. "He was the clown of the group, always fooling around, always searching for the next party, the next cool thing. No one was that surprised when he played guitar after college. We *were* surprised when he got his PhD." Denver's smiled was wistful. "Pressure from Daddy. Not sure it was the best move. He seems edgy."

"You don't think he's happy at BOLD?"

"I don't know. Just something about him seemed off tonight."

"And the others? Barbara?"

"We met her through Jatin. They dated, and she became like a little sister to the fraternity. Always hanging around. I think Chase had a thing for her. They're very close friends."

"Are they together now?"

"Barb is married."

Denver disentangled himself from Camilla and stood up. "Xavier was the studious one of the group. Straight As, always studying. Focused to a fault. He liked the good life. He's become jaded, as you could see. And Jatin? Just an all-around good guy. Dependable. The one you went to with your problems."

Megan pictured them all as teens. Hopeful. Optimistic. Full of bravado. "And where did you fit in?" she asked. She stood up as well, moved closer, and put her arms around his waist.

Denver returned the gesture with a soft kiss. He stroked the hair back from her face.

"I guess I was the bad boy. Trouble and I were well-acquainted."

"Mmm . . . I always did like a bad boy."

"Oh, yeah?" Denver lifted her up, swung her over the makeshift enclosure. "I've changed my ways since college."

"I hope not too much."

"There may be a little bad boy left." He pressed against her.

Megan laughed. "Don't you have to get home to the dogs?"

"Aye, I do." Denver hopped over the

34

fence. "And I promised I'd take Dillon to the kick-off event early tomorrow. He's a shy kid, kind of awkward, and Aunt Eloise thought he might do better with me. Want to come along?"

Megan answered by kissing him. "Pick me up at seven? You can have breakfast with Bibi and me."

"I'll be here."

Megan weighed her next words carefully. "You're sure your friends are the right ones to help these kids? I don't mean to sound mean, but empathy didn't exactly seep from their pores."

"I know what ye mean. Truth is I don't feel like I know them that well anymore. College was a long time ago. I've seen them here and there in between, but not often. Life throws curve balls and people change to catch them — or to avoid getting hit. But Pioneer Village vetted them, and BOLD has money. As mentors in science and business, maybe they can teach these kids something."

Camilla snorted and they both looked down at the pig. Her tiny tail was wagging.

"In the meantime, we have a mystery on our hands," Denver said, his voice softening. He reached down to give her a last pat. "Who is Miss Camilla?"

"Indeed." Megan watched Camilla, thinking about troubled kids and self-obsessed adults and orphaned pigs. "And why was she locked in a storage facility?"

THREE

Saturday morning greeted them with early sun and a blast of cooler air — a perfect day for a hike. Denver arrived at 6:10. By then, Megan had fed the chickens, checked on and fed the goats and Camilla, and given Clay and Porter her requests: namely, get Alvaro, the cranky chef at the Washington Acres Café, ten pounds of salad greens for today's Green Goddess special.

Clover Hand, Clay's sister and Megan's store/café manager, had become a vegan. As a reformed junk food junkie, Clover was struggling. Everyone was trying to support her new lifestyle, even Alvaro, and although he never said a word, Megan noticed at least one appetizing vegan item on the menu every day.

"What's 'Green Goddess?' " Bibi asked. They were sitting around the kitchen table, eating Bibi's buttermilk pancakes. "I think Alvaro's gone mad. Yesterday I saw him grilling tofu."

"He's doing it for Clover," Megan said between mouthfuls. She knew Denver was anxious to get Dillon, and she was eating as fast as she could without offending her grandmother.

"I don't know why that girl can't do anything in moderation." Bibi's smile softened her words. "What's in Green Goddess and does that mean the old man will have me chopping vegetables all day?" Bibi flexed her hand in front of her, running a finger along swollen knuckles. "I can't handle a knife like I once could."

Denver, who had been unusually quiet throughout the meal, said, "I have no doubt you can still handle a knife, Bonnie."

Bibi graced him with the smile she reserved for angels and newborns. "Well, thank you . . ."

Was her grandmother blushing? Megan shook her head. "Green Goddess is a mixed salad. Greens, avocado, green peppers, scallions, broccoli, some crunchy cabbage. Alvaro tops it with toasted walnuts and pumpkin seeds and a creamy avocado-ancho-chili dressing. He made a sample earlier this week." Megan stood and placed her dishes in the sink. When she saw Bibi staring at her she said, "It was delicious."

"I'd be in the bathroom for a week if I ate all that fiber."

"Bibi!"

"What? Denver's a doctor. He doesn't care. Right, Denver?"

Denver smiled, but the gesture didn't quite reach his eyes. "Aye, I am a doctor and I know everybody uses the bathroom."

Bibi laughed. Megan shook her head. Her grandmother was feeling saucy today, clearly. That meant she and Alvaro would spend much of the day arguing.

When the dishes had been cleared and the vegetables set out for Clay to bring to the café, Megan joined Denver in his 4Runner.

"Are you going to tell me what's bothering you?"

Denver pulled out of the farm's long driveway and on to the road. The trees were heavy with new growth, and the bright green leaves fluttered in the breeze. Megan rolled down her window, enjoying the scents of late spring. Denver was good about listening to others' problems — he did it often enough while attending to the animals in his care, or while making his large animal rounds — but he wasn't always one for sharing. He and Bibi had that in common.

Finally, he said, "I don't know about this charity thing, Megs. Chase texted me this morning. He was already complaining about the event. Doesn't seem quite the attitude to have before even starting out. Is it really safe to have these kids out there in the wilderness with a bunch of people who don't know what they're doing and don't want to be there? Ye know what I mean?"

"I think it'll be fine, Denver. It's the Pennsylvania woods. Not a dangerous jungle." Megan touched his arm. "They'll never be too far from civilization. Or a cell tower."

"I guess."

"There's a bunch of them. What can go wrong?"

"Kids can get lost or hurt. Or they can come away hating nature for the rest of their lives because they were forced to spend a long weekend with a jerk who made them feel miserable."

"You really are worried. What happened to your optimism from last night?"

"I got home, and Chase called me. He was drunk and surly."

"Oh."

"Ye don't get drunk the night before something like this. There are kids to think about."

"And his company's reputation."

Denver grunted. He turned the SUV onto a tree-lined road, breaking into a sharp curve. His aunt's house was about five minutes away. Megan glanced at her phone. They had some time to spare. Dillon and Eloise weren't expecting them until seven.

"Do you want to pull over and talk about it?" Megan asked.

"What's there to talk about? Chase's hung over and complaining and he's going to go anyway because his boss expects it of him. Got to move up that ladder, right?"

Denver looked more than angry. He seemed enraged.

"Look," Megan said, "he's an adult. Barbara is an adult. These kids — Dillon included — will be fine. It's not your fault Chase is an idiot."

Neither spoke while they made their way up the steep, narrow road. The houses along this stretch were larger, grander, than the ones in other parts of Winsome. Stone farmhouses with stately barns and acres of pasture. New, multi-winged Colonials built to look like they were crafted in the 1700s — with all the amenities of modern life, and twice the square footage. And at the end of the road, on a ten-acre lot, sat Denver's aunt's property, with it's gorgeous white Colonial, oversized barn, fenced-in pastures, and horses. It was an impressive, grand, and lonely place, Megan thought. One that could be overwhelming for an adult much less an unaccustomed foster child.

"Let's get Dillon," Megan said.

Denver placed a hand on her arm to stop her. "Sorry for being so morose."

"They're your friends. You feel responsible."

"Megs, there's —"

But Denver couldn't finish. His aunt rushed outside carrying a pile of camping gear.

Breathless, Eloise Kent said, "You're going to be late. Here are his things. Sleeping bag and pad. A backpack with snacks and water. A first aid kit. A journal." His usually reserved aunt and Winsome's retired pediatrician seemed flustered and out of sorts. "Extra chargers." She threw up her hands. "Everything on the list and then some."

Denver slid out of the 4Runner and took the gear out of his aunt's hands. "Did you send the good China and the fine silverware?"

"No, but I did send a spork."

"I was kidding."

"I know."

"There's no getting a smile out of you today, huh?" He placed the gear in the back of the SUV and gave his aunt a kiss on the cheek. "Relax, Aunt Eloise. Dillon will have a good time."

Eloise glanced behind her, toward the house. "He doesn't want to go."

"Just the jitters." Denver gave her a reassuring smile. "He'll be fine."

Eloise nodded, but she looked unconvinced. Aside from Denver's sister, who lived in Scotland, Eloise was his only living relative. Both Denver's parents were dead. He was protective of his aunt, and Megan knew he didn't want to let her down. The fact that she was stressed would only add to his worries.

"Where's Dillon?" Megan asked. "I'll help him get the rest of his stuff."

"No need. There is no 'rest' — this is it."

Even as she said the words, the front door opened, and a young man came lumbering out. Dillon was tall, over six feet, and heavy-boned, with the peach-fuzz mustache of adolescence. He stared at the ground as he made his way to the SUV, his face expressionless, size twelve feet shuffling along.

"Dillon, you remember Dr. Finn. This is his friend Miss Megan."

Denver and Megan shook hands with the boy. His hand was sweaty, his grasp firm.

"Okay, then," Eloise said. "Do you have everything, Dillon?"

Intelligent eyes seemed to focus inward

43

on the question. "I think so, ma'am."

"If you need anything, Dillon, anything at all, please call me." Eloise touched his arm tenderly.

"Yes, ma'am."

A bird flew overhead, circled, and landed on the fence. Dillon watched it, his expression softening. Eloise's dog, an older Golden Retriever, trotted over and stood by the boy, tail wagging. Dillon bent down, gave it a gentle rub behind the ears, and stood back up reluctantly.

"Remember, Dillon, this is for your future. Make some connections. You never know where this will lead."

He nodded, then slipped silently into the backseat of the 4Runner. When he was belted and the door was closed, Eloise leaned in. Voice barely audible, she said, "He's a sweet boy. Doesn't show much emotional range, but that's understandable." She moved closer. "Poor boy. Mother is dead, father is in prison." Eloise walked away, not even bothering to connect the dots aloud.

"Hey there, champ." A man slapped Dillon on the shoulder. "Looks like you're paired with me."

The man shifted from Dillon and locked

his gaze on Megan. "You must be Denver's new flame. I'm Xavier Jones, former fraternity brother and long-time friend." He held out an exceptionally hairy hand. His shake was damp and weak. "Nice to finally meet you." He glanced at Denver and smiled. It was a great job, bro kind of smile — one Denver didn't return.

Xavier bounced up and down on his heels. He was short and stocky, with an island of dark hair surrounded by a sea of sunburned scalp. He wore the confidence of someone whose life has always gone as planned, and he pinned that confident stare on Dillon, who seemed to shrink from his attention.

"Ready for the fun?" Xavier asked.

Dillon nodded, his focus once again on the ground. The event was starting at the Lyle Lake State Park main parking lot, and a dozen students were milling about. A few were talking to adults, but most, presumably residents of Pioneer Village School, were grouped next to a large white van. Every once in a while, one would sneak a furtive glance toward the adults standing by the park's welcome display.

"Do you know the other boy in the tent with us?" Xavier shared a name.

Dillon mumbled something and nodded.

"You *do* know him?" Xavier leaned down

and tilted his head up, so he was peering into Dillon's face. "Speak up. Rule number one in business. Use your voice or lose your voice."

Dillon swallowed. His Adam's apple bobbed. "Yes, sir."

" 'Yes, sir,' you agree or 'yes, sir,' you know this kid?"

"Both, sir."

Xavier stared at the boy for a long moment. He made an exasperated face and glanced at Denver, looking for agreement.

Denver shot him a reproachful look, touched Dillon's arm gently, and said, "Come with me." To Megan, he said, "I'll be back in a moment. Will you be okay?"

Megan nodded. She watched as the two walked off toward the trail map that hung on a post by the bathrooms.

Xavier also followed their progress before turning his attention to Megan. "That kid will be fun to have around." He nodded toward the larger group standing by the school van. "Part-y time."

Megan made sure no one was in earshot. "You do realize these kids haven't had easy lives. It's the reason they need you to begin with. Social skills are *not* their thing."

Xavier's expression darkened. "Hey, I get it."

46

Megan frowned. She'd just met Xavier and already she was ready to move on. "I hope so."

Xavier pointed at Denver, who was deep in conversation with Dillon. "So, you snagged Daniel. Nice."

"I wouldn't say I snagged him."

"He's a catch. Handsome, educated. Too bad about his wife."

Megan didn't respond. This guy was supposed to be Denver's friend, but his tone was anything but friendly. Jealous of Denver? Or just awkward himself? Megan looked around for someone else to talk to and actually felt grateful to see Chase and Barbara making their way in their direction.

"Ready?" Barbara said. She wore black yoga pants, a tight, maroon performance t-shirt, and hiking boots. Her long, dark hair was held back with a scrunchie. A black sweatshirt was tied around her waist. She carried a water bottle and took small sips, watching Xavier over the rim.

Xavier shrugged. "Sure. Why not."

Chase looked worse for wear, his lank hair greasy and a day's worth of dark shadow on his face. He was carrying cooking equipment in an open box, including a small coffee pot, several plastic dishes, an aluminum pot, a tiny cast iron frying pan, and two

47

ceramic coffee mugs. A utility knife hung from his pants.

When he saw Barbara looking at his equipment, he said, "Boys have to eat."

Barbara shook her head. She reached down and touched her toes, stretching. "You'll regret that. Stuff is heavy."

"Seriously? Look around. This isn't exactly the Alps. I'm putting it in the backpack. I'll make the kid carry some of it." To Megan, he said, "Overdid it last night," as though it were something to be proud of.

"Who do you have?" Xavier asked.

His question was directed to Barbara, but it was Chase who answered with the name of his charge.

"Just one?" Xavier asked.

"Yeah."

Xavier smiled. "Lucky you."

Barbara looked annoyed. "We're here for Harriet and for BOLD." Her attention strayed. She glanced across the parking lot, where Martine was talking with two teen girls and an older woman in jeans, who Megan assumed was a teacher or chaperone. "This is important to Harriet and for BOLD Pharmaceuticals." Looking at Megan, she said, "Harriet owes everything to Pioneer. Her kid and all."

48

"Is Harriet from Pennsylvania?" Megan asked.

"She was originally. Her kid did some stupid things. Was going to go to juvie but Harriet worked this out so she could go here. She had serious emotional and behavioral issues. Paranoia. Poor judgment. Other stuff. Harriet says her daughter literally wouldn't be alive now without Pioneer Village." She took another sip from her water bottle and locked her gaze onto Megan's. "Sometimes things do work out."

"Looks like this will work out too." Megan tilted her head up toward the cloudless sky. "You couldn't have asked for better weather."

"For sure," Barbara regarded Chase with an apprising stare. "Go take two Excedrin and get back out here. Look alive. Please." She shifted her attention to Xavier, taking in his button-down plaid shirt and pleated shorts. "And you look like you're going to a church picnic. Don't you have anything more practical to wear? Martine will be taking photos."

"I have a t-shirt."

"Put it on. Lighten up. We *will* have a good time." It was an order, and Xavier responded with military salute.

When both Chase and Xavier had left,

Barbara sighed. "They mean well. They really do. I'm afraid I roped them into this. Harriet was so gung-ho about the idea, and I couldn't very well tell her that no one wanted to give up a weekend to traipse in the woods of Pennsylvania with delinquents."

Megan said, "No, I don't imagine she would have appreciated that."

"They'll benefit in the long run. Especially Chase." She glanced around. "Have you seen Jatin?"

"No."

"I wonder where he is." She looked at the large watch strapped to her wrist. "He should have been here twenty minutes ago."

"Traffic?"

Barbara made a face. "In this Podunk town? I don't think so." Realizing she'd just insulted Megan's home, she added quickly, "I wish I lived here. Fresh air. No traffic. It's awesome."

"What's awesome?" Denver had returned. He put his arm around Megan and pulled her close. "Ready, Megs? I think we can head out. The kids are in good hands. Staff have arrived, and Barbara here will keep everyone in line."

Megan searched the lot for Dillon. She spied him near the white van, standing with

50

two other teens. "Dillon's feeling better?"

Denver said, "He's fine."

"Okay, then." Megan said goodbye to Barbara, although she was already on her phone, searching, Megan assumed, for the missing Jatin.

When they reached the 4Runner, Denver started the vehicle. "Don't you wish you were going with them?"

"Honestly? Yes. I wish *I* could take the kids *instead of* them."

Denver smiled. "At least then they'd have fun. You and Clover? Much better than this crew."

FOUR

"How's the construction coming along?" Merry Chance, the owner of Winsome's only nursery, took a dainty bite of an omelet, dabbed at her mouth with a paper napkin, and placed her hands in her lap. "When will the inn be ready?"

Megan wiped the long counter at the back of the Washington Acres Larder & Café. Merry asked regularly about the progress on the former Marshall property. Megan wasn't sure if she was genuinely interested — or if she was tired of looking at the town eyesore.

Megan said, "If not this year, hopefully next."

"Have they broken ground yet?"

"They started on the new barn, which will house the educational center. The old Marshall house is in pretty bad shape. We had hoped to renovate it and use it as the inn and kitchen, but we're waiting on reports from the inspectors and structural engineer."

Merry pursed her lips, forehead knitted into a matrix of thinker's creases. Well into middle age, she had the sort of ageless quality some women retain, with clear ivory skin and jade-green eyes. Today she seemed tired. "Is it a good idea to build the barn? What if the house has to be torn down?"

The old Marshall place had sat abandoned for decades. Megan had wanted to buy it for years, but it was only last year that she found the funds to afford the property. Only years of neglect had taken their toll on the house that was once, long ago, part of the Washington Acres farmstead, and Megan was afraid fixing the impact of that neglect would take time and more funds than Megan had.

She leaned against the counter, dishrag in hand. "If it has to be torn down, we'll tear it down. We can still use the barn for the farm and educational outreach. I'm hoping some portion of the house can be saved, but if not, we will rebuild it when funds allow."

"That's exciting."

Megan didn't think Merry looked remotely excited. The eyesore was going to get worse before it got better.

"Megan, order's up." Alvaro sounded cross. But then, Alvaro always sounded cross.

Megan grabbed a plate of cinnamon French toast and a tiny pitcher of maple syrup from the counter. She served it to the lone man at one of the copper-topped tables. He mumbled a thank you. Megan refilled his coffee without being asked and slipped a bill next to the cup.

Back in the kitchen, Alvaro was cleaning up from the breakfast crowd and beginning the night's specials. The prior summer, Megan had opened and wood-fired pizza farm on the farm property. The pizzas, with all their locally-sourced ingredients, had been a huge success, and it was open again this summer. Last night, the pizza farm had served a large crowd, and Alvaro was balancing the café's menu with the pizza farm's wood-fired offerings so they wouldn't compete.

Megan read the board. Mango curry, served with or without chicken, coconut sticky rice, and micro-green salad with peanut or avocado dressing. Three-cheese panini with early season tomatoes and arugula, and homemade kettle chips. Wild mushroom pot pie with a puff pastry crust.

"I think you outdid yourself." Megan spun

around, ready to see Alvaro wave away her compliment or hear her cook utter some complaint. Instead he was staring past her, into the store.

"What's wrong?" Megan followed his gaze. She saw Bobby King walking toward the back of the shop with purposeful strides.

"Damn," Megan said under her breath. What now?

Bobby walked around the counter, entering the kitchen uninvited. "Megan. Have a moment?"

"I don't suppose you're here for breakfast."

"Afraid not." He nodded toward the small office Megan had set up in the back. "Please."

Megan followed him into the cramped space and closed the door behind her. "Please don't tell me something happened to Bibi."

"Oh, gosh, Megan. No. She's fine, far as I know. Actually, I need to find Denver."

"Did something happen to his aunt?" Not again, Megan thought. The woman had suffered an attack at the hands of a psychopath almost two years ago. She seemed to have finally recovered.

"No, it's not Dr. Kent."

"Then what's going on?" Megan's stomach twisted. She remembered the Pioneer Village School. The hike. "Did something happen to Dillon?"

"Look, I can't say anything until family has been contacted. But I need to find Denver. He's not answering his cell and his office manager isn't picking up either. Just the answering service, and that guy's as useful as a paper hammer."

King was a tall man, well over six foot. Large hands were fisted by his sides. His square jaw was clenched, his ruddy face almost crimson. Someone had died. Megan knew it by King's reaction alone.

Megan opted not to push it. "It's Sunday, Bobby. Denver's off. He's kayaking at the lake."

"Do you know when he'll be back?"

"Before dark."

Bobby walked around her and grabbed the knob. "I don't have time to go searching for him myself or the human power to send someone. You hear from him, send him my way. And in the meantime, please don't say anything. To anyone, not even Bonnie."

"You know you can trust me."

Bobby's nod was curt. "I know, Megan. It's why I'm here."

Megan called, but as expected, she got

Denver's voicemail. She didn't wait for Denver to call her back. She left Alvaro and Clover alone to cover the store and headed up the valley toward the small lake where Denver tended to go when he was feeling contemplative. The lake was north, along the field-flanked back roads that led to the Lehigh Valley, and tucked deeply into the woods. It took her forty minutes before she turned into the small boat launch area, which consisted of enough parking for maybe four cars. A slime-covered, three-foot ramp provided access to the clear water.

Denver's SUV sat alone in the lot.

Megan climbed out of her truck, still wearing her café clothes — a white blouse tucked into a pair of dark jeans and comfortable clogs. She made her way to the ramp and looked out at the water but saw no sign of Denver. The banks of the lake were overgrown with trees and shrubs. The water extended out to the left and the right of the ramp, but with the curve of the banks and the thick foliage, Megan couldn't see more than fifty yards in any direction, and the banks were too thickly vegetated to hike along the shoreline. She considered calling for him, but she didn't want to scare him.

She folded her body on a large rock by the boat ramp and waited, enjoying the feel of the sun on her face. She couldn't recall the last time she'd just sat somewhere — nowhere to be, no one hounding her for something. She reminded herself that something was wrong, someone was hurt or worse — otherwise Bobby King would not have shown up at her door. Suddenly the sun felt too hot, the air constricting.

About fifteen minutes later, Megan heard the rhythmic splash of Denver's kayak paddles. She saw the nose of the boat come into view, and then the whole craft. Denver sat inside with his Golden Retriever perched between his legs. The dog was staring into the water. Denver's focus was off in the distance. While Megan waited for him to come within earshot, she studied him from afar. Broad, strong shoulders. A deep chest. Thick auburn hair, just a little more red than brown. A handsome man, more rugged than beautiful. So different than her late husband, Mick, in that sense — but with the same quiet strength, of character and of build.

"Denver," she called. "Denver!"

He looked over, startled, and grinned when he saw her waving by the ramp. With deft strokes, he turned the boat toward shore.

"What are you doing here, Megs?" he

asked. He hopped out of the boat and pulled it up the ramp. Swirls of muddied water lapped at strong calves. "I don't suppose you came to kayak." His blue eyes pierced her own, a shadow falling across his face. "Something happen?"

The Golden Retriever jumped out of the kayak with a splash and waded out into deeper water. Megan watched her swim, envying the dog's ability to immerse herself, quite literally, in the moment.

"King's looking for you."

With a grunt, Denver picked up the heavy boat and hefted it over his shoulder. He whistled for the dog and trudged up to the 4Runner. He placed the kayak on the roof rack and began securing it. Megan joined him, and together they tied it to the four corners of the vehicle.

"Did King say what he needed?" Denver's tone was neutral, his face impassive. Megan knew that meant the waters were churning deep below the surface.

"Wouldn't tell me." Megan helped Denver with the cords. "I think it may be one of your friends." Megan glanced over at him, relieved to see his expression had softened.

"I heard from Chase not long ago. Sent a photo of himself in the woods. Fooling around, as always. I'm sure everyone's fine.

Would have said something if bad things were afoot."

"What time did you get the text? Maybe there was a delay. Reception is sometimes poor in parts of the park."

Denver nodded. "Maybe. One way to find out." Kayak tied down, he pulled his wet bag open and removed his phone from a baggie inside. With a glance at its face, he frowned. "No reception here, either. Let's drive a bit."

Megan followed the 4Runner in her truck. A few miles away, Denver pulled into the parking lot of a mom and pop convenience store and climbed out of the SUV, leaving his car running for the dog. Megan joined him.

"Six missed calls," Denver said. "Two from King, one from Barbara, and three from my aunt."

With dawning horror, Megan remembered that Jatin had been missing yesterday when they started out. "Is it possible Jatin never showed? That something happened to him?"

Denver was already dialing. He reached King and did more listening than speaking. When he hung up, he looked like he'd just seen a demon.

"Well?" Megan said softly. She walked over and touched Denver's arm lightly. "Are you okay?"

"Chase. He's dead." Denver shook his head. "Murdered."

"I don't understand. You said you'd just heard from him."

"I don't know details, Megan. Just what little Bobby said. Chase was stabbed to death." He looked at her, his face stricken. "The only person with him at the time was Dillon."

FIVE

It was nearly two by the time Megan and Denver arrived at the Winsome police station. They were immediately ushered into an austere, windowless room and asked to wait for King. He marched in fifteen minutes later carrying two cups of black coffee, his expression grim.

"Sorry, Megan. Didn't know you were coming too. Want my coffee?" King proffered the paper cup. Megan declined.

"Okay that she stays?" Denver asked. "Just for moral support."

"That's fine for now." He glanced at Megan, obviously weighing his words. "Maybe she can offer some insight. Being a former lawyer and all."

Confidentiality issues, Megan thought. Which must mean Dillon's involved.

Sure enough, King's next words gave her chills. "The boy found the body."

"Damn," Denver muttered. "Dillon's been

through enough, Bobby. Do you know about his past?"

Bobby nodded. "Father is in prison. Accused of killing his mother." King rubbed his temple with a beefy paw. "Look, this is a rough one, I get that, but before I can tell you anything, we need to ask you some questions. On the record. Any objection?"

"None at all." Denver sat straighter in the chair.

"Not here. One of my officers will talk to you." His expression was apologetic. "She'll want to know where you were this morning."

Denver nodded. "Chase was a friend. I understand. You need to be thorough."

"Your aunt too. It's just routine. You get it."

Denver said, "Not exactly our first rodeo."

King nodded. None of them needed reminding that Chase's body was not the first to turn up in Winsome. King started to stand as the door to the room opened. A red-haired, heavily freckled officer entered.

"If you could go with my officer, that would be great." King turned to Megan. "Can you stick around?"

"I'm with Denver, so sure."

Megan watcher Denver leave. Silence hung between King and her, a silence filled with the dread of resignation. Both parties knew that a murder in Winsome meant news media, shock, rumors, and panic. Especially an unsolved murder.

Megan waited for King to speak. He'd want to keep the lid on this for as long as possible. But he knew she was discreet. If he wanted to talk with her it was about something other than discretion.

Finally, he said, "We got a messed-up kid here, Megan. I didn't want to say anything to Denver until we go through the official protocols and get his statement, but Denver's right. Dillon has been through a lot. He could be a ticking time bomb." King paused. "I'm glad you're here, though."

His shrug seemed almost shy. It was such a young gesture, one that reminded Megan that their Chief was not that much older than a kid himself. She felt fondness for King rush through her. Fondness and a strong sense of protectiveness. They'd been through a lot together. She was glad he consulted her, even unofficially.

Megan nodded, meeting his gaze with a half smile that, she hoped, conveyed empathy. "What can I do?"

King sat forward in his chair. He folded his hands on the scarred wooden table wedged between them. "Thing is, this kid

— Dillon — found the body. At least he says he did."

"You don't believe him?"

"You know as well as I that it's not my job to believe or disbelieve. It's all about establishing facts."

"Fine, Bobby, but you know what I mean. You have some reason to think he's lying?"

After a pause, King said, "I have every reason to believe Dillon is lying."

"Ouch."

"I'll say." King stood up and walked to the door. He opened it, glanced into the hallway, and pushed it shut again with more force than was necessary. "Denver's aunt. A potential media blitz. Winsome's collective mental health. It's a nightmare. But Dillon . . . no investigator wants a kid like Dillon to be their chief suspect."

"And poor Chase," Megan said, thinking of the man she saw the day before. "Having him die, and in our beloved Lyle Lake State Park, no less, is a nightmare, period."

"Yes."

Megan motioned toward the chair opposite her. "Sit, Bobby. There's a reason you wanted me to stay. What is it?"

King turned the chair backwards and straddled it. "The victim was found with the murder weapon. A utility knife. We've identified it as Chase's utility knife."

"Were they alone?"

"From what we can tell, the victim —"

"Chase."

King nodded absentmindedly. "Chase. Had been alone. The kid split off from the group and wandered down into a clearing by the pond. Chase went after him. They were gone for a short while — some witnesses say five minutes, others twenty — when screams erupted. Three of the adults went to find the source of the screams while the others stayed with the kids."

"Chase had been screaming?"

King shook his head. "No. They found Chase on the ground. He was already dead." King swallowed, hard. "It was the kid who was screaming." He closed his eyes. "For his mother."

Megan remembered what Eloise had said. The boy's father was in prison, mom was deceased. Megan felt bile rise in her throat. "Oh, Bobby."

"Sad, right? Heartbreaking. Problem is, he was covered with the victim's blood."

Megan frowned. "That doesn't necessarily make him guilty."

"No, it doesn't. But take a troubled kid with a family history of domestic violence, add an isolated setting, and give him the means — access to the murder weapon — and the opportunity, and you have a problem on your hands."

"You need motive too, Bobby. Why would Dillon want to do that to a man he barely knew?" Her face contorted in horror. "Could it have been self-defense? Have you *asked* him?"

"That's the other thing." Voices could be heard on the other side of the door, and King lowered his own. "The kid won't talk."

"Won't say anything until he has an attorney? Or won't talk at all?"

"Just won't talk." King's young face sagged. "It's like he's comatose. Just stares out into space, silent."

"Shock?"

A curt nod. "He's at the hospital now being evaluated. We've asked for a psychiatric evaluation. It will take time."

Megan let all of this sink in. Dead businessman in Winsome for a charitable deed. Troubled teen at the scene of the crime, screaming for his late mother. A killer? Or an unfortunate witness?

"Where was the staff? The other people from BOLD?"

King said, "They were up at the campsite involved in their own groups' activities when this happened. No one was paying much attention." King pulled a beefy hand through limp blond hair. "Denver will be back any minute, and I'll share some of this with him. But I want Denver and Eloise Kent to know I'm not the enemy here, Megan. This kid looks guilty. And maybe he is. You didn't see him in that hospital room." He shook his head as though ridding himself of the memory. "This big kid rocking like a child. If I know Eloise, she will fight me tooth and nail to protect Dillon's confidentiality. She's stubborn. I want the truth, not a scapegoat." His gaze was beseeching. "I'd appreciate if you'd help me get through to them."

"I can't convince Eloise to do anything she's uncomfortable with. She's a pediatrician. Her concern will be for Dillon, Bobby. You know that."

"I'm just afraid in her effort to protect him, she'll make things worse."

Megan understood. Bibi could be the same way with Megan's father, Eddie — so determined to protect him that her actions hurt him in the end. "I'll see what I can do. No promises."

The door handle jiggled, and King hopped out of the chair. "She needs to know we're on the same side. I want him protected too. From the media. From those who will assume guilt." The door opened. King turned in the direction of the entryway, and said, "And from himself."

SIX

Denver was quiet during the drive to his aunt's home. Eyes on the road, jaw rigid, hands wrapped around the steering wheel so tightly his fingers were white sausages, he maintained a speed that would have him losing his license if any police in Winsome were monitoring the roads. Megan sat beside him, resisting the urge to speak. She knew he needed his space. She also knew she didn't have the right words. How do you express sorrow in a situation like this? Denver would be blaming himself — right or not.

Denver pulled up to the old farmhouse, parked next to Eloise's three-year-old BMW, and jammed the 4Runner into Park. With the vehicle still running, he sat back and let out a long breath. Megan studied her hands, the side of the barn, the hills in the distance — the same hills that delineated the edges of Lyle Lake.

Unable to stand his silence any longer, she finally said, "None of this is your fault, Denver."

"Ta, Megan. I wish I could agree."

"How are you to blame?"

He turned to face her. No reproach, only sorrow. And exhaustion. "Aunt Eloise asked me if Dillon should be involved. I said yes, let the boy take part. I assured her he would be fine."

"She would have sent him anyway? It sounded like a great opportunity. Mentoring? The possibility of college tuition? How could she say no?"

He shook his head. "It wasn't like that. Dillon didn't want to go. She urged him to go, because I told her I thought it would be good for him. Because Chase and Xavier and Jatin were my friends, she listened to me." He put his head in his hands. "And when Chase called and told me Barb had approached him, I urged him on too. 'It's in my backyard,' I said. 'I'll get to see you,' I said. And now the bloody bastard is dead."

Seeming to realize what he just said, his eyes widened. "I don't know what happened out there, Megs, or why, but had I not gotten involved, Chase might still be alive, and Dillon would not have been anywhere near him."

Megan sat next to Denver for a long while, in silence. When she spoke, it was with firm conviction. "Denver, stop. This line of thinking is unproductive. One, your aunt is a pediatrician fully capable of making informed decisions. Had she felt this was a bad idea for Dillon, she wouldn't have sent him. I'm certain of that." And she was. Dr. Kent *was* a stubborn woman. She'd lived alone much of her life, and she was accustomed to being the boss. "Two, the Chase I met at the restaurant was an opportunist. He was going to do this, one way or another. Winsome, PA or Walleye, Kansas, he was going." Megan pulled Denver's face gently toward her. "Don't fool yourself into thinking that Chase — or any of them — came here for you."

Megan watched Denver's eyes close, his face relax. Hard truths, but he needed to hear them. When he opened his eyes, they were clearer.

"I only met Dillon a few times, mostly during dinners at Eloise's house or when I was over to see to the horses, but the boy seemed shy. Kind. I watched him with Eloise's colt, the one who startles, and Dillon was gentle, even when he thought no one was looking. A gentle giant."

Megan nodded.

"I don't think he killed Chase. Why would he? He didn't even know him." Denver turned off the ignition, and the interior of the SUV started to warm up immediately. "But if not Dillon, then who could have done something so heinous?"

Megan opened the vehicle door. She paused to collect her bag. I guess that's the question, she thought. Who wanted Chase dead? And why?

Eloise was on the phone in the kitchen when they walked into the home's large center hall. She barked something into the receiver before ending the call abruptly when she saw Megan and Denver. She placed her cell on the kitchen island's marble top and greeted them with a half-hearted hug.

"I guess you heard."

Denver nodded. "I had to make a statement at the station."

Eloise frowned. "What did they ask you?"

"How I knew the victim, his whereabouts and itinerary while in town, where I have been the last six hours. The norm, I would imagine."

"Surely they don't suspect you." Her tone was indignant.

"Just doing their jobs." Denver glanced

around the large, immaculate kitchen. His eyes fell on a man's coat draped over one of the stools at the marble-topped island. "Someone here?"

"I'm afraid that belongs to Dillon. I was packing up some of his belongings for the hospital before his agency called."

No hint of emotion in her voice, which concerned Megan more than histrionics would have.

"Is someone from the school going to visit him at the hospital?" Megan asked. "I would think they have a staff psychologist, someone who could talk with him. This had to have been very traumatic."

"They do, Dr. Star. And he will visit eventually, when the dust settles. I'm afraid it's about to get much more traumatic." Eloise sat heavily on one of the stools. Her voice remained flat, but Megan could see the flush creeping along the edges of her ivory skin, the tremor in her hands. "The police suspect him of murdering your friend, Denver."

"We got that sense from Bobby." Denver's voice had the ring of alarm. "Have they arrested the boy?"

"No, nothing like that. He's at the hospital being treated for shock. He'll have a psychiatric evaluation. A youth defender is being assigned." Her shoulders slumped. "He's nearly catatonic, so I don't know what they think they're going to get out of him."

Denver shot Megan a concerned look. "Eloise, how are you? This has to have been traumatic for you as well."

"Do you really think my comfort matters right now?" Her tone was sharp, and Megan took an involuntary step back. "I'm sorry," Eloise said immediately. "I don't quite know what to do. What does one do to help a boy in this situation? I can stitch up wounds, treat pneumonia, diagnose viral infections, but this type of emotional pain? It's not so easy to cure."

Her voice trailed off. Denver put an arm around her. "I imagine you do what you would do in any health crisis situation in which there is no obvious cause. You treat and monitor the symptoms. In this case, once the shock has been addressed, the symptoms will be emotional. If what you say is true, he'll feel embattled and alone. Support and friendship will be the tonics you can provide."

Eloise nodded. "How did you get so wise?"

"I was lucky enough to have a good aunt in my life."

Eloise picked up the jacket. She held it to

75

her face and took a deep breath, looking distracted. "When Dillon first arrived, I wondered what I was going to do with this kid. He's not much of a talker. He'd walk around looking morose, picking at his food, remaining largely in the shadows. He likes to read. And play video games. That's about it." She stood. Once at the window overlooking the barn, she turned. "Then I saw him with the horses. They listened to him. Even that wild little filly, the headstrong one that threw you, Denver. She let him ride her."

Eloise put on the faucet and ran the water for a moment, holding two fingers under the spigot. She was lost in thought. Without washing or doing anything else, she shut off the water and dried her hand with a small towel.

"The clinical part of me says he could have done it. Violent father. Deceased mother, with whom he was very close. Who knows what he witnessed in that house. Pent-up anger, they'll say. All those months of 'yes, sir,' and 'yes, ma'am,' and he finally broke. Maybe that Chase Mars did something to upset him. Maybe Dillon had a psychotic episode, though he has no history. Maybe he confused Chase with his dad."

"Or maybe he didn't do it," Megan said.

Both Denver and Eloise turned to her.

"Yes," Eloise said softly. "The other part of me says that's right. I've gotten to know Dillon, perhaps as much as he'd let anyone in. I don't think he's capable of an act of violence against anyone or anything."

Denver studied his aunt. After a pause, he said, "I'm sorry I urged him to go. If he hadn't —"

Eloise laughed. It was a bitter, high-pitched laugh, full of malign amusement. "Denver, I love you, but let's be clear. I wanted your opinion, of course, but if I didn't think he should go, he wouldn't have gone. Period. So don't blame yourself. This is on me."

"This is on whoever did the act," Megan said. "Period." She looked at Denver. "What about the others? Barbara, Xavier, Jatin . . . have you connected with them?"

"Just by text." Denver leaned against the island. "They're being questioned by King and his officers. I think Xavier is still there. Dillon was his charge, so I imagine King wants to understand why Dillon was off by himself in the first place."

"They're teens, not first graders," Megan said.

"True. But it was a mentoring event. And these kids have special needs." Denver

77

shrugged. "That's the last I heard. Obviously, the rest of the event has been called off. My friends are all staying at the Bucks County Inn, so I'll connect with them there later."

The phone rang, startling Megan. Eloise picked up the cell and stared at screen. With the same maddening calm, she answered.

"Dr. Kent." A long pause. "Oh, I see. So soon?" Another lengthy silence. "That's fine." She clicked off.

"Dillon?" Denver asked. "Is he responding?"

"On the contrary. That was his social services agency. They're placing him in the psychiatric unit. They feel that's the best place for him right now, all things considered. They want me to bring his clothes to the hospital."

"We can take them over," Denver said. "Or at least go with you."

Sadness shadowed her features. "That would be nice," she said before disappearing into that center hall.

78

SEVEN

Winsome's closest hospital was six miles away, a distance Denver once again covered in record speed. Megan sat in the back, next to a medical kit and a box full of leashes, treats, and dog toys. Denver was of the habit of stopping to rescue stray and lost dogs and cats, and he kept everything from small cages to extra towels and blankets in his vehicle. Today he made room in the rear for Dillon's belongings, which amounted to one small suitcase and a duffle bag of books and comics.

At the hospital entrance, they were greeted by a stern-looking woman in a beige suit. She let them know Dillon was on the fifth floor but reiterated three times that he was not allowed visitors.

"No problem," Eloise said. "We're simply bringing him his belongings."

The nurse on the fifth floor was warmer but just as adamant. "You can leave everything here," he said. "I'll make sure Dillon's agency gets the belongings when they arrive." He glanced toward a uniformed officer standing guard by Dillon's hospital room. "Technically he's under police custody. I don't think we can let you in there."

"I'm his foster mother, and a doctor as well."

The nurse smiled apologetically while tapping on the clip board he was holding. He was a tall man, well over six foot, and he loomed over even Denver. "You understand procedure."

Megan and Denver exchanged a look. Megan hoped this wouldn't get ugly. There'd been enough ugly for a while.

"Can you call Chief Bobby King of the Winsome Police Department?" Megan asked. "I'm certain he will okay a brief visit."

"I don't think so." He glanced back at the uniformed officer. "We have our orders."

"Please?" Megan said. She held the nurse's stare. "He's a kid. I know he's not responding. Maybe seeing Dr. Kent will help." The nurse's expression softened, and Megan said, "Just a call. We have Chief King's cell number. I can call him for you."

The nurse glanced again at the officer. "Fine. Give me the number. I'll call."

Megan obliged, and the nurse walked

away to make the call, his back to them. Moments later he came back looking chagrined. "The Chief said it was fine. But as part of Dillon's medical team, I'm saying only you —" he looked at Eloise, "— and only for five minutes, tops."

Eloise didn't wait for him to change his mind. She thanked him and strode into Dillon's hospital room. Megan watched her disappear from view.

"Thank you," Megan said.

"I feel bad for the kid," the nurse said. "He's had a parade of officers and doctors in there. Maybe seeing someone who cares about him will make a difference." He squinted at Denver. "But I heard what happened." He shook his head. "Crazy world."

"What did you hear?" Megan asked.

"I can't talk about the patients." The nurse flushed. "I just heard what was on the news. Someone was murdered." He shrugged a shoulder in the direction of Dillon's room. "And this patient is in police custody."

Megan knew exactly what he was implying. "That could be for his own protection," Megan said. "He was a witness. When he becomes responsive, they may want someone here to take a statement. It doesn't mean he had anything to do with what happened."

The nurse didn't look convinced. He glanced at the clock on the wall. "I'm afraid time is up."

Before he could evict Eloise from Dillon's room, Megan heard voices coming from the room. It was Eloise — and a lower voice. Dillon's voice.

The nurse's eyes rounded in surprise. He beelined for the door. Denver held up a hand. "Can't you give them some time?"

"I have strict instructions." He didn't have to say more. The uniformed police officer, an older man with a bushy mustache, had heard the boy's voice as well and was entering the room.

I guess that will end any conversation on Dillon's part, Megan thought.

Seconds later, Eloise was back at their side. Her eyes were watery, but her mouth was pressed into an unyielding line. "You go," she murmured. "Leave me here. I'll get King or someone to drive me home."

"What did he say?" Denver asked.

"Nothing of consequence."

The tear on Eloise's cheek said otherwise.

Camilla was a welcome distraction.

"She looks good." Denver was kneeling in the small pig's pen. "You're doing a fine job of caring for her, Bonnie."

Bibi looked away, but Megan could see the edges of her mouth turned up in an almost-smile.

"Let me see you, little lassie." With a gentleness that belied his strength, Denver picked up the animal. He looked her over and placed her back on the ground. She squealed, then ran in circles, small tail waving. Denver smiled, bringing out his dimples. "She's a cute one. What will you do with her?"

"The owner will turn up," Bonnie muttered.

"Oh, I don't think anyone is inclined to give the pig back to someone who kept her in a storage unit. Inhumane and against the law," Denver said. "Someone named Saul Bones, no less."

"Maybe we could keep her?" Megan glanced at her grandmother, who had picked up a broom and was suddenly engrossed by a need for cleanliness. "Bibi?"

"We'll cross that bridge if we need to."

"We'll keep her," Megan mouthed to Denver.

Denver smiled again. "Okay, then, Bonnie. We'll see what happens. In the meantime, some fresh air and more good food for this wee one."

"Too much food and she won't be so

wee," Bibi said. But she grabbed a handful of fruit and vegetable slices from the Tupperware container on the floor and fed them one by one to the pig.

"Come for a walk?" Denver said to Megan. "I think Camilla is in good hands."

Megan followed Denver out of the barn and up toward the old Marshall property — now her property. When the Marshalls moved out and abandoned the property, they stopped all maintenance. The large yard had gone to seed and was a meadow full of thistle and grasses and wildflowers. The old house stood as it had for the past several decades, parts of it worn, parts in disrepair. The fascia was crumbling, the piers holding up the front porch had long since rotted away, and Megan knew from previous visits that the interior was mice-infested and marred by vandalism caused by the occasional intruder. Fixing the house itself would be a project. And they were still awaiting the engineer's reports.

The new barn, on the other hand, consisted of a large hole in the ground and a poured foundation. The bones of the building would be going in soon. Megan couldn't wait. The barn would give them a place for community programs, healthy cooking classes, gardening club meetings. Clay's vision of making Winsome a hot spot for sustainable agriculture and locavore living had become her own. Even Bibi shared the passion.

Right now, the place looked like a war zone.

"I can see it, you know." Denver took Megan's hand. "What this will be."

Megan smiled. "And what exactly do you see?"

"The finished inn. The barn. Bibi teaching classes on bread-making and baking her signature scones. Lively discussions about types of turnips and the absolute best color for a broccoli head." He picked Megan up and swung her around. "And maybe a few dogs and wee ones running around."

Megan felt herself go stiff. "Wee ones? As in goats or pigs?"

Denver must have felt the change in her demeanor. He put Megan down on the ground. "Wee ones. Kids."

"Whose?"

"Ours." Denver's eyes narrowed. "Is that so bad, Megan?"

Megan turned away, her eyes suddenly moist.

"Whoa. How did we get here?" Denver asked. He touched her shoulder. "What's wrong?"

85

"Kids, Denver? Kids?" she said softly. "It's a big step."

"I didn't mean to upset you." When Megan didn't answer, Denver said, "Let's forget I mentioned it. It was just a fantasy. A vision."

He marched on, toward the woods. But there was an iron in his voice that wasn't lost on Megan.

Megan felt badly about snapping at him, but they never really discussed marriage much less a family. "Denver . . ."

He stopped walking. "What?"

What? Megan wasn't sure. Once upon a time, she'd envisioned a home with her late husband Mick. A few kids. Sadie. Maybe a cat or two. A secure job in a law firm. Mick as a career soldier, or perhaps retiring to open a business of his own. She never in a bazillion years saw herself on a farm back in her hometown of Winsome, with two dozen animals and a Scottish vet as a boyfriend. Megan considered herself a rational person, and she knew she was being unfair. Irrational even. Even if Denver's vision included *their* children, he had a right to that expectation. They'd been together more than two years.

And although Megan was reluctant to admit it in case fate snatched it away — she was *happy.* No, more than happy. At times, she felt true joy in her life. But with children inevitably came worry and heartache and even loss. Parenting, loving someone that much, demanded courage and faith, and since Mick's death, Megan was afraid — terrified, really — that she was low on both. Deep down, she was afraid suffering that kind of loss again would break her.

Denver's expectant look passed, and he turned to walk away, this time back toward the farm. "Wait," Megan said.

He stopped.

"I love you," Megan said.

"But?"

"No buts, Denver. I love you." She moved alongside him and took his hand. "One day at a time?"

He stared into her eyes for a long while, searching for something. Megan wanted to look away, but she held his stare, feeling on some gut level that he was taking her measure. Finally, he squeezed her hand.

"I love you too."

EIGHT

The café was crowded. Death had a way of bringing people together, and the loss of a stranger didn't change that. Megan waded through the people standing in the back of the Washington Acres Larder & Cafe, searching for Clover. She found her in the kitchen with Chef Alvaro and Emily, a family friend and their sometimes help. Clover was lecturing Alvaro about the importance of keeping vegan mayonnaise and butter around for guests.

When she saw Megan, she let out an exasperated sigh. "Is it too much to ask, Megan? Some Vegannaise? Geez, Alvaro can make his own." Clover glanced at the older chef with affection, softening her words. "Although I appreciate the mango curry. It's delicious."

"Alvaro's been pretty accommodating," Megan said. And he had. Megan knew the chef considered Clover a surrogate daughter, and although it wasn't his way to fawn over anyone, he was altering his menu options to please her. While Alvaro preferred locally raised meats, he was about as vegan as Bibi, who viewed chicken broth as a condiment.

That said, Megan liked the idea of expanding the café's options to cater to the plant-powered crew. No harm in differentiating themselves, and it was something she could get behind. She encouraged the change.

Megan said, "Clover, two minutes of your time?"

Clover glanced out at the crowded café. Every table was full, and customers were milling about between tables, talking. Dishes were lined up on the counter, ready to be delivered, alongside a tray of water glasses. "I guess. We're kind of busy."

"I can handle the tables," Emily said. She was writing out slips, tallying orders by hand. "I'm almost done here." She nodded toward one of the copper-topped tables. "Besides, no one seems to be in much of a hurry."

And indeed, they didn't. This was a wake of sorts, Megan knew. A way for the people of Winsome to reassure each other, get information, and deal with the presence of death in their midst once again.

Clover followed Megan into the cramped back office. "What's up?"

Megan sat behind her desk. Clover, with her long, dark hair and penchant for mini-skirts, tended to look younger than her years, but now in her mid-twenties, Megan knew she could be counted on in a pinch.

"I need you to increase your hours this coming week. Take a few of my shifts. Support Alvaro and Bibi. Will that fit with your schedule?"

"Sure, okay . . ." Her voice trailed off, making the word into a question.

"You heard about Chase Mars?"

"I heard he was killed up by Lyle Lake."

"Yes, in the park. While on a mentoring retreat as part of a corporate nonprofit initiative. He was Denver's friend."

Clover nodded. "I'm so sorry to hear that, Megan. If it's any consolation, Bobby's nowhere to be found ever since."

"I imagine he has his hands full with this one."

"I don't think Chase's friends have been very cooperative." There was an increase in the volume coming from the café, and Clover's attention followed the sound. "Maybe they're here now?"

Megan listened. It did sound like more

people had arrived. Voices she didn't recognize.

"Anyway," Megan said, in a hurry to get back out into the café, "Denver's going to need me this week. He's pretty upset about Dillon and about his friends. I'd like to do a little searching on my own. Between the farm and the construction and now this, I think I may need support at the café."

Clover grinned. "By searching you mean sleuthing?"

Megan smiled. She'd been known to dabble.

"I can do whatever you need me to do." Clover opened the door to the office. "Winsome folks pull together in bad times. Besides, doesn't seem like I'll be seeing much of Bobby anyway."

"Anywhere to sit?" Xavier looked around the small café. "Quite a crowd for a such a small establishment."

Megan glanced around. Where to put them? The tables were full, the counter was jammed. No one seemed ready to leave. She remembered the extra tables and chairs they kept locked in the back for catered events. "Give me a few minutes," she said. "In the meantime, the menu is on the board."

True to her word, Megan was back

91

quickly. She'd pulled a square folding table from storage and wiped it down. She placed it in front of the aisles of the store portion of the building and covered it with a white cotton tablecloth. Clover unfolded two chairs and went back for two more.

Barbara sat in one of the chairs. "Have you seen Denver?" she asked.

"He's on a call," Megan said. "He's dealing with some emergency or another."

Xavier coughed. "Convenient timing."

"I'm sure the animals planned it." Megan was about to say more but she bit her tongue — literally. "I'm sorry about Chase," she said instead. "About everything you must be going through."

"You have no idea," Xavier said. "It's been hell on all of us."

Clover had returned with the two additional chairs, and Martine and Jatin took their seats. Martine looked tired. Her face was pale, the skin around her eyes and mouth flaky and dry. She wore minimal makeup, and without it her pale eyes seemed ghostly.

Jatin looked no worse for wear, but he was quiet, allowing Xavier to speak for him. Of all of them, Megan felt for Barbara. Her dark hair fell about her shoulders in greasy waves, and her eyes looked listless. She seemed devastated.

"What can I get you?" Megan asked the group.

She jotted down their orders, which ranged from coffee for Barb to mango curry for both men. Martine wanted nothing but water.

"I'll be back shortly with your food."

Martine's hand shot out. She grabbed Megan's Washington Acres apron. "Have you heard anything?" she asked. "Anything at all about the kid? About who the police think did this to Chase?"

Megan paused long enough to meet her gaze. "I'm afraid I don't have any news."

"This is a PR nightmare." Martine's eyes pleaded with Megan, but for what, Megan wasn't sure.

"Chase is dead, and you're worried about PR?" Barbara shook her head. "He'd *dead,* Martine. He's not coming *back.*" Barbara's voice became choked, shrill. She reached in a red Prada bag and pulled out a wad of tissues. "He didn't deserve that."

"She feels guilty because she convinced him to come," Xavier explained. His face said she should feel guilty.

"That's understandable, but it's not your fault." Megan turned toward Jatin. "How were the other children besides Dillon? I imagine this was horribly traumatic for them as well."

Eyes blinked with surprise at the question. Finally, it was Barbara who said, "I guess they were okay. The school got involved pretty quickly and picked up the children. All but Dillon, of course."

"Why did Dillon take off in the first place?"

Barbara looked pointedly at Xavier. "Ask Mr. Sensitivity here."

"Don't look at me." Xavier raised heavy brown brows. "The kid has issues, that's apparent. All I did was ⸺"

"All you did was tell him he was an unathletic loser and he'd best get with the program if he wanted to succeed in life." Jatin spewed the words with disgust. His focus turned to Megan. "Dillon didn't want to take part in a trust exercise. He was afraid to fall." He glanced at Xavier, eyes narrowed in anger. "You insulted him in front of his peers, Xavier. What kid wouldn't get upset?"

"A kid with the drive needed to succeed." He glanced around the table and then up at Megan. "What? Wasn't that our job? Hard truths. Mentoring. What kind of mentor would I be if I told him the world was made of sugar plums and he could get by just staring at his shoes? It was a trust exercise, for god's sake. A simple one."

"The exercise was over and everyone had gone their own way," Barbara said. "Chase must have seen Dillon head to the lake and followed him. No one is quite sure."

Jatin said, "Had Xavier been doing his job, we would be in the woods right now, getting some great photos, eating s'mores, and looking at the stars. *Not* mourning our friend."

Xavier slammed a fist down on the table. "Enough."

Jatin shook his head, stood up. "The restroom?"

Megan pointed toward the back of the café.

When he left, Barbara said, "As you can see, tensions are high. Maybe if you hear from Denver, send him our way? We're at the Bucks County Inn. I have no doubt we'll be there for a few days. We could use the distraction and the support." She sniffed, wiped away a tear. "I have to deal with Chase and his . . . family. And the police, of course."

As Megan walked away to place their order, she couldn't help wondering a few things. What was the deal between Jatin and Xavier? And why did Xavier seem so unaffected by his friend's death?

■ ■ ■ ■

Bibi was visibly shaken. "I don't understand people these days, Megan," she said. "The man was doing a good deed. And now this?" She put her face in her hands and shook her head, a crack in her normally stoic demeanor. "Are they sure he was murdered?"

Megan thought about a utility knife. About a ruined life. Two ruined lives. "Yes, I think it was clear."

They were in the kitchen at Washington Acres. Megan had returned home after the dinner rush to have a bowl of soup and a conversation with Bibi. Her grandmother had found out about Chase's death earlier, from Merry Chance, who always liked to be the first person to share news. The more shocking, the better. If they crowned people for gossip-mongering, Merry would be a queen.

"He was such a young man," Bibi said. She studied her hands, knuckles swollen from arthritis and years of physical labor. "Too young." She stood up and placed her half-eaten bowl of vegetable soup by the big farmhouse sink. "Do they have any idea who did it?"

"Not really."

Bibi turned to face her. "What about the boy? What's his name? Eloise's foster child."

"Dillon."

"Yes, that's it. Poor child. Merry made it sound as though he's the killer."

"Merry needs to mind her own business once in a while."

Bibi smiled. "That will never happen. If she returns as a ghost, it will be to bring news of the afterlife."

They both chuckled. Sadie, Megan's mixed-breed rescue dog, rose from her spot under the table and sat in front of the sink. With a dog's sense for leftover food, she begged by the half-full soup bowl until Bibi finally caved and placed the bowl on the floor. The dog lapped at it gratefully, and Bibi gave Megan a look of reproach as though *she* had been the one to break the rules.

They both watched Sadie eat. Finally, Bibi glanced at the clock on the kitchen wall. It was almost nine at night.

I'm going to clean up in here and go to bed," Bibi said.

Megan started collecting plates from the table. Bibi held up a hand.

"I'll get this. Why don't you finish the farm chores while there's still a little daylight left? I'd rather you not be out there in the dark with —"

She didn't finish her sentence. She didn't need to. Here we go again, Megan thought.

Megan collected some vegetable and fruit scraps from the compost bin for the animals and a ginger cookie for each of the goats — their favorite. As she was leaving, Bibi pressed something into her hand. It was a package wrapped in wax paper.

"For Camilla. I made her special pig cookies. They're good for her."

Megan squeezed Bibi's shoulder. She knew better than to say anything. Just like Bibi would never admit to giving table food to the dogs, she'd deny spoiling the farm animals. But small acts of kindness were Bibi's way.

The night air was heavy and humid. The sun had gone down, and the horizon glowed in the distance, a fiery explosion of pink and yellow. Megan trotted across the courtyard to see to the chickens first. Safe in their chicken tractor, they were already in for the night. She made sure the house was secure — fox in the area had a taste for chicken — and headed for Camilla next.

A noise in the distance startled her, and Megan jumped. She heard rather than saw something moving her way. It took a moment to see the white fur, the massive head. It was only Gunther, her Polish Tatra Sheepdog, doing his own nightly rounds. Like Great Pyrenees, Polish Tatra Sheepdogs were bred to watch over sheep and other livestock. Gunther had been bought by a local farmer who mistreated him. Rescued by Denver, he came to live with Megan when still a puppy. Since then, he'd earned a spot as a reliable farm hand and steadfast friend. Megan allowed him his freedom on the farm as well as a warm spot in her bed.

More frequently, he preferred to stay outside with the goats. Tonight, Megan was happy for his company.

She reached down and patted his head. "Good boy, Gunther. What's happening?"

The dog walked beside her as they visited Camilla, gave her Bibi's treats — which she devoured with all the grace of a ravenous wolf — and moved on to the goats.

Megan found Heidi and Dimples asleep. They lay next to each other, tucked between bales of hay. When Megan entered their enclosure, Heidi jumped up to greet her. Dimples did the same, only she ran for Gunther and play-butted his chest.

They were pygmy goats, unable to do much harm even if they wanted to. Other than eating things they shouldn't. Gloves.

Bibi's hats. Their entire crop of strawberries. Naughtiness aside, Megan ended most nights with a visit to the ladies. She found some semblance of peace in their midst.

So did Gunther, apparently.

Megan was just settling on a bale of hay when her cell phone rang. A local number, but one she didn't recognize. "Hello?"

"This is Martine." Hesitant, high-pitched voice, slight whine. "From BOLD Pharmaceuticals. Denver's friend."

"Yes?"

"I'm . . . I'm looking for Denver. I hope you don't mind that I called."

"I'm afraid he's not here." Megan paused, wondering what Martine wanted with Denver. And how she got her number. "Is there something I can help you with?"

"No." A long pause. "But thank you."

"Look, Denver's working. He's dealing with a breach birth and it could be a while before he's finished, and by then he'll be exhausted. Are you sure I can't help you?"

Martine took so long to reply that Megan thought she'd hung up. With a deep sigh, Martine said, "I can't talk here. Can you meet me somewhere?" She was silent for a moment. "But I don't know where. I have no idea what's even open in this town."

"You're at the Bucks County Inn?"

100

"I am, but we can't talk here."

"Okay." Megan thought about this. Normally she'd consider a friend of Denver's to be a friend of hers and invite her to the farm, but these were not normal times. While Martine's motives may be benign, Megan couldn't put Bibi or the farm at risk. "Do you have access to a car?"

Martine grunted a yes. "If this is too inconvenient . . ."

"There's a Starbucks about four miles up the road from your inn. They're open until midnight." Megan glanced at her watch. "Meet me in twenty minutes. And I'll text Denver, asking him to meet us if he becomes free."

Martine agreed. Megan was sure it had little to do with the prospect of talking to Megan — and everything to do with the hope of seeing Denver.

NINE

In keeping with her promise to Martine, Megan texted Denver. She didn't hear back, which was no surprise. He was up at a farm and could be there half the night. Megan changed from her work jeans and t-shirt into a pair of gray linen pants and a matching tunic, slipped on sandals, and ran a comb through her dark hair. Why she cared what she looked like, she wasn't sure. Maybe the fact that this was a woman from Denver's past. Maybe because she was half hoping Denver *would* show up. In either case, she was out the door and on the road in ten minutes and at the Starbucks in twenty-two.

Martine wasn't there.

Megan sat in the truck, engine off, and watched the traffic speed by on Route 611. She wondered what Martine wanted to talk about, and why it couldn't be discussed at the bed and breakfast. The presence of the others? Or fear of the police. No matter, whatever it was would have to wait.

Megan was about to turn the key when a silver Volkswagen Jetta pulled into the lot. The driver was a woman. She wore a black scarf over blonde hair. When she got out, Megan recognized the slim build, the hesitant walk. She watched as Martine entered the coffee shop before climbing out of the truck herself. Martine slipped onto a bench at a table in a shadowed corner.

Megan waved a greeting. At the counter, she ordered two teas. She met Martine at the table, offering an herbal Chamomile tea and what she hoped was a friendly smile.

Martine looked at her through heavily made up eyes. She kept the scarf draped over her head, covering her hair a la Jackie Kennedy Onassis. Her black sheath dress and heels were reminiscent of Jackie O as well. A smear of red lipstick marred her front teeth, and mascara stained the pale skin under her eyes. She watched Megan take a seat with large eyes, her expression despondent.

"Thank you for meeting me. I guess Denver couldn't make it?"

"I haven't heard back from him."

Martine nodded. She stared at her cup for a moment before tearing open the tea wrapper and placing the bag in the steaming water. She watched it sink.

"Thanks for meeting me." She gave Megan a shy smile. "I was at a loss. I can't trust anyone, don't know where to turn."

"What's happened, Martine?"

"I think I'm just being paranoid."

"You called me for a reason."

"Jatin never showed up before the event started," she said finally. "I guess he just sort of appeared at some point, but I don't know when." She ran a manicured nail across the table, continued studying her tea. "I'm not sure what to tell the police — if anything. I'm not sure if it matters."

"Did anyone else notice he was gone?"

"Barbara." She shrugged narrow shoulders. "Barb was worried at first, when we were waiting to take off, but then the groups started going, one by one, not together, and hers took off before his. I left with the second wave. To get photos of the girls. Especially the girls." Her smile lacked humor. "They wanted the female students captured on film."

"For good PR."

"Of course. It may seem like I was just a tagalong, Megan, but you have to understand that in a twisted way, I was the main feature. The sad truth is that without a rendering of the event, without the right pictures, the right spin, this would simply be another nonprofit outing."

"For BOLD to profit from it, they needed you there to capture the kids, the hike, the selfless volunteers."

Martine sat back in her chair. "It's the way of the world right now. Look at your friends on Facebook. Do they really live the happy lives they portray, with loving spouses and well-dressed children who never whine or complain? They don't post the picture of Daddy after he's taken care of vomiting children for three days, or Mommy when she gets back from a three-day work trip and the house is a wreck." Martine tapped her fingers on the table to emphasize her points. "We all tell a story. It's a matter of whose story is most compelling."

From her tone, Megan couldn't tell if this was a mission she believed in, or whether she'd simply become pragmatic over time.

"And Chase — where did he fit in with this story?"

"He was one of the company's best visionaries, believe it or not. Some would say he had no conscience, which allowed him to think up ideas others would censor. Others felt he could lead the company into the future. That's why he was promoted to

Strategy after such a short tenure with the company." Martine took a small sip of the tea. "I was to focus on him. Barbara wanted to do a piece on his rags to riches story."

"Rags to riches?"

Martine nodded. "Poor family. Scholarship student. After losing his way to drugs and debauchery in the music industry, he put himself through graduate school. A real success story."

Megan thought of the crude and obnoxious man she'd met at dinner. "Chase as the face of BOLD?"

"Just one face of BOLD. We are building out an image of diversity. Another reason for the outing."

"Tell me, Martine," Megan said, thinking of Martine's comment — that some thought Chase could lead the company someday. "With Chase gone, who serves to gain?"

"That's just it. I don't know."

"Would Jatin move up with Chase out of the way?"

"I don't see how. He's in Finance. He's great at his job, but BOLD never has the finance guys running the show. It's always a scientist."

"What did Jatin say he was doing when Chase was killed?"

"I was so focused on getting good camera

angles that I didn't pay any attention to where anyone was. Who knew —" her voice cracked, "— who knew that would happen?"

Megan gave Martine a moment to collect herself. Eventually, she said, "Whatever whereabouts Jatin gave the police, I'm sure they checked them out. Chief King seems young, but he knows what he's doing."

She nodded, looking unconvinced.

"You still seem upset."

Martine took a deep breath, steeling herself for something. "Jatin and Chase had an argument the night before. Chase's room was next to mine. I . . . let's just say I could hear the shouting."

Megan considered this. "Did you catch what they were fighting about?"

Martine frowned. "I'm not sure. Maybe money. I wish I could say for sure."

"And you think —"

"I don't *think* anything," Martine said quickly. "That's why I wanted Denver's opinion. I do remember listening to them — I couldn't help it, honestly, because they were so loud — and thinking that Jatin was angrier than I'd ever witnessed before. He's usually a pretty quiet guy." She took a sip of her tea. "I like Jatin. He's probably the politest of that group. But when I heard them . . . and then what happened to Chase. I can't

107

even imagine, but I was worried."

"I understand."

"Do you?" Martine looked at her quizzically. "I'm not sure I would. And frankly, now that I'm saying this all aloud, I realize how silly it sounds. Of course, Jatin would never have hurt Chase."

"Yet someone did."

Megan looked up, startled by the voice. It was Denver, who'd somehow managed to come in without being seen, probably because she and Martine had been so engrossed in their conversation. He was wearing a gray Colorado State t-shirt pulled tight across chest muscles. His auburn hair was tousled, his face chiseled under a dusting of beard. His blue eyes looked concerned, annoyed even.

Denver slipped into a seat next to Megan. He said, "Martine, someone killed Chase. Everyone is a suspect at this point. If you heard something, you need to tell King. Let the police sort it out."

Martine stared at him, eyes wide, as though he were larger than life. Megan studied her boyfriend, seeing him through the eyes of this stranger. Storybook handsome. Strong hands, neatly clipped nails scrubbed clean, the dried strip of mud above his left brow, the sheer weight of his presence.

Denver said curtly, "What were Jatin and Chase discussing? Did ye hear any of the details?"

She shook her head. "That's just it. Had I heard something specific, I'd know what to do. It was simply shouting. They could have been arguing about whether to have eggs or muffins in the morning."

"But you know they weren't, or you wouldn't be here." Denver leaned in toward her, and Martine didn't move. "They wouldn't have been shouting over nonsense."

Face pale, eyes narrow, Martine looked ready to cry. "I don't want to get Jatin in trouble if it's nothing."

"Jatin didn't do anything, but let him answer to King," Denver said.

"For all you know, he already told King all of this," Megan said. "And you're torturing yourself over nothing."

Martine looked unconvinced. "King is a fair man?"

Megan nodded. She pulled her cell out of her purse and speed-dialed the chief. He answered immediately.

"What's up, Megan?"

Megan explained the situation.

"Be right there." King hesitated. "Stay

with her, okay? Just until I can get there? I don't want her to get cold feet."

Megan agreed. She was watching the way Martine Pringle was staring at Denver. Megan didn't think Martine would go anywhere as long as Denver was present too.

"What do you make of all of that?" Megan asked.

She and Denver were back at his house, sitting on the back deck of his bungalow, looking at the stars and playing with his five rescue dogs. The Golden Retriever asked repeatedly to play fetch with Megan, and after a half hour of throwing the tennis ball into the dark abyss of the backyard, Megan finally told her to be still.

"I don't know what to make of it. I've known Jatin nearly as long as I've known Chase and Xavier. He's probably the best of the bunch, as morals and integrity go."

"You don't suspect him?"

Denver rubbed his eyes, shook his head. He took a long swig of beer from a bottle he kept on the table between them. "I don't know what to think. I meant what I said to Martine. I guess everyone is a suspect."

"She seemed pretty upset."

"She's a hell of an actress."

Megan's eyebrows shot up. "You don't like

her much."

"Can you tell?"

Denver was sinking into a funk again, so Megan opted to shift topics. "How is Dillon? Have you heard anything more from Eloise?"

"They transferred him to the psychiatric unit at the hospital where he'll receive a full evaluation. He's still not talking."

"But he spoke to Eloise at the hospital. We both heard him."

The Golden Retriever nudged Denver's arm with the ball, and he gave in to her, throwing the object nearly into the woods. "She says it was nothing. That he mumbled a few words about being in the hospital and going home."

"But it means he can talk. He's not truly in some catatonic state."

"Aye." Denver finished his beer, placed the empty bottle on the table, and sat back in his chair. "I suppose that will be part of the evaluation. Poor laddie." Denver lapsed into a heavier brogue. "As though he hasn't been through enough."

Megan said, "And I'm afraid things are only going to get worse."

Denver nodded. He reached across the table and took Megan's hand. He stroked her fingers with his own in long, gentle caresses. "I wish there was a way I could help him. And Eloise," Denver said. "She's so upset right now. I don't know that I have ever seen her so upset. And Dillon . . . I don't know what to think, to be honest."

"It must be excruciating for Eloise," Megan said. "Taking in a boy like Dillon, someone who's been through so much. Setting him up in a special school, trying to provide him with a safe and loving environment, and now this. One way or another it will have an impact."

"True," Denver said, squeezing her hand. "If he is innocent, and I have to believe he is, he witnessed something atrocious."

Again, Megan thought. How much could one kid take? She didn't know much of Dillon's history, but she knew his father killed his mother. Could that have caused him to explode and do something heinous? Although she also wanted to believe him incapable of murder, she wasn't as convinced.

"I'm tired, Megs," Denver said. "I think I need some sleep and some perspective."

He *sounded* tired. Megan knew the life of a country vet meant middle of the night calls. Denver sometimes traded on-call shifts with neighboring vets, but there were only so many large animal veterinarians in

112

this part of Pennsylvania. He was rarely assured a full night's sleep.

"I'm heading out," Megan said. She stood and stretched. The Golden made another attempt to engage Megan in ball-throwing, but it was half-hearted. Even she looked tired.

"You could stay," Denver said. "It's nearly midnight."

Megan looked out into the dark yard and the woods beyond. Bibi would be home asleep, guarded by Sadie and Gunther. The thought of driving home now was unappealing. The thought of being curled up next to Denver until morning — most appealing.

Megan smiled. "Let me text my grandmother. I think I'll stay."

TEN

By Tuesday, news of Chase's death had reached the media, and Winsome was besieged by journalists. Megan left the café for Clover, Emily, and Alvaro to cover, and decided to focus on the farm. Selfishly, she needed to be away from the commotion. The café, as the only real hang-out along Winsome's cobblestoned, historic main drag, Canal Street, had become a hotspot for reporters. Most were simply taking up tables, using the space to type up notes and make phone calls, but occasionally questions were asked. Megan, more in the know than anyone else at the café, didn't want to be put on the spot.

It was a beautiful June day. The sun overhead shown bright against a backdrop of lapis lazuli. The massive barn, its newer portions — the part that housed the pizza farm — deep red, contrasted beautifully against the greens of the forest beyond. The

114

only noise came from the construction on the adjoining property, and even that amounted to the comforting murmur of voices and an occasional hammer.

It should have been a peaceful scene. And it would have been — without murder in the background. Chase's murder, the cold way he was stabbed, stuck with Megan and intruded on her thoughts. It was an act of anger, rage. Dillon was large enough to do it. Given his background, he could have been angry enough to do it. But why Chase? And from what Megan knew, Chase had gone to the lakeshore to help the kid. To bring him back to the group.

Then again, Megan had seen Chase in action. Who knows what he'd said in his effort to *help*?

Megan was harvesting kale. She pulled leaves from the plants lined up in the long beds outside. Dinosaur, Red Russian, Siberian, Tuscan . . . keeping the varieties in separate coolers of ice-cold water, which she pulled behind her on a wagon. Alvaro needed the greens for a stuffed puff pastry dish he was making. Garlic, spices, herbs, sautéed greens, roasted mushrooms, all covered with a layer of golden puff pastry. Another nod to Clover, but sure to be a hit.

She clipped another Red Russian leaf and

placed it in the cooler, taking the time to inspect the plant. As the weather got warmer, the kale suffered. This plant was healthy, no signs of aphids. Satisfied, she moved to the next plant.

That's when she heard it: a helicopter overhead. News sign emblazoned on the side.

Megan looked up, watched it move on, toward the west. In the direction of the hospital where Dillon currently resided. He was still a teen; surely, they couldn't disclose his name or any information about him. Unless he was being charged with a crime. As an adult.

Megan pulled off her gloves. She took the coolers back to the barn, used the hose to clean the leaves thoroughly, and packed them in accordance with variety. She'd have Porter, her farm hand, drop them off for Alvaro.

Megan considered the conversation she'd had with Martine a few days earlier. She hadn't heard anything more from the woman, or from King for that matter. Things had been eerily quiet. She fished her phone out of the pocket of her jeans. She flipped from CNN to local stations. Nothing new on the murder.

Finished with this chore, Megan went in

search of Porter. She'd take a break for the afternoon. King wanted her help keeping Eloise Kent cooperative. That meant she needed facts. If the reporters were going after Dillon, something must have transpired. She needed to figure out what.

King was out, and his next in charge wouldn't tell her anything. Megan left the police station and headed to the Bucks County Inn. Plan B: she'd try to meet with Martine or one of the others. She thought of calling Eloise, but Denver said she hadn't been answering her phone. She was busy procuring resources for her foster son, he said, and would be hard to reach.

That also sounded like a bad omen. But Denver didn't know more.

The Bucks County Inn was a neat stone Colonial tucked back off the road, a few miles from Winsome proper. Megan had looked at the inn's website before coming over. The main structure housed half a dozen en suite guest rooms. Two outbuildings — a small cottage and a barn — offered a cozy couple's retreat and a small apartment, respectively. If Martine had heard Chase and Jatin arguing through the walls, that meant she was in the main house.

Inside, two matching desks flanked a large

center hall entryway. Wide-plank pine floors, a navy area rug in front of the doorway. A white-muzzled Schnauzer with a Scottish plaid collar padded over slowly and greeted her at the door. Soon after, a white-haired older woman in a Scottish plaid skirt, white cardigan, and white sandals joined the dog and welcomed Megan with a warm smile.

"How can I help you, dear?"

"I'm looking for Martine Pringle. I understand she's staying here."

"Oh, yes. Poor thing." The woman walked toward the desk on the left and shuffled through papers. Pulling one from the pile, she glanced up at Megan. "Your name, dear?"

"Megan Sawyer."

The woman smiled again, highlighting warm green eyes and a set of dimples. "The Washington Acres lady! So nice to meet you. I'm the Inn's owner." She picked up the phone, dialed, and waited. When no one answered, she put the receiver back in the cradle. "I'm afraid Martine isn't answering. She must have gone out for a bit." She frowned. "Come to think of it, I didn't see her at breakfast this morning either."

"Could she still be sleeping?"

"I guess. I don't normally keep track of

my guests, other than to make sure every-thing is locked up in the evening once all of the guests are back." She lowered her voice. "Of course, these aren't normal times, are they?"

"No, they're not." Megan paused, listen-ing for footsteps and sounds overhead — anything indicating someone else was here. "Martine came home last evening?"

"Martine never left, to the best of my knowledge. Her Volkswagen is still here. Her friends didn't mention anything." Concern flashed across the innkeeper's pleasant features. "You don't think she left without paying?"

"Oh, gosh, no. Given everything, I was afraid —"

"Oh! Yes, I should have thought of that." The woman's face flushed crimson. "Sorry. It's been a long week. We've had the police by almost every day. I can tell you, that's never good for business."

"How about the rest of the group? Bar-bara and Xavier and Jatin. Are they around?"

"They left earlier, after asking me to set the apartment aside for their boss. Appar-ently, she will be flying in from California and staying with us as well." She picked up the phone again. "Let me try Martine one

119

more time."

When again no one answered, the innkeeper used a key on a ring attached to her skirt to open a desk drawer. From inside, she pulled an old-fashioned looking brass key. She held it up. "Let me check on her."

Megan nodded, concerned. Martine had been agitated on Sunday night, but neither Megan nor Denver had talked with her since Martine had met with Chief King. Megan didn't know what had come of that meeting or whether there had been backlash against Martine. Maybe she was now a pariah from the others from BOLD. Maybe she was missing.

The innkeeper came down the long staircase, shaking her head slowly back and forth. "I have to admit, I was a little worried." She strode back to her desk, the Schnauzer leaving her post by the door into the kitchen to join her. "She's okay. A little out of it, but okay. I told her you were here, and she said to give her ten minutes. She's going to get dressed and she'll be down."

The innkeeper placed the key back in the desk. She looked out the window before turning her attention to Megan once again. "One thing," she said. "Martine asked that if the others return, you not mention Sunday. Whatever that means." The look on her

120

face said she'd love to know *what* that means.

Megan nodded, giving her nothing.

Clearly disappointed, the innkeeper cleared her throat. "Would you like some hot tea while you wait? Some nice orange pekoe? Or maybe English Breakfast?"

"That would be lovely."

"Come with me to the kitchen. I'll show you around."

Megan followed her through a rear doorway and into a large dining room. One large farmhouse table filled the space with twelve matching chairs around it and a matching buffet behind it. A giant flower centerpiece scented the air with the perfume of lilies and hyacinths. The dining room looked out onto a large veranda set with four smaller sets of tables and chairs. From the dining room they opened a door into an annex — the kitchen.

"I don't have guests back here. Or the dog. Code violation, you know." The woman turned on a spigot over the large stainless farmhouse sink and filled a teapot with water. She motioned to the kitchen, which, unlike the rest of the house, was filled with stainless steel and white tile. Modern, clean, and efficient.

"It's lovely."

"Thank you, dear. I normally serve home-made granola, yogurt, fruit, and sweet breads for breakfast. Sometimes pancakes on the weekends. And once in a while I'll make a dinner if someone asks. I love to cook." She smiled shyly. "Can't compete with your Alvaro, though. He's gotten himself quite a reputation."

"I lucked out when he came to the café."

"You did, dear. Hold on to that one."

Megan smiled. She was anxious to talk to Martine, but she appreciated the tour of the competition. Their inn, if it ever got off its feet, would have a large commercial kitchen with teaching space. Not as high-end as this, perhaps, but similar.

The innkeeper placed the teapot on the gas stovetop. She began rummaging through the Sub Zero refrigerator. "These guests — the people from BOLD — they like snacks in the afternoon. I've been making them cheese and crackers. Would you like some, dear?"

"I'm fine, thanks."

"Mind if I put a plate together while we chat?"

"Not at all." Although Megan wondered what they would chat about. She didn't have to wonder long.

"This group — are they friends of yours?"

The woman pulled three plastic-wrapped chunks of cheese from the refrigerator and placed them on the stainless-topped island. She added an unwrapped summer sausage and a bottle of mustard. "They seem very nice."

"I don't really know them. Some of them went to school with my boyfriend."

"That nice Dr. Finn?" Then, after a glance at Megan, "Don't look so surprised, dear. Those of us in the hospitality business keep tabs on the competition. Plus, there was that murder last year. You and Dr. Finn were in the news."

"Yeah, it was a rough year."

"I'll say." She unwrapped a hunk of cheddar and placed it on a serving plate. The teapot whistled, and she paused to fill two mugs with boiling water. "Here you go, dear. Honey or cream?"

When Megan declined both, the innkeeper returned to her cheese tray and the topic at hand. "They're an interesting group of people. A few of them really keep to themselves. Martine. That Barbara."

"Barbara, really? She seems pretty outgoing."

"Has said maybe a dozen words since she arrived. Not like that Xavier. Orders the others around. Always has a complaint."

Her mouth tightened into a small knot in the bottom center of her face. "I don't mind telling you this," she whispered, "because you're in the trade, but some guests make you happy to be in the hospitality field. Others wish you had gone into accounting like your mother suggested."

Megan laughed. "And Xavier does the latter."

She answered with a deeper frown. Megan watched as the woman sliced a large slab of Gouda from a wheel and placed it on the tray. The innkeeper studied the tray, returned to the refrigerator, and came back with a roll of goat cheese and some fig jam. "Xavier likes variety." Her tone told Megan just what she thought about *that*.

Megan laughed. She looked into the hallway to see if Martine was nearby. With no sign of her, Megan stood as close as she could to the innkeeper without seeming odd. "Did you notice any tension between members of the group on Friday night?" she asked.

Only the woman didn't look surprised by the question. She put the knife down on the counter and placed her hands on her hips, her expression thoughtful. "Now that you mention it, I had a guest complain about noise."

"Noise?"

"Bickering. Loud bickering. When I asked for the room from which it was coming, they told me room four."

"Whose room is that?" Megan asked, suspecting she already knew.

"That's Barbara's room, which is why I was surprised. She's so quiet. I asked several times to be sure the guest had heard right, but he and his wife were adamant."

"A male voice along with Barbara's?"

"I didn't ask, and he didn't offer."

Megan considered that. "It was definitely Friday night?"

"Yes." She gave a firm nod. "The couple was celebrating their tenth anniversary. They stopped on their way to New York City. Coming up from Delaware."

"Is it possible Barbara had her speaker phone on? That the voice they heard was a caller — not someone in the room with her?"

The innkeeper tilted her head. "You know, I didn't ask that, but they seemed quite adamant that there were people in the room." She paused. "And the woman said someone slammed the door. Hard. It dislodged a vase in their room and it crashed to the floor."

"Did you ask Barbara or Martine the next day?"

The innkeeper nodded. "I brought it up with Barbara because the noise was coming from her room. She flat out denied it. Said someone must have heard wrong. That she went right to bed and slept soundly until morning."

Megan was processing this when a small voice said, "Megan?"

Megan looked over in time to see Martine slipping around the corner. She wore her blonde hair loose around her shoulders. Straight and fine, it lay flat against her face. Dark denim jeans were pressed to a fine crease, and a frilly rose-colored blouse fell at her hips. A floral belt around her narrow waist pulled it all together.

"How are you, Martine?"

Martine didn't answer, but she didn't need to. Her ivory skin was alpine white. Eyes were red-rimmed, with bruised hollows underneath. She looked as though she'd lost ten pounds off her tiny frame in days. Megan felt a wave of sympathy course through her. Martine looked like she'd been through hell.

Megan had to wonder whether there had been more between Martine Pringle and Charles Mars than either had let on.

"Can we talk for a few minutes?" Megan asked.

"Sure." To the innkeeper, Martine asked, "May I take an apple?"

"Of course, dear." With a knowing glance at Megan, she handed Martine an apple from a basket on the counter. "Your fellow colleagues are expected soon, Martine. You may use the veranda if you'd like. It's quiet. Or if you want more privacy, there is a guest study on the second floor, past the library table."

"That would be wonderful. Thank you."

Martine dug into the apple as she led Megan back into the public area of the house and up the grand staircase. Megan admired the chestnut railings, the sheer width of the steps. She looked up. The staircase continued to a third floor, but Martine stopped on the second.

"This way," she said. She continued down a wide hallway adorned with eighteenth century artwork and paused at room two. "Hold on for a second, okay? I need to grab my phone."

Martine opened the door, and leaving it wide open, ran inside. Megan could make out a neatly made bed covered with a navy blue-patterned quilt, a stately oak dresser, an upholstered chair, also navy, a window seat, and a closet door. The rest of the room was blocked by a wall, behind which Martine disappeared. Megan presumed it was the en suite bath.

Seconds later, Martine returned with her cell phone and a sweater. "Chilly in here." She locked the door and continued down the hall, past a narrow secretary that housed stacks of paperbacks and hardcovers — the library table — and rooms three and four.

"Which was Chase's room?"

"Room one," Martine said. She pointed down the hall. "The police have been through it. Room's empty now."

"I'm surprised you all stayed here."

Martine opened the door to a small room. Inside sat a cheery Queen Ann style desk, matching wooden chair, and two plaid upholstered wing chairs that shared a coffee table. More eighteenth century artwork on the walls. A navy-blue area rug. The faint scent of musky male aftershave lingered in the air, mixing with cigar smoke and the faintest hint of lemon cleaner. These were old smells, as worn into the woodwork as the oils used to dust and polish.

"I don't think this room gets much use," Martine said. She sat on one of the upholstered chairs. Megan chose the wooden desk chair, but she turned it around, so it was facing Martine.

"I wanted to check on you. See how things went with King."

"They went as well as could be expected. I talked, he listened. I asked him if his people already knew about the argument, he was noncommittal." She shrugged. "Traitor to friendship, but civil duty done."

Megan smiled. "I'm sure Chief King followed up with Jatin."

"I have no idea. Jatin doesn't seem to be speaking to me. Or any of us, for that matter."

"Did he go with the others to get Barbara's boss, Harriet?"

"I have no idea. Barbara texted me and said they were heading out, did I want to come. I stayed behind. Worked for a while on some damage control. Contacted the social worker in charge of Dillon's case to see how he's doing, handled some media requests. Took some happy pills and went to sleep."

"That's actually what I wanted to talk to you about: Dillon."

"What about him?"

"The news crews are in town. Many are hanging out at my café, so I know they're all over this story. It feels like *maybe* something broke, but nothing's been said. I saw the chopper headed toward the hospital where Dillon's been admitted. I thought, maybe —"

"If you're wondering if I spilled his name to the media, the answer is no. He's a minor."

"That's not what I was going to ask."

"What then?" Martine crossed her arms over her chest, looking suddenly defensive.

"I thought maybe the police found some new clue, something to point to a killer."

"Oh." Martine took an audible breath. "What I know about Dillon, I'm afraid it's not much. The social worker was not very forthcoming. Said Dillon is under a doctor's care, and that all inquiries should be directed to the police or the hospital staff." She sighed. "That's about when I took my happy pill."

Megan could understand the social worker's position. The agency that placed him wouldn't disclose information, and neither would the police or the hospital. Not to Martine, at least. Megan had been hoping there'd been a break in the case. One that didn't involve Dillon.

Didn't sound like it, though.

"Tell me, what does 'damage control' look like in a situation like this?"

Martine let out a strained laugh. "I can

honestly tell you I've never been through this before, so it's hard for me to know. Rather than publishing photographs of the happy campers and doing all of the media and social media outreach I would normally do, I'm left on the defensive. Fending off inquiries, making brief statements. Talking with our lawyers."

"Your lawyers?"

"The company organized this event. Those kids suffered trauma. Not our fault, certainly, but the second guessers are already out there. Were our employees vetted? Did we have adequate staff on site? Did we knowingly allow kids with mental health problems to participate, putting themselves and others in danger?" She frowned. "We're preparing for the worst."

Megan's mind was stuck on the words "with mental health problems." Didn't all of these kids have problems of some sort? Wasn't that why they were in the school in the first place?

"I sound cold," Martine said. "I've been stuck here for days with nothing but this situation to dwell on. I don't know who to trust, and no one is telling us anything. I can't get away from them." She motioned toward the hall and, presumably, her co-workers. "It's enough to drive anyone crazy."

Megan heard a car pull into the driveway outside. She walked to the window and peeked outside. A black Tahoe was parking next to her truck. After a few moments, Barbara climbed out of the driver's side. Xavier and a tall woman Megan didn't recognize joined her.

"I think your friends are back," Megan said.

"They're not my friends." Martine threw her head back, exposing a slender neck and a lacy rash above her collarbone. "And nothing will get better with Harriet here."

"But she's the big boss."

Martine nodded, stood. "Dr. Harriet Mantra. One of BOLD's founding members."

"This charity event was her brainchild, right?"

Martine sighed. "Yep. And now that brainchild is dead. And Harriet is livid."

Eleven

Martine slipped back in her room, leaving Megan to negotiate her way back down to the center hall. The innkeeper was there, checking in Harriet. Xavier and Barbara were huddled by the desk, waiting. The friendly Schnauzer seemed wary of the stranger. She was leaning away from her and against Barbara's leg. Barbara rewarded her with a quick pat.

"Megan," Xavier said, managing to sound surprised and sarcastic at the same time. "What brings you to the beautiful Bucks County Inn? Did our dear friend Daniel send you?"

"I thought I would check on you, see if you were okay."

"No Denver?" Barbara's smile had all the energy of a dead battery. "We haven't seen him since Saturday."

"He's been caught up with his practice and his aunt."

"Oh, I'd forgotten that the boy was her foster child. She must be terrified, having lived with a killer under her roof." Before Megan could respond, Xavier nodded toward the new woman. "This is Dr. Harriet Mantra, CEO and Chief Strategist at BOLD."

As though on cue, the woman finished with the innkeeper and turned. Up close, she seemed even taller — close to six foot. She had long, thick, straight black hair, slightly frizzy on the ends. Expertly applied makeup tried to shave ten years off her fifty-five or so, and the monotone pantsuit succeeded in trimming ten pounds. More striking than beautiful, Harriet Mantra had a strong jaw, handsome features, and a pair of piercing eyes. These eyes bore into Megan's with an intelligent ferocity that was almost intimidating.

Almost. Megan had spent too much time in a courtroom back in her law firm days to be easily cowed. But she recognized someone used to moving mountains — on their own terms.

"Megan Sawyer." Megan held out her hand. The return grip was firm, Harriet's skin smooth and dry.

"Megan Sawyer? Are you with the law firm we hired?" The glance Harriet threw at

Barbara asked the same question: Why is this woman here?

"No, I'm not."

"Megan is a friend of a friend," Barbara said. "A local business-owner and the girlfriend of a college friend."

Harriet's expression said if Megan wasn't with the police or a lawyer, she'd already dismissed her as irrelevant.

"Nice to meet you, Megan. You've heard all about what happened to Charles. We have some business to attend to. I'm sure you understand."

"Of course."

Barbara and Xavier exchanged a look. "Good to see you, Megan," Barbara said. "Please tell Denver not to be a stranger."

Harriet was already walking toward the veranda, which would lead out to the barn apartment. Her bags stood next to the desk, probably for the innkeeper to handle. Harriet had her hand on the knob leading outside, and without turning around, she said, "Please make sure Ms. Sawyer doesn't tell anyone where we're staying. The press are here — I saw the vans on our way in. It would be unfortunate if they discovered our whereabouts. This lovely inn would become a zoo."

Megan said, "I'm still here, Dr. Mantra. I

can hear you. And I won't be the one who tells reporters where you are."

"Good." Harriet pushed open the door. "Xavier, my bag," she called over her shoulder.

When Harriet was out of earshot, Xavier looked at Barbara and laughed. Barbara didn't look so amused.

"She's an acquired taste," Xavier said. "Absolutely brilliant. She took the company from a few scientists to a real competitor. Unfortunately, with that amount of brilliance comes a degree of narcissism."

"A degree?" Barbara shook her head. "You'd better get the bags to her. Otherwise, we'll both be getting irate text messages."

"That bad?" Megan said once Xavier had gone.

"Worse. That was her *good* behavior. Only certain people can work with her because BOLD considers her a lawsuit risk." Barbara shook her head. "I can see why her daughter avoids her at all costs." She closed her eyes. "And why there was so much tension between them growing up. So much so that Harriet sent her across the country."

"There must be good schools like that in California."

"Harriet has family here. Plus, in my opinion — so don't repeat it — I think she

136

wanted her daughter away. As in miles and miles away."

Interesting. Megan had assumed Harriet's daughter had been a ward of the Commonwealth, like Dillon, but if Harriet had a choice, perhaps the school was private. "That means the school accepts paying students?" Megan asked.

Barbara nodded. "As a matter of fact, I think it's mostly students who pay tuition. Does that matter?"

"No," Megan said quickly. "I was just wondering about Dillon. How did he get in — and who was footing the bill?"

"Maybe that nice doctor? The one who fostered him?"

"Maybe," Megan said. She doubted tuition was cheap, and that seemed above and beyond even Eloise's willingness to be altruistic.

Barbara said, "Anyway, Harriet's daughter was facing a pretty big choice. A special school or real, hard time — meaning a lock-up facility. A few too many thefts and a fire, at least that's what I heard."

"And the judge let her go to a private school? With that much on her record, it sounds like juvie would have been appropriate."

Barbara smiled. "Good to know people in

137

high places. When Harriet wants something, it generally happens."

Megan knew how that worked. A few words with the right people and the wealthy executive's daughter was flying first class to Philadelphia. Meanwhile, some kid with half her record would celebrate his birthday in lock-up.

Maybe it was time to visit Pioneer Village School.

"It's a messed-up world," Barbara said. She looked out on the veranda and watched as Xavier made his way back to the inn. He was carrying towels and a heavy white terry robe. His eyes were angry squints.

When he neared the entrance, Barbara said, "Harriet thinks the linens are dirty."

"And she's making Xavier return them?"

Barbara nodded. "Been there, done that." She watched as Xavier dropped a towel, kicked it, and picked it up with two fingers, looking disgusted. Barbara laughed. "A crazy, awful, messed-up world."

Pioneer Village School was located seventeen miles West of Winsome, in a small hamlet called Blessings, Pennsylvania. Megan drove along a series of back roads, watching the bucolic countryside give way to forest and the occasional abandoned fac-

138

tory or store reclaimed by nature. Her interest in the school had been piqued by her conversation with Barbara. She hadn't expected it to be in such a remote location.

Megan thought she'd been everywhere in this part of Pennsylvania, but she'd never been to — or heard of — Blessings. Indeed, the town was more of a village. Sneeze, and you'd miss the town center, which consisted of a Victorian home reinvented as the town hall; a narrow, stone Catholic church; a luncheonette advertising $3.99 breakfasts; a Chinese take-out restaurant; a post office; and a bank. Further down the road, Megan saw signs for a bird sanctuary and nature center, and three miles beyond that was the driveway of what Megan presumed to be the Pioneer Village School.

Two stone black bears and a large rock surrounded by pink and white impatiens marked the entrance. No sign announced the school, but the street number — 555 — matched the address she'd found online.

Megan made a left and followed the driveway down a short, tree-lined drive until she reached the parking lot. She pulled into a visitor's spot and looked up at the sprawling structure before her. The school was built of brick. A central square stood sentry, jutting forward toward the parking lot, three

three-story arched windows only deepening the building's intimidation factor. Two wings emerged from either side of the central portion, their windows plain rectangles topped with arched stained-glass panes.

No barred windows, no barbed wire fencing. It was an imposing building, and the exterior lacked warmth, but it didn't scream "institution." Megan got out of the car. As she walked toward the entrance, she wondered what it would be like to be a student here, to drive up that drive for the first time. She wondered what it had been like for Dillon.

How his life must have changed overnight. One day, two parents. The next day, both are whisked away. Strangers became his world.

The front door was unlocked, and Megan pushed it open carefully. It led her into a wide vestibule. On one side, a young woman with a bright red pixie haircut sat at a large Mission oak desk. She was small and slender and consumed by the big piece of furniture. A phone was positioned on her left side, a computer was chained to the desk in front of her, and it was hard to miss the suspicion in her eyes as Megan approached the desk.

"Dr. Star will be with you shortly." Clipped British accent. Her tone was less than welcoming.

"I'm here —" Megan said.

But the woman was already on the phone.

Megan leaned over the desk. "Really, I'm not —"

The woman waved her hand and shushed her. She murmured something into the phone, hung up, and returned to her computer, dismissing Megan. Megan realized she had no good reason for being there — other than curiosity and a strange feeling that the school was somehow tied to all that was going on — but she hadn't been shushed in a professional setting in forever, and she would be damned if she was going to be forthcoming with the receptionist after that.

A few minutes later, a startlingly handsome man in his fifties wearing pressed khakis and a button-down blue gingham shirt walked into the reception area. He nodded at Megan and motioned for her to follow him. Together they walked down a wood-floored hallway and into a spacious office. A wooden plaque on the desk said, "Dr. Star." Two banks of filing cabinets and a printer and printer stand, plus two black upholstered chairs, made up the contents of the office. No photos, no personal items. One large arched window overlooked a manicured lawn and a set of tennis courts. The lawn was pristine; the courts had seen better days.

Megan recognized his name from a conversation with Eloise. This was the school's psychotherapist.

"The kids here don't tend to enjoy tennis," Dr. Star said, following Megan's gaze. "They're more into video games than physical games, which is why we jumped at the chance to get them outside and hiking. Nature has a way of healing." Dr. Star turned and studied Megan. "What do you want to know, Ms. Lewis? My receptionist tells me you've been very persistent. I'll be candid, but I'd appreciate it if you wouldn't drag the school into the fray. These kids have been through enough."

"I'm afraid I'm not who you think I am."

Megan watched as Dr. Star's eyes narrowed, going from cautious to outright distrustful. "Come again?"

"It's a case of mistaken identity. I just want information about the school. I'm not Ms. Lewis — whoever that is."

Dr. Star sat back in his chair and, to Megan's surprise, started to laugh. "Ah, well, you didn't look like the fiend my receptionist made Donna Lewis out to be." He stood, leaned over the desk, and shook

Megan's hand. "My apologies. My staff can get impatient. Your real name, then?"

Megan told him. "It's a lovely setting."

"Yes, it is. As I said, we hope the woods have healing properties for our kids. Sometimes that works, sometimes it doesn't." The phone buzzed, and Dr. Star picked it up. "Ah, it seems you made an error. Yes . . . bring her down . . . that's fine." He hung up. "Do you have a child for whom the school might be a good fit?"

"I know someone who could benefit."

"Not your child."

Thinking of Dillon, Megan said, "No, not mine."

"There are brochures at the receptionist's desk. We don't do interventions, so if there are parents or guardians who would need to be brought on board, that would have to happen outside of us, and they would need to contact us personally." His smile was apologetic, and he held Megan's gaze for a few beats too long. "You understand."

"I'd just appreciate a better sense of what the school does so I can tee it up to my friends."

"The doctors here, they play with kids' heads, that's what they do," said a voice behind Megan. "But only if they're rich." Megan turned in her seat and saw the red-haired receptionist standing next to a short, stout woman with silver hair, dressed head to toe in blueberry blue. "Dr. Star? Donna Lewis from *The Bucks County Times.* You're a hard man to pin down."

The receptionist looked stricken. The doctor smiled.

He said, "I'm glad you managed to find me."

"I'm sure you are." Donna Lewis seemed to notice Megan for the first time. "I see someone else got to you first."

"Ms. Sawyer was just leaving." He shook Megan's hand, his gaze warm. To his receptionist, he said, "Can you give Ms. Sawyer some brochures? Maybe provide a high-level overview of the program? I'll need some time with Donna."

As Megan left the doctor's office, she could hear Donna say, "It's about time you agreed to see me, Dr. Star. After the atrocity your student committed, you owe the community information about exactly what goes on in this hellhole."

TWELVE

"What goes on here," the receptionist said, "is old-fashioned treatment." She slid two brochures across the desk to Megan. "Cognitive behavioral, mostly. We have a psychiatrist on staff when we need her."

"For pharmacological treatment?"

"If absolutely required." Connie tilted her head. "That's not our primary treatment modality."

Megan skimmed through the brochures: glossy, small print, lots of photos of the woods. A shot of the tennis courts looking new and neat. Selling a fantasy to parents? Come here and we'll pull your child out of her or his head and into the real world of fresh air and mainstream sports? Megan's eyes settled on one line: children of high-intellect.

A school for gifted children? Gifted children with emotional issues?

Megan said, "My nephew, he has special

needs. Specifically, his IQ is . . . higher than average."

"Is it above 135?"

"I believe so. Is that a problem?"

"That's the threshold for admission." She met Megan's gaze with unexpected sympathy. "The IQ requirement can be a problem. Some kids would benefit from the program, but they just don't meet the testing rules. A point or two will keep them out." She shrugged. "We've been lobbying Dr. Star for years to provide other avenues — other tests — for admittance. Unfortunately, he feels this is an absolute prerequisite for the type of treatments here."

This made a certain sense, given Dillon's intelligence. Megan smiled. "Well, hopefully he's bright enough. Appreciate your time."

As Megan headed back outside, she heard the receptionist say, "What's your nephew's name? In case his parents call —"

Megan kept walking and pretended she couldn't hear her.

Megan snapped off a garlic scape, lifted it toward the dying sun, and squinted. "What does Alvaro plan to make with these?"

"He sautés them with other spring veggies and serves them with mashed potatoes, homemade cranberry relish, and roasted chicken. Sometimes he makes vegetable pot pie." Clover picked one and held it to her nose. "I think these may be my favorite of all the spring vegetables. And to think, most people don't even know what they are."

"Which is why we'll bring them to Saturday's farmers market." Megan started snapping them off and tossing the fronds into a bowl. They were long and thin with a curlicue on the end. Bibi was making a salad, and Megan loved fresh scapes raw.

"Makes sense." Clover plopped down on the ground and watched Megan pick vegetables for the salad. She traced a finger over the scape in her hand, her expression pensive. Finally, she said, "Bobby's not sleeping."

"Because of this case?"

"I guess." Clover frowned. "Bobby won't say it, but I think he kind of identifies with this kid."

Megan glanced up. "Dillon?" They seemed worlds apart. Bobby was from a conservative family. He and Clover still lived near them in a house they rented from his parents. Megan wasn't quite seeing the parallels.

"You were gone from Winsome when Bobby was a teen, but based on what I've managed to piece together from Bobby and

147

his parents, he went through a bad spell after his grandfather died. Truancy. Anger issues. Bullied at school." She shrugged, tossed her long hair over her shoulder. "He's having nightmares, talking in his sleep. He's been through a lot as Chief, but I haven't seen him this shaken before."

Megan mulled this over. He did seem particularly agitated when he visited her a few days back. Sympathizing with a potential suspect? Or conflicted over the direction the case was taking?

Megan made her way to the lettuce bed. She picked a large handful of baby lettuces and cut a head of Romaine. She added these to the bowl of garlic scapes.

"Has he said anything? About Dillon? About the investigation?"

"Only that it looks bad for the kid."

Megan said, "He's still in the psych unit."

"Yes, but who knows for how long. I heard that Denver's Aunt Eloise is working with the placement agency to get him help — and a good lawyer."

"Not a public defender?"

Clover cleared her throat. "The kid has money."

Megan's eyebrows shot up in surprise. "I just assumed . . . I guess I was wrong to do so."

148

Clover unfurled herself. Standing, she raised her arms over her head and stretched. "Eloise would know more, but she probably won't tell you. I bet if you do some digging, though, you can find out more about Dillon's family. His dad was a big shot in the wrestling industry. They lived north of here. Near Allentown."

"I'll have to look into it." Megan glanced around the farm, thinking about what else she wanted in her salad. Thinking about Dillon and his parents. Thinking about Bobby and Winsome. "Did Bobby say anything about the Pioneer Village School?"

"Like what?"

"I don't know. Just curious if he mentioned it."

"I'm sure he and his officers were there, but beyond that I don't know anything." Clover looked toward the barn. "Can I meet this pig of yours before dinner?"

"Sure. Want to take Camilla some apples? She loves them."

"Of course!"

"Head to the kitchen. Bibi probably has a pile sliced up for the pig." Megan smiled. "She'll tell you they're for a pie. Don't believe her."

Clover laughed. "Your grandmother always was a secret softy."

Denver joined them for dinner. Clover stayed because King was out again, working on the murder case. Bibi placed the salad on the table along with two homemade dressings and a loaf of sourdough bread. She dished out grilled cheese sandwiches to everyone except Clover. Avocado toast went in her spot at the table.

"Bonnie! You remembered." Clover hugged her. "I love avocado toast."

Bibi fought a smile. "You're going to waste away on this diet."

"It's a lifestyle, Bibi, not a diet."

Denver slid into his spot at the table. Megan noticed the shadows under his eyes, the extra growth of beard on his face. Perhaps Bobby King wasn't the only one not sleeping.

"Denver," Bibi said. "I'm glad you made it. Have some salad." She heaped salad on his plate, then cut him a thick slice of sourdough. "Butter?"

"A sandwich, salad, bread, *and* butter, Bonnie? Are ye trying to fatten me up?"

"I'm helping you keep your energy up."

"She's trying to tell you that you look tired." Clover shoved a piece of bread in her mouth — sans butter. "And she's right."

"I've had a few night calls."

"Is that it?" Clover eyed him over her toast. Softly, she said, "Or maybe it has something to do with what happened at the park."

"Clover," Megan said, "pass the salad, please?"

"Speaking of what happened, that man came into the café again today, fists swinging," Clover said to Megan, oblivious to the tension in the room. "Xavier? Went after the other one. I think his name is Jatin?"

Denver looked suddenly alert. "What happened?"

"I have no idea. One minute Jatin was sitting at a table, drinking coffee and eating a slice of pie, and the next Xavier was there. He shouted something, the place got quiet, and Alvaro asked them to leave."

"Did they?" Denver asked.

Clover nodded. "Jatin was already half out the door. Xavier gave Alvaro some lip and then he disappeared too."

Bibi poured maple vinaigrette on her salad. She put the Mason jar down and said, "This town feels like it's going to explode. I went to Bridge last night, and the murder was the only thing we discussed. What happened, who did it, why." The look she gave

Denver exuded empathy. "Of course, everyone assumes the boy did it."

"Of course," Denver said.

"I can't see a young man doing that, not without great provocation," Bibi said. "Boys turn anger outward, girls inward, if you ask me, so I could see a boy getting that angry. But not for no reason. A punch, a tantrum? But that?" She shook her head vehemently, side to side. "Not without a major incident beforehand."

"And if there had been a major incident, you would think someone would have heard something," Clover said.

Megan wasn't so sure. The area was wooded, and the rest of the students were involved with other activities. She stayed quiet, though — and watched Denver.

"Bonnie," he said calmly, "what if I told you the boy had a troubled past. That he witnessed his father harm his mother in a way that led to her death? Would that change your mind about him?"

Bibi sat back, away from the table. "I'm not an expert in child psychology."

"But you've seen a lot in your eighty-five years, Bonnie."

"Sadly, yes, I have. And people never fail to surprise me — for the good they do, and the evil."

152

Denver said, "Please. What do you think?"

Megan reached across the table and took Denver's hand. His former friend was dead, his aunt's foster son a potential murderer. Megan sensed he didn't know in what ring to toss his hat, if any at all.

"I think a young man capable of such an angry, heinous act would either be fully without conscience or would have given some indication of severe mental illness or anger issues before now. I don't know him, but I know Eloise. We haven't always seen eye to eye, but I respect her as a doctor and a person. If she believes this boy, I believe her. And from what I have heard in Winsome's version of Whisper Down the Lane, the boy is no psychopath."

Denver nodded. "Aye, I would agree."

Bibi leaned forward, eyes on Denver. "With all he went through, he's an easy answer to a hard question. But while the town and press are focused on him, someone else may be getting away with murder."

Denver didn't want to talk about it, so Megan kissed him goodbye and let him go. It broke her heart to watch him climb into his 4Runner, but she knew any pressure would be resented and result only in his retreating further. This was his way: stew

153

until ready to talk. She understood; it was her way too.

Back inside, Megan brought the laptop downstairs and set it up on the kitchen table. She could hear the murmur of Bibi's game show coming from the sitting room. Sadie and Gunther lay at her feet, one next to another, and Gunther was snoring gently. The window was open, and the air flowing in was cool and welcome.

Megan pulled up a search engine and typed in what little she knew about Dillon's family. It didn't take long to find the headlines: major news in Bethlehem, Pennsylvania, a minor blip on the national radar.

Former pro-wrestler injures wife in household incident.

Pro-wrestler indicted for domestic abuse.

And the saddest: *Child looks on as mother takes fatal fall.*

The facts were stated pretty consistently. Randy "Titus" Brown, former pro-wrestler, was arguing with his wife. She fell down the stairs, landing at the bottom, near her then thirteen-year-old son. He called 911. Her neck was broken. She died at the hospital hours later.

What was at issue was whether the father pushed the mother. The boy said no, but he didn't see the actual fall. He came running

154

when he heard her scream. Angry text messages leading up to the incident swayed the jury that Susette Brown was, at best, pushed by her husband in anger, and that it was possible her death had been premeditated. Titus got life in prison, and with no relatives willing or able to take the boy, Dillon went into the system.

Not only was Dillon viewed as a problem child, but he was the son of a pro-wrestler. No wonder the media was all over this one. His name had been leaked by someone, and despite his age, the press was bringing up his parents' ordeal again. What a hell to have to re-live.

Megan was about to close the laptop when she remembered her chat with Martine. She wondered what Xavier's fight with Jatin had been about . . . and what had him so angry he'd shouted in public.

Too tired to do much else, Megan looked up BOLD Pharmaceuticals. The "About Us" page read just as she'd expect a relatively new start-up to read. Lots of glossy promises, lots of caveats in small print. It looked like they were working on some encouraging new drugs for Multiple Sclerosis and Parkinson's disease. Megan expanded her search, looking for BOLD in the news. A few press releases, many scholarly articles in medical journals. Again, what she would expect.

She expanded further, using each of the people who worked at BOLD. Chase's name brought up articles on his murder — so many that she switched to Jatin out of sheer frustration. Nothing on Jatin, Xavier, Barbara, or Martine jumped out at her — just the normal work profiles, and for Chase, Barbara, and Martine, private social media pages.

Bibi came in to say good night, and Sadie followed her upstairs. Frustrated, Megan turned off her computer — it was time for her and Gunther to do night rounds and go to bed. On impulse, she switched her laptop back on and searched for Dillon Brown. Not an uncommon name, and her search turned up with many hits. She started to narrow it, and finally found his Instagram account under DDBrown — Dillon David Brown or, as his profile stated, Dungeons and Dragons Brown.

Dillon had uploaded four photos: two of Eloise's dogs, one of a horse, and one of him standing by a tall, brunette woman with broad shoulders and a tired smile. There was no mistaking their relationship — this was his mother, Susette Brown. He had been younger in the photo, maybe twelve.

They were standing arm-in-arm outside. The multi-colored leaves in the background said it was autumn. Both wore long-sleeved dragon t-shirts. Dillon was grinning, a plastic sword in one hand, a wand in the other.

The Renaissance Faire?

A young boy playing fantasy. Hardly the profile of a murderer.

Gunther put his great, white head on Megan's lap and whined. He wanted to check on the goats and Camilla, his internal body clock as well-tuned as any instrument. Megan shut off her laptop, for the night this time.

But as she slipped on her sneakers, she thought about Bibi's wise words. Psychopath or anger management issues? The boy in that photo clearly loved his mother. Could that have been enough to trigger an outburst? But why Chase? Photos of Titus Brown bore no resemblance to the handsome Chase Mars. Titus was tall and thick, with a barrel chest and pockmarked face. Chase was all-American handsome. Personality similarities? She didn't know.

Megan opened the door, and she and Gunther slipped out into the breezy night. She paused on the step, hearing something from afar. The hair on her neck stood at attention, and she felt Gunther stiffen beside her.

She heard it again and relaxed. Just an owl, hooting from deep in the woods.

THIRTEEN

The news came with a phone call from Denver the next morning. The psychiatric evaluation was complete, and Dillon Brown was deemed well enough to be released from the hospital. Eloise was picking him up later that day, and Denver would be accompanying her. Did Megan want to go too?

Yes, she did.

Megan spoke with Clay and Porter and reviewed the farm chores for the day. It was time to plant the fields of organic corn seed, a labor-intensive job. She'd help until she had to leave, and after that, Porter and Clay would finish. Raising corn without pesticides or herbicides meant clean beds and plenty of attention, but the result was worth it. Fresh, sweet, crisp ears, and because organic corn was harder to come by and harder to raise, a premium price.

Clay had invented a small seed-dropping motorized car that he would use once the bed was ready. Bibi loved watching it roll over the soil, and she'd no doubt pull a lawn chair up for the fun. In the meantime, the three of them would be out there making sure the beds were weed-free and well nourished.

At noon, Megan went inside for a sandwich and a shower. She changed from jeans and a t-shirt to a pair of pressed black pants and a plum-colored wrap shirt. She gave Bibi a kiss on the way out, but her grandmother grabbed her arm gently to stop her.

"Your Aunt Sarah called," she said. "She mentioned that she'd like you to come by later."

"She could have called me directly."

"She knows how busy you are."

"I am pretty tied up, Bibi."

"I know. I told her that." Bibi pushed a piece of hair away from Megan's face and studied her granddaughter. "You look like your mother," she said — warmly. Then she changed the subject again quickly. "Sarah has some information she thought might help. She's working on a book and will be around all day. Go when it's convenient."

"Information that will help with what?"

Bibi shrugged. "She didn't say, but I'd guess it has something to do with Denver's friend and that boy, Dillon."

Sarah Birch, Megan's great-aunt on her father's side, was an enigma in Winsome. A famous mystery author with numerous awards to her name, Sarah chose to live quietly in her cottage on the outskirts of Winsome. Some called her a modern-day Agatha Christie, and while everyone in Winsome knew who she was, they were willing to keep her identity and whereabouts secret — all the while relishing having a celebrity in their midst.

Megan had just discovered her aunt a few years ago. Their relationship had been a rocky one, but the more Megan let her guard down, the more she came to respect — if not like — her aunt.

"Fine," she said, kissing the top of Bibi's head. "I'll swing by later this afternoon."

"Here." Bibi handed Megan a flat Tupperware container. Inside, Megan could see the swirled tops of chocolate-frosted cupcakes. "I know the boy is going home." She shrugged. "All kids like cupcakes."

"These look amazing." Megan hugged her grandmother as tightly as she dared. "Maybe you could visit him once he's home," she said. "I have a feeling Dillon might like that even more than these cupcakes."

■ ■ ■ ■

Megan and Denver waited in the visitor's lobby on the psychiatric wing of the hospital while Eloise met with the hospital staff and the placement agency. Denver was quiet, but his knee bounced up and down, and his hand gripped Megan's own. They stared at a muted talk show on the television, neither of them talking.

"Is this a good idea?" Megan whispered.

"I can't say I'm thrilled."

"Where are the police? Is Bobby here?"

Denver shook his head. "Dillon hasn't been arrested, the hospital says they have no reason to keep him, and the only other alternative is a group home or a different foster home. Eloise put her foot down and said she wants him back with her." He let go of Megan's hand. "What do you think, Megs?"

"I'm not sure having him at Eloise's home is wise. What if he acts out? Can she handle that?" Alone, Megan thought, with the boy on ten acres. It was one thing to believe in his innocence. It was another to bank on it.

"I know. That's my worry too."

"If you want to stay with her, your dogs can stay with me."

Denver smiled. "Eloise will have none of that. She wants the home as normalized as possible for Dillon."

"Eloise never struck me as the maternal type."

"Aye, I know. This boy has struck a chord with her."

Megan watched as a couple walked into the visitor's room. They both looked worn and pale. They sat together on a couch, entwined around each other, their blank expressions reminiscent of refugees. Megan felt a surge of sympathy. How quickly life can turn.

Eloise walked in and waved to Denver and Megan, her mouth set in a stern line. Denver and Megan rose and followed her to Dillon's room, past the uniformed officer that still stood guard outside his room. "For his protection," Eloise whispered. "Not because he's dangerous."

They found the boy standing by his bed. A small duffel bag, open on a chair, had been stuffed with pajamas and a blue terry robe. One arm and the head of a Teddy bear stuck out amidst the clothing.

Dillon's eyes were half closed. His shoulders slumped, his head was hung nearly to his chest. His entire persona screamed of dejection. Megan brushed aside a deep urge to go to him, to hug him. When she and Denver entered the room, he looked up from underneath his mop of hair and nodded ever so slightly.

"Hello, Dillon," Denver said. "Are ye packed and ready to leave this place?"

Dillon nodded. Eloise zipped up the duffel bag and turned toward the nurse, a young man in his thirties.

"Do we have a safe way out of here?" she asked.

To avoid the press, was the part she left out. But the nurse seemed to implicitly understand what she was asking, and he nodded. "We'll take the service elevator. If you want, you can have someone pull a car around back, near the dumpsters."

They all agreed this was the best plan. "It's why we took Denver's SUV," Eloise explained to the nurse. "The press have seen me coming and going. They don't know my nephew."

The man smiled. He turned that smile to Dillon and said softly, "Will you be okay, son?" He meant the words kindly, but at the mention of the word "son," Dillon flinched. The nurse frowned. "I'm sorry," he said to Eloise. "That was insensitive."

Eloise's smile was wan. "It's okay — you meant no harm. Dillon has a lot to deal with." She turned to Dillon. "Dr. Finn will get the car. Megan, Nurse Anderson, and I will escort you out the back door. It's just for your privacy, Dillon. When we get home, you'll get to see the dogs. They've been waiting for you."

At the mention of the dogs, Dillon's face relaxed. Just a little bit.

Denver left the room. The psychiatric wing was a locked area, so he wasn't worried anyone would follow him from the room. To be careful, though, he told Megan he'd planned a circuitous route back to his car.

Megan and Eloise grabbed Dillon's insubstantial belongings. As they left the room, Eloise stopped. Dillon was wearing a black hoodie, and she faced him and pulled the hood up, shielding his face from public view. Before she turned to leave again, she tilted his head back slightly with her hand and forced him to look her in the eyes.

"I know you didn't do anything wrong," she said quietly but firmly. "You're safe with us, Dillon."

Dillon blinked twice, his eyes watery.

Eloise smiled. "Come on."

He walked between the two women, out to Denver's car. He slid in the back next to Eloise, his duffle bag clutched like a shield.

He was silent for the entire drive to Eloise's farm.

"Look at that," Eloise said, "Those dogs love him."

The adults watched from the kitchen window as Dillon played with Eloise's three dogs. He threw a ball. One retrieved it while the other two danced dog circles of joy around his feet.

"How will you cope, Aunt Eloise?" Denver plopped down on an island stool. "With the press. With his emotional needs. With school."

"School is out for the summer break, so it will just be tutoring and therapy appointments. I'm retired now, so I can get him where he needs to go."

"And his other . . . issues?" Denver held his aunt's gaze. "Even if he had nothing to do with what happened, he found Chase. That has to have made a deep impression."

"Are you asking about counseling?" Eloise asked sharply. "I think I know what he needs emotionally. I said he has therapy, and they have him medicated. Too medicated, if you ask me."

"You may not be in the best position to make those decisions. It requires a degree of objectivity that a parent — including a foster parent — may not have." Denver glanced at Megan for confirmation, but she wasn't so sure he was right.

"I appreciate your candor, Denver, but I'm not in the mood to have you questioning my decisions as well. Dillon has therapy with the school psychologist twice a week, and a weekly psychiatric appointment. If he requires more, I'll procure those services."

Eloise was a tidy, well-dressed woman whose cool reserve was well known in Winsome. That reserve was on display now, but her nephew seemed nonplussed.

"As long as you have help," he said.

"I have all the help we need."

Megan watched as Dillon rolled on the ground with the dogs. His entire demeanor had changed, and in that moment, he *looked* like an average teen boy.

"Eloise," Megan said, turning her face so she could both watch Dillon and talk to Denver's aunt, "it will be hard getting him out, won't it? With the press in town and so many people interested in his whereabouts."

"Perhaps —"

Megan, hearing the defensive tone creep into Eloise's voice again, raised her hand. "I just had an idea. Why don't you bring him to the farm for some visits? He'll be free from reporters' watchful gazes. I'm watch-

167

ing him with the dogs, and I think he would be good with my dogs and the goats and now the pig." Megan told Eloise about their newest household member. "We could use some help, and maybe time with the animals would be therapeutic."

Eloise's expression brightened. "I think it's a fabulous idea."

Denver looked less than enthusiastic. "Megan, do you think that's wise?"

"I think it will be good for him. And for the animals."

Denver's frown said he thought otherwise. Megan knew he was thinking about her safety. If Dillon came to the farm it meant he'd know where she lived. Megan just wasn't buying Dillon Brown as murderer. The boy she was watching would benefit from the animals — and Bibi.

"It's settled, then." Eloise clapped her hands. She lifted the lid off Bibi's Tupperware and stared into the container of cupcakes. "Your grandmother always was thoughtful."

"I think she agrees with you about Dillon. What he needs right now."

Eloise shot Denver a caustic glance. "I'm glad someone is on our side."

"What is your problem?" Megan asked

168

Denver on the way back to Washington Acres. "You were pretty surly with your aunt. Where's that fighting Scottish spirit."

"Eloise may be living with a dangerous boy. I say boy, but he has the size and strength of a man."

"Eloise is a grown woman and a doctor. I think she can take care of herself."

Denver turned onto Canal Street, his jaw clenched.

"You're that worried about her."

"I don't know what to think, Megs, and it's driving me crazy. I had dinners with Dillon before all of this, and he was quiet but mannerly. Not someone who would do such a terrible thing. Chase could be obnoxious at times, sure, but he had no enemies, Megan. Someone went out of their way to kill him, to stab him with his own knife." Denver glanced at her. "The only person who makes any sense is this kid. And now he's living with my aunt. I don't want to think he could be guilty — just the notion is making me ill — but I have to think of Eloise."

"Don't you think if the police thought he was guilty, they would have kept him locked up?"

"I don't know what is bloody wrong with King, but I would have thought they'd have arrested someone by now."

"Have you talked to Chase's family, Denver?"

Denver was silent.

"Denver?"

"Yes. I spoke to his mother and his sister after Barbara called them. They were bereft. His ex-wife, Diana, too."

"Your friends say you haven't been by at all."

"I've been busy." Another glance at Megan. "He was my friend. I knew this was a bad idea. I knew it, but I did nothing to stop it."

"Pull over."

"No —"

"Please, pull over."

Denver drove until he reached Merry's nursery. He pulled into a spot at the back of the lot and killed the engine. "What?"

"You're getting everything jumbled in your head. Emotions like grief and fear are scary, Denver. They make us feel out of control. None of this is your fault, and Bobby King is an excellent detective and chief. If he felt Eloise was in danger, he wouldn't have allowed Dillon to go back to her house."

Denver stared straight ahead.

"Are you listening?"

"Yes, of course. Eloise and my sister are all I have, Megan. Aside from you, they are my family. Chase was one of my oldest friends. What am I to do with all of this? I can't protect Chase, but I can protect Eloise. Can you trust me on that?"

"Of course, Denver, but Eloise feels like she needs to protect that boy in her care. Maybe you need to trust *her* on that."

Denver put his head back against the headrest and sighed. "Life is so bloody complicated." He glanced into the rearview mirror and what he saw made his eyes widen. "Bloody hell."

Megan turned around in time to see Merry Chance running across the lot toward Denver's SUV.

"Merry," Denver said much too enthusiastically when Merry approached Megan's window. "What has you running across the lot like a gazelle in heat?"

Merry didn't laugh at the comparison. "I heard the boy has been released to your aunt's care. Is that true, Denver?"

"Now is that what the rumor mill is saying?" Denver squinted at Merry and bit down on his lip. "What happens with the boy is not my business."

"It's your aunt's safety I'm thinking about," Merry said. Megan could tell by the

171

confused expression on her face that she wasn't sure whether to be amused or offended. "He could be dangerous."

"Aye, so I have heard." Denver smiled at Megan. "My aunt is a grown-up. If she is keeping up with her responsibilities as a foster mum, I'm sure she knows what she's doing."

"I sure hope so." Merry looked around the lot. A new car had pulled in — a BMW — and Merry eyed it eagerly. "Well, I had best get back to business."

"You'd best," Denver said. "Before that customer leaves."

He and Megan watched her return to the store.

"You're awful," Megan said.

"She's awful." Denver leaned over and kissed her. "But ta, Megs. For talking sense to me."

Megan returned the kiss. "Anytime."

"If I can't protect my aunt, what *can* I do?"

"Help her with Dillon. He could use a reliable male in his life right now. Be open-minded about what happened with Chase. Maybe figure out what's going on with your friends at BOLD."

Denver arched his eyebrows in surprise. "BOLD? What do ye mean, Megs."

172

"The argument between Jatin and Chase. The argument between Xavier and Jatin. Martine's concerns about Jatin. There seems to be one consistent thread here."

Denver's frown deepened. "Jatin."

Megan nodded. "And now the head honcho is in town, which only makes things more interesting."

FOURTEEN

The visit from King that Megan had been half-expecting came later that day. She had stopped by the café to check on things there before keeping her promise to Bibi and heading over to her Aunt Sarah's home. She'd found the café busy but under control and decided to stock shelves in the store. The canned foods were running low as was the pasta and rice. Normally she saved stocking for after-hours, but with the café so busy and the farm in full swing, it was a job that had been ignored. And it offered some blessed relief from all the worry.

Megan was placing organic black beans on a shelf next to pinto and kidney beans when she heard someone behind her. She'd been thinking about Chase and was jumpier than usual. She spun around to come face to chest with Bobby King.

"Didn't mean to startle you." King grabbed two cans from the package at

Megan's feet and placed them on the shelf. "Can we talk?"

"Sure. I'm almost done here."

She and King worked together for a minute to finish emptying the case of black beans. When the last can was stocked and the cardboard had been placed in recycling, Megan turned to the police chief who, she noticed, was conspicuously dressed down in jeans and a t-shirt.

"Taking the day off?" she asked.

"Can we talk outside?"

"You don't want to just use my office?"

"I'd rather not."

Megan glanced back toward the café. She didn't recognize half the people. It was a weekday, so it was unlikely to be tourists. Press, she figured — at least some of them. King's reason for avoiding the office. They'd have to walk through the café.

Outside, the day was hot and muggy. Megan's linen top clung to her within minutes, and the air felt soupy and smelled faintly of ozone and car fumes. Clouds had gathered overhead, and the angry state of the sky harkened rain. Good for crops, not so good for business.

"Where'd you want to go?"

"Let's walk down by the canal."

Megan tried to match the Chief's long

175

strides. Within a few minutes, they reached the paved canal path. The recreation trail had been one of the positive outcomes of the Historical Society's attempts to revitalize the town's center. The canal trail. Historically accurate lampposts. Wooden benches. New cobblestones. Sign restrictions. Winsome's small town center *was* attractive — even if the price tag had been daunting. Today she followed King west on the trail, toward the more wooded section of town. She struggled to keep up.

When they were out of site of the main street, King slowed down.

"How are things going with the investigation?" Megan asked.

"The State Police are taking over," King said. "Even the damn Bureau of State Parks is involved."

"The murder happened on state park land. I guess that makes sense."

King kicked at a stone on the pathway. "I figured we'd have some jurisdiction issues, but with all this press, the state guys are being pretty possessive." He looked up toward the hills in the distance. "The park is still closed while they comb for evidence."

"All probably normal procedure, Bobby." Megan knew King was well aware of procedure, but he looked so down, she wasn't sure what to say.

"Yeah, I know."

"Then what's bothering you?"

"The boy, I guess. These state folks, they're all about closing this case — and fast. We're working together still, but at some point, they may push us out altogether. I need to be fast and decisive."

"I wouldn't expect anything else from you."

King smiled. "Thanks, Megan, but reassurance isn't what I'm after."

"Then what are you after?"

"Just the truth."

Megan laughed out loud. "Good luck with that."

"Tell me about it."

Sweat had beaded along Megan's forehead and the back of her neck. Spying an empty bench under a maple tree, Megan pointed. "Let's get out of the sun."

When they were both seated, King said, "What I can't get straight in my head is the series of connections we have going here. Chase and some of the other BOLD crew are Denver's long-time friends. He went to college with Chase, Xavier, and Jatin, right?"

"They were fraternity brothers. Barbara was friends with them too."

"Not Martine?"

"She came later."

"This group of people from the same company came here not because of a former close friend, but because of a school. And the connection to that school is the boss's daughter, who was a student several years ago."

"That's right. Dr. Harriet Mantra, Barbara's boss. Her daughter was a student, and she wanted to give back."

"So she sets up this mentoring program with the aim of helping other Pioneer Village kids go to college."

"Right."

"And Eloise's foster son just happens to be a student at the same school."

"Right again."

King watched a hawk circling overhead. "And you don't think these are weird coincidences?"

Megan considered the question. "If no one had gotten hurt, we wouldn't have thought twice about any of this. According to Denver, Chase called him to let him know he was coming to town and why. It was only after Denver found out about Chase that Eloise told him Dillon would be on that camping trip too." Megan paused. "What I didn't understand is why Harriet's daughter was in school in Pennsylvania

178

rather than California and how Dillon, a ward of the Commonwealth, was able to attend as well."

"That's an easy one to answer. The school is private. It's a program for children with high IQs and emotional problems. Eloise knew about it because of her medical practice. Presumably this Harriet Mantra found out and chose to send her daughter there in lieu of some state-run school."

"Yes, that's what I think."

King still looked concerned. "I asked Denver why his friends were here, and he seemed oddly anxious. Not like him."

Megan fanned herself with a paper from her purse. "When we had dinner the night before the camping trip started, Denver was pretty shaken up. Chase was obnoxious. Denver hadn't seen him in a while. I think he was expecting him to be less . . . Chase-like. He felt like the trip was a bad idea, that Chase and the others didn't seem very altruistic. That maybe the kids weren't going to have a good experience. You know how much Denver likes the outdoors. He was worried they'd ruin it for the teens." Megan shrugged. "I think he feels responsible. Not because he did something, but because of his connection with the parties. I suspect this would have happened with or

179

without him, though. BOLD wanted its photo ops."

King was quiet for a moment. "That was why Martine was there," King said. "To capture this on film."

Megan sat back against the bench, stretching her legs out in front of her. "Yeah, it was to be a big PR opportunity."

"Do you know why?"

Megan glanced at King. "I assumed because they could. New pharma company does good in the world, blah, blah, blah. Earn some good will."

"BOLD isn't a public company."

"Maybe they intend to take the company public at some point."

King didn't respond right away. His gaze remained on the horizon. Megan could feel the tension coming off him in waves. "BOLD has been around for a few years. Hardly a newcomer."

"So?"

"Something doesn't fit, Megan. You and I have worked through enough of these puzzles to know there are no real coincidences. I'm trying to figure out who benefitted from Chase's death. Who, besides Dillon Brown, would have wanted him dead?"

Same question Megan had posed earlier. She nodded for him to go on.

180

"The State guys are looking at the kid as suspect number one. His family's legacy lives on. But that park was full of other people that day, including several of Chase's coworkers. The murder instrument was Chase's own knife. Any one of them had access to it."

"You looked at Jatin?"

"Martine told me about the argument between him and Chase, if that's what you mean." King extended his arm, flexed his hand. "Jatin claims he was scolding Chase for getting drunk the night before the event. I have no reason to disbelieve him."

Megan told King about Clover's description of an argument between Xavier and Jatin at the café. "Jatin again. What do you make of that?"

"That my girlfriend is holding out on me."

Megan smiled. "She's worried about you, Bobby. Says you're not sleeping."

"Because I'm not."

"Wearing yourself out isn't the solution for solving this case."

"Tell that to my brain." He slapped his hands down on his legs. "Jatin, huh? The way I see it, one of three things happened. One, the kid killed Chase. He had access to Chase and the weapon. What we don't know is what his motive would have been — or if he needed one."

"He was found with Chase?"

"He was screaming. His screams brought the others running. They found him in the water, doubled over, still screaming. He wasn't with the body, but he was close enough."

Megan said, "You couldn't determine if the splatter on him was consistent with what you'd see if he'd wielded the knife."

"He was soaking wet. Most of the blood had been washed off. He denies anything other than finding Chase, and right now we have no strong evidence to the contrary. His prints were on the knife handle, but so were a half dozen other people's. And part of the knife was submerged. Not the best crime scene for forensics. No witnesses. No cameras. And most of the prints gone."

"No surveillance going in and out of the park?"

King's eyes narrowed. "You're thinking of the kiosk where you leave day trip payments."

Megan nodded. The park had a cheap day use fee and visitors were supposed to place their money and envelopes in a slot in a locked kiosk. "Visitors are supposed to write their license plate numbers on the envelopes. That could provide a clue."

King smiled. "If only it were that simple. No security — completely an honor system. Shh. Don't tell anyone. And almost no one includes license number. We went through them; nothing helpful."

"Right. And we're assuming the killer would follow the rules. What're the other possibilities? You said you had three."

King said, "Two, it was someone from BOLD. Like Dillon, they each had opportunity. Motive is again an unknown."

"And three?"

"A stranger. Someone who happened to be in the park and acted because they could."

Megan frowned. "That was a lot of rage for a stranger."

"Who knows what goes through people's minds. Could have been someone with whom Chase had an altercation, could have been a road incident and the person stalked him to the park." King frowned. "Road rage gone wild."

"Stranger things have happened." Megan sighed. "There's a fourth possibility. That whoever killed Chase followed him to Pennsylvania for the purpose of murdering him."

"Someone not affiliated with BOLD?"

A child on a tricycle and a woman running beside him were coming toward them down the path. Megan waited until they'd passed before responding.

"They could be affiliated with BOLD — or not. Chase wasn't an easy guy to be around. Imagining that he had enemies isn't that hard."

King nodded. "So I've heard."

Megan watched the Chief as he watched the boy on the tricycle. She and King had been through other murders together, sat vigil through many sleepless nights. She wasn't surprised he was confiding in her. Besides her connection to Denver, she'd become and unofficial sounding board, a friend. She wouldn't let him down now.

She said, "Your theories all ring true. If it were me, I'd start with Chase's life. What was he into? Who did he hang around with? What did he do for fun?"

King looked briefly amused. "Besides work?"

Megan watched the receding backs of the boy and his mom. "There are twenty-four hours in a day, Bobby. No one can work all of the time."

FIFTEEN

Sarah lived in a fairytale cottage on the outskirts of Winsome. Tucked into the woods, her home was a small Tudor dream. Megan parked and climbed out of her truck. She figured Sarah would be inside, writing at her dining room table, one or more cats sleeping by her computer. She decided to take a moment to wander around the yard, admiring the perennial gardens and tiny fairy villages, while collecting her thoughts.

Despite years of legal training, despite hours spent cross-examining witnesses and answering to surly judges and caustic plain-tiffs' counsel, Megan was intimidated by her aunt. Sarah Birch was no people pleaser, and her ideas about the world were often . . . different.

Aunt Sarah, a sworn bachelorette, lived a charmed life these days. She came and went as she pleased. With few human demands aside from her career, her perspective on life was, to Megan, often overly black and white, and conversations between the two of them could get heated. Megan steeled herself for whatever topic Sarah wanted to discuss today — no doubt, it would be incendiary.

After a few minutes, Megan knocked on the kitchen door. Sarah answered immediately. Her tall, solid form was dressed in an ankle-length maroon cotton skirt and matching lace-trimmed top. A gray sweater had been tied neatly around her neck, and chunky silver earrings hung from her lobes. Her long, thick gray hair had been wrestled into one chunky braid. Striped maroon and navy-blue readers hung from a navy lanyard around her neck.

"Megan," she said, stepping back. "Come in. I assume Bonnie gave you my message? Thank you for stopping by."

"No problem." Megan stepped over the threshold and into a firestorm of paper. There were stacks on the kitchen counters, on the dining room table, and from what Megan could see, on the living room floor and every available furniture surface. "Looks like you've been busy."

Sarah laughed — it was deep and guttural and rather infectious. "Understatement. Two book deadlines, different stages in the editing cycle. I like to print off my manuscripts and read them in hard copy. I'm old-fashioned that way. Somewhere along the line, I got my edits mixed up and I'm just now sorting through." She waved toward the living room loveseat, one of the few places where you could still see fabric. "Come, have a seat."

Sarah sat cross-legged on the floor across from Megan. One of her cats, a large orange tabby, took up residence in her lap.

"Dr. Star called me," Sarah said. "Benjamin Star. Ring a bell?"

"The psychologist at Pioneer Village School?"

Sarah nodded. "He and I have known each other for a while. I used him as a reference when I was writing a book. Remember *Murder at Lehman Hall*? The school in that book was fashioned after Pioneer Village. Benjamin and I met a few times, I bought him dinner, he gave me great insight into schools for the gifted."

Megan let this sink in. Her aunt — and her aunt's wide network — never ceased to amaze her. Nevertheless, why would she know Megan had visited the school?

"Don't look surprised, Megan. Benjamin called me after you left the school. He recognized your name from events last year.

187

Didn't take him long to connect the dots. He called me thinking that you had a relative you wanted to be considered for the school."

"You didn't dispel him of that, did you?"

Sarah smiled. "No. Your secret is safe. I know full well you went there because of the murder. You wanted to see what the fuss was about, and why Eloise Kent put the boy in that school to begin with."

"I'm afraid I didn't get very far in my quest for information."

"No, you wouldn't. Benjamin is very careful about patient privacy. Although I don't see where the school fits in, perhaps I can help you?"

Megan squirmed in her seat. She was expecting an argument. She wasn't expecting her aunt to be helpful. "Has the school had any history of issues?"

"What kind of issues?"

"Kids with violent tendencies? Allegations of abuse?"

"Not that I know of."

"How do kids get into that school?"

"It's private. Most students pay tuition. Those who are worthy of admission, that is."

" 'Worthy of admission?' You make it sound like a prestigious prep school, not a school for kids with delinquency issues."

Sarah raised her pointer finger and wiggled it back and forth. "Not so fast. Very few of the kids have criminal histories or tendencies. They have to be smart, and they have to have what Benjamin calls adjustment problems. Social anxieties. Phobias. Some of the kids have Asperger's or Attention Deficit Disorder. There is a range, but generally these students are functioning and non-violent."

"Kids like Dillon Brown."

"Yes, kids exactly like Dillon."

"Dillon clearly has some adjustment issues likely stemming from family trauma. But if he's there, he would by definition also be smart."

"Benjamin doesn't bend that rule."

"So I've heard." Megan rubbed her eyes. "Dr. Harriet Mantra, a principle at BOLD Pharmaceuticals, wanted this mentor outing as a way of paying the school back. She wanted each kid to have a mentor in the worlds of science or business. She was even offering full college tuition to kids who stuck with the mentoring program through the end of high school."

"Yes," Sarah said, "I'd read that. She was especially interested in attracting students to STEM careers."

"Right. All very good. But if the school is private, why would these kids need scholarships? Does their parents' ability to pay tuition mean they have money — and could pay for college? It feels like an empty gesture."

"Not if it gave the company exposure."

Megan had been thinking the same thing. More and more, this appeared to be a publicity boon for BOLD more than an actual attempt to pay back a school.

"Don't get me wrong," Sarah said. "The school can accept some underprivileged youth, and it uses a scholarship fund for those kids who can't pay and who otherwise meet the criteria."

"But Mantra wasn't offering to add cash to the scholarship fund, or to send poor kids to college. She said she'd send anyone who couldn't afford it and finished the program to college."

"Convenient. Most of the kids who go to Pioneer Village are from wealthy families." Sarah stretched her long legs out in front of her, disturbing the cat. He jumped up onto the loveseat and made a spot for himself behind a stack of files. "Harriet Mantra, huh? I suppose her daughter was Cat Mantra?"

"I don't know."

"Well, Cat was one of the few students who did have a history of criminal behavior."

"That meshes with what I've heard about Harriet's daughter. Mantra basically chose this place to avoid juvie for her daughter."

Sarah nodded. "Sounds like Cat. Only reason I know about her is that Benjamin confided that a particular student was causing issues. He didn't name names, of course, but I read the papers and it was easy to put two and two together. Cat would run away frequently and cause problems with the locals."

"That must have sparked tension between the town and the school."

"You would think, but I suspect money was flowing, if you know what I mean."

"Not quite."

Another cat was slinking behind Sarah. This one was a sleek silver tabby. She looked young, and when she pounced on Sarah's back, Sarah grinned. "Matilda," Sarah purred, "did you finally come out to say hello?" She lifted the tabby onto her lap. "Found this one outside. Just a wee kitten. Romeo over there wants nothing to do with her, but she's starting to come out of her shell."

As though proving the point, Matilda leapt

off Sarah's lap and onto Megan's. She curled into a tight ball, one paw out, and purred.

"Don't pet her," Sarah said. "She doesn't like attention. Wants things on her own terms." Sarah grabbed a pillow from a chair behind her and tucked it under her knees. "Where were we? Ah, the school and money. Did you happen to see the bird sanctuary? After someone from the school vandalized the town's small bird watching area, everyone was upset. Gorgeous birds, I hear. Something about the plant life."

Sarah readjusted again. "Iced tea?" she asked Megan.

"No, thanks."

"Suit yourself. Anyway, two months later this bird sanctuary appeared. There's a heated observation house with benches and windows, bird feeders for dozens of species of birds, gardens, and a part-time 'ranger.' " Sarah put air quotes around the word ranger. "No one said Cat's parents footed the bill, but after that the townspeople of Blessings stopped bitching about the school."

"And Cat graduated?"

"My research finished mid-way through her senior year. I have no idea what happened to the girl, but I did see that a nature

192

center went up in Blessings as well. Co-incidence?"

"Hmm. Harriet Mantra credits the school with saving her daughter, yet it sounds like the kid's behaviors continued throughout school."

Sarah said, "Sounds that way. That was years ago. Maybe something clicked, and Cat went on to make something of herself. Stranger things have happened."

"For sure." Matilda started kneading Megan's leg with her claws. Megan tried to move her, so her claws would dig into a less tender area, and the cat jumped down, indignant.

"Told you. Mind of her own." Sarah stood and stretched. "Did I help?"

"You did — thanks."

"Will you leave Benjamin — Dr. Star — out of it, then?"

Megan looked up, surprised. "What do you mean?"

"No need to talk with the school if your curiosity is satisfied. They hardly need the attention right now."

Megan could feel her face heat up. Typical Sarah. "Is that why you called Bibi? To keep me from the school? Was this some type of quid pro quo with Dr. Star?"

Sarah's smile tilted toward condescending. "Hardly. I told you, your secret is safe. But that horrible reporter from *The Bucks County Times* did a terrible piece on the school this morning. Did you see it? I feel I owe Benjamin, and if you show up asking questions, it's bound to attract more attention."

Megan took a deep breath. "Has it occurred to you that perhaps the school is complicit somehow? From what you've told me, they took Cat — a kid with delinquent tendencies — and then possibly participated in the cover-up when she vandalized parts of the town. What if the school is doing that now? What if there is more to Dillon's story than they're willing to say?"

Sarah seemed unmoved. "Nonsense. Don't make a simple situation more complicated than it needs to be. I need to get back to editing, Megan. Can you see yourself out?"

"Did you hear a word I said?"

"Of course. Did it occur to me? Yes. Do I believe it? No. Benjamin Star is a wonderful man. Caring, intelligent, generous. He understands that bright kids have special needs, and he views himself as protector and advocate. The world could use more Dr. Stars."

"That doesn't mean the school isn't

194

somehow involved. That at the very least, they're hiding information about Dillon."

"That man died because someone was very, very angry at him. An adult did that, Megan. I write mysteries for a living, and there is no mystery here. Look for a grown-up with a grudge and you'll have your killer."

"You're *that* sure?"

"Yes." Sarah opened the back door, ushering her niece out with a saccharine smile. "I'm *that* sure."

"Everyone has an opinion," Megan said to Bibi later that night. They were eating vegetable soup and freshly-baked sourdough bread, and Bibi had asked about the Chase Mars murder. "Some seem to feel it's Dillon, others that it's absolutely not. I'm just trying to deal in facts."

Bibi dunked a small slice of bread into the little amount of broth left in her bowl. "The police are on it?"

Megan told her grandmother about King's visit to the café earlier that day. "That's the thing, Bibi, this occurred at a state park. Bobby doesn't feel like he has control of the investigation. I think he's worried they're going to steamroll the boy because he's easy and they want this closed."

"He's a child. Surely that won't happen."

They both ate, aware that much worse things happen all of the time.

Bibi finished her soup and pushed the bowl away. "How well did Denver know this man, Chase."

"Very well, years ago. They hadn't really stayed in touch."

"So effectively he was a stranger?"

"I guess, at least on some levels."

"As you learned with Thana Moore, people change." Bibi frowned, clearly thinking about the murder that had occurred the year before. "Or maybe they become more themselves over time." She picked at a piece of bread, twisting bits between arthritic fingers before popping them into her mouth.

Megan nodded. "We meet people at a point in time. Sometimes we grow together, other times we grow apart. My sense is that Denver and his friends — all of them — grew apart."

Bibi waited until Megan was also finished before clearing the bowls from the table. She and Megan washed dishes and cleaned the kitchen side by side, a comfortable routine made more comfortable by silence.

When the kitchen sparkled and the clock on the wall read 8:37, Bibi announced she was turning in early. "Have to keep my girlish complexion," she joked. "Besides, I feel tired. Maybe sleep will meet me half way."

Megan kissed her grandmother good night. She wasn't tired. She would return to her computer and information about Chase Mars.

It was 9:18 when Denver called. "Ready for some company?" he asked.

"Always," Megan had just homed in on an article of interest and was lingering over a photograph.

"You sound distracted."

"Do I?" Megan scanned the page. She needed another source — and bingo, she knew where to find it. "Can you come now?"

"Wow, I'm glad you want to see me —"

"Bring your social media passcodes."

Pregnant pause, then, "Is this some kinky new game, Megs? Because I've had a long day of animal husbandry and surgery and —"

Megan laughed. "Not a kinky new game. Just found something interesting. Come now?"

"I'm at your service."

Denver arrived at 9:44. He smelled clean and male, like bath soap and spicy after shave, and Megan resisted the urge to fall into his embrace. Instead, she pulled another chair over to her laptop and directed him to sit.

"Take a look at this," Megan said.

"What am I looking at?"

"This is an archived article about what it's like to be a roadie. Look at the last two paragraphs."

She watched Denver skim the words, reading over his shoulder.

"Okay, they quoted Chase. He played with The Rolling Stones. We all know that — he talked about it incessantly."

"Keep going."

When he got to the grainy photos at the end, he squinted at the screen. Running a hand through his tousled hair, he said, "I don't see what this proves."

"Look at the photo again."

After a few seconds of staring at it, his eyes narrowed further. "Huh."

"Right?"

Between the final two paragraphs was a photo of the musicians and roadies who toured with the Stones on that particular evening years ago. Chase was in the picture, carrying his guitar. Next to him, staring up at Chase's face like it was the face of God, was Martine Pringle. Her hair was a frizzy mass of waves, her eyes heavily made-up, and she was wearing an off-the-shoulder top. Megan might have missed her, but her name was listed in the caption under the photo.

"Chase never mentioned that he knew Martine," Megan said.

"No, and Martine never mentioned it either."

Denver glanced at the laptop screen again. "And clearly they knew each other. Look at the way she's ogling him." Denver shook his head. "She was crazy about him. Seems strange that neither of them mentioned knowing one another, at least to me."

"Maybe not. Can you pull up your Facebook page?" Megan waited while Denver found his page and plugged in his password. "Clearly you're not on here often." The photo of him was years old, and his cover image was a black rectangle.

"I'm not fond of social media."

"I see that. But you're friends with Chase on here, right?" When Denver nodded, Megan said, "May I?" He handed control of the page to her.

Megan searched through his fifty friends. He and Martine weren't Facebook friends, but she found Chase on the list. "You know he's divorced, right?"

"Yes. He and his wife Diana split a long time ago. They got married right out of college. They're still good friends."

"Did they divorce while he was traveling as a musician?"

Denver said, "I don't really remember, but I think it was after that. You think his relationship with Martine broke up his marriage?"

Megan sorted and skimmed and followed the dots until she had what she was looking for. Photos Chase had been tagged in, visible only to his friends. Photos from Martine. Chase made no mention of the woman on his site, but she had catalogued her time as a groupie with numerous photos, many of them quite good. She tagged Chase in over a dozen, and most of the pictures were dated after his marriage.

"How would you feel if I was on the road with a man who looked at me the way Martine is looking at Chase in many of these pictures?"

"Like I want to punch the guy in the face."

Megan laughed. "How stereotypically manly man of you." She turned to Denver, her expression somber again. "Can you friend Martine?"

"Why?"

"Then we can see what she's posted aside from her tags of Chase."

Denver's expression darkened. "Again, why? I don't want to encourage her, Megs."

Megan had seen the way Martine looked at Denver as well. She seemed to attach strongly to men — something that made Megan wonder. Denver had a point, though. If Martine was feeling pressed, now wasn't a good time for Denver to encourage her, even with something as simple as a friend request.

Megan said, "Never mind."

Denver stared at the screen. "You're investigating again?"

"I'm thinking through the patterns."

Denver pulled Megan onto his lap. He kissed her. "If you dig enough around the edges of Chase's life, who knows what you'll find."

"Including bits about one Daniel 'Denver' Finn?"

Another kiss, but his demeanor had changed. "Maybe."

"I'll take the risk."

"I'm an open book."

"Are you?" Megan stood. She grabbed Denver's hand and pulled him upright. "Come with me."

"Here?"

"I understand the barn is nice this time of year."

Denver smiled. "You're full of surprises."

The night air was still warm and muggy. Stars shown faintly overhead in the muted light of a waxing moon, tufts of haze like cotton candy here and there in the night sky. Megan tugged on Denver's hand, clinging to it until they reached the barn's small office. Inside, she kept the light off but fell against him in the dark.

"Don't disturb Camilla," she murmured. "I hear she's a light sleeper."

"You smell nice," Denver whispered against her ear.

Megan reached up, wrapping her arms around his neck, thoughts of Martine and Chase vanquished for the night.

SIXTEEN

"Hold your hand out straight." Megan placed her own hand flat and showed Dillon how to feed the goats the apple slices. "They have strong jaws, and they're very happy to put your fingers in the back of their mouths. Don't let their size and cuteness fool you. They have the ability to break a small finger." She smiled to soften her words. "Just keep your fingers out of their mouths and you'll be fine."

Dillon didn't need to be shown twice. Within minutes he and the goats were the best of friends. Megan and Eloise stood against the pen wall and watched them play. The tiny goats clearly adored the boy, and it was nice to see him smile.

"Want some tea?" Megan asked. "I think Dillon is just fine for now."

Eloise looked torn. "I know I'm being a worrywart," she whispered. "I feel like I can't let him out of my sight. He's probably sick of me by now."

Megan smiled. "You're not a worrywart, Eloise, but he *looks* like he's doing better."

"Less moping, although he still doesn't talk much." Eloise walked over to Dillon and whispered something. He nodded, and Eloise said, "Tea it is. Dillon will keep an eye on the goats."

"There's a super friendly pig in the barn, Dillon. Her name is Camilla. I bet she'd like some company as well."

"Does she bite?" Eloise asked.

"Camilla? No, she's a sweetheart. She may try to crawl into your lap, though. If you want to meet her, I'll let my farm manager know. His name is Clay. He can make introductions."

Dillon gave a solemn nod. "Okay," he mumbled.

"Well, that was one more word than I got out of him all morning," Eloise said as they headed through the courtyard toward the farmhouse. "He just doesn't communicate."

"How's he been otherwise?" Megan asked.

"Same, I guess."

Megan placed a quick call to Clay to ask him to keep an eye on Dillon. To Eloise, she said, "Any breakthroughs?"

"Breakthroughs?" Eloise stood by the kitchen window, her gaze on the barn.

"Would you consider nightmares, unexplained shakes, and fits of immobility to be breakthroughs?"

Megan filled the teapot and placed it on the stove. "It sounds like he could use some help."

"He's getting help. I just don't know if it's enough." Eloise turned away from the window, but only for a moment. "His therapist thinks he has post-traumatic stress disorder. From what happened with his parents, and now . . . this."

"That makes sense."

"It doesn't make it any easier to help him. To know what to do."

"The therapist should be able to guide you."

"He's doing his best, but I can't help but think he's out of his element as well."

"Have you seen a change since . . . since Dillon found Chase?"

Despite the heat, Eloise wore a pair of gray dress pants, a gray tank, and an ivory cardigan. She pulled the open cardigan tight against her now, as though warding off Megan's question . . . or the very fact of Chase's murder.

"He's never been a chatty kid, but the nightmares are worse, and the fits of immobility, as I've been calling them, are new."

Eloise sighed. "The police questioning him every freaking day doesn't help."

The tea kettle whistled, and Megan poured the hot water into a tea pot containing Earl Grey tea. While it steeped, she pulled some of Bibi's ginger snaps from the cupboard and placed them on a plate. "Think Dillon would like a snack?"

"Yes — his appetite is one thing that hasn't changed."

"We can bring him some treats after tea. The goats and Camilla love ginger cookies too."

"Is that good for the animals?"

"Is that good for the humans?"

Eloise smiled. "Touché."

Megan poured two cups of tea. When it became apparent Eloise wasn't leaving the window, Megan put the tea on the table near her and the cookies next to the cup. *When in doubt, feed people* — that seemed to be the Birch family motto.

Megan said, "Maybe Dillon just needs time."

"You know, when he finally did speak, he was very clinical with the police about what happened. He told them he saw Chase lying there, went over and picked up the knife, checked Chase for a pulse, and then he realized Chase was dead. He said he freaked out. He told them all of this in a strange monotone, as though he were relaying what happened to someone else." Eloise picked up the teacup and her hand was shaking so badly that tea sloshed over the side. "It was strange to hear him talk that way."

Megan sat at the table. She mixed raw honey into her tea, thinking about Brian "Brick" Porter, her farm hand who suffered from PTSD from his time in the military. He would often talk about his time overseas in a flat manner, as though describing events on television. "I'm no psychologist, but it sounds like maybe that's the only way he can deal with this. Separating himself emotionally by pretending, perhaps, that it happened to someone else. Isn't that common with PTSD patients?"

"That's what his therapist says."

"You don't buy it?"

It was a while before Eloise responded. "I guess. Despite what I told my nephew, sometimes Dillon spooks me."

Megan put down her teacup. "Spooks you how?"

Eloise tapped her fingers against the windowpane. "I'll hear a noise at night. When I get up, I'll find him . . . standing by the window, or outside on the porch . . . almost like he's in a trance."

"Maybe he's sleepwalking."

"Maybe." Eloise turned around. "I'm a doctor, Megan. I'm familiar with night terrors, sleepwalking, PTSD. There is something about Dillon I just can't put my finger on. It's as though . . . as though he's only half there most of the time."

"He's been through a lot, Eloise."

"I know, I know." Eloise's face reddened. "I don't know how to explain it. He says the right things — when he talks. The animals love him. I've never seen anything but kindness toward the horses or the dogs." She scrunched her features. "Yet I can't seem to reach him."

Megan regarded Denver's aunt. She didn't know the woman well, but she did know Eloise had been Winsome's primary pediatrician prior to her retirement a few years ago. Certainly, she'd been there for Denver after his parents died. Maybe this was guilt talking. Dillon was in her care when the murder occurred. Or maybe this was personal: deep down she was frustrated that she couldn't give the boy the home he needed. She was frustrated that he wasn't responding to her attempts to help him, and it made her feel helpless.

Or maybe there *was* something going on with Dillon.

"Eloise, if Dillon were your patient instead of your foster son, what would you think?"

"I would think he's dealing with grief. I would send him to a —"

Before Eloise could finish her sentence, Clay came into the kitchen through the porch door. He glanced from Megan to Eloise and back to Megan again. "Have a moment, Megan?"

Eloise's eyes widened. "What's happened with Dillon? I knew I shouldn't —"

"Nothing with the boy, Dr. Kent." To Megan, he said, "Bobby's here."

"Bobby?" Megan frowned. "What does he need?"

Clay shrugged. "He asked me to find you."

"Thanks, Clay." Megan turned to her guest. "Eloise, I may be a few minutes."

Eloise had already placed her tea cup in the sink. "I think that's our cue, Megan. I'm going to fetch Dillon, and we'll be off."

Megan studied Denver's aunt. "Will you be okay?"

"We'll be fine."

Megan placed her own cup in the sink and rinsed her hands. "I'd love for Dillon to come back. He can help me with the animals."

"Perhaps." Eloise looked distracted. "Tell my nephew I'll call him."

"He'd like that."

Eloise gave a curt nod. Megan followed her outside and watched as Eloise disappeared into the barn to get Dillon.

"She okay?" Clay asked, his gaze also on the barn.

It was Megan's turn to shrug. "How okay can you be in a situation like this?"

"True."

"Where's Bobby?"

"In his car, taking a call. He said he'd be back in a few."

Megan waited while Eloise and Dillon walked through the courtyard and down to her car. They paused to say goodbye.

"Thanks," Dillon mumbled.

"Did Camilla behave for you?"

The tiniest hint of a smile. "She was fine."

Megan's eyebrows shot up. "Just fine?"

Dillon looked down at his shoes, a pair of brand new Nike sneakers. "Pretty nice pig, I guess."

Megan laughed. "As pigs go, she's a winner. Come back again, Dillon. We could use the help."

He looked up at Eloise. "Would that be okay, Dr. Kent?"

"I don't see why not."

A door slammed and out of the corner of her eye, Megan saw King climb out of his car. Eloise must have seen it as well, because she placed a hand on Dillon and urged him to their own car, saying goodbye as she went.

When Eloise and Dillon were safely in her Lexus, Clay whispered, "I guess having the boy see Bobby would be upsetting."

"He'd think he'd done something wrong." While King walked toward them, Megan asked, "How did he do with Camilla?"

"Great. Camilla treated him like a long-lost littermate."

"Megan." King crossed the final few yards of the driveway with giant steps befitting his height. "Sorry to bother you."

"No bother. Want to come in for some coffee?"

"No time." He looked at Clay. "A few minutes?"

Clay took the cue. "I'll be in the green-house if you need me." He gave King, also his sister's boyfriend, an appraising glance. "You've lost weight."

"It's this case."

"My sister is worried about you."

When King didn't respond, Clay left. His slim form sprinted toward the greenhouses beyond the barn.

"What's up, Bobby? Clearly, you're not

here about Dillon. He was just here with Eloise."

"I saw him from my car. Friendly visit?"

"Friendly enough. Thought time with the animals might do him some good."

King rocked back on his heels. His gaze meandered toward the old Marshall property and the half a dozen workers hammering away at the new building. "Time with other people might do him some good. Not so sure he and Dr. Kent are the best fit."

"She seems to genuinely care about him. And she is a doctor."

"I guess."

"That's not why you're here, though."

King met her gaze. "No, it's not. We had an issue this morning at the inn where the BOLD employees are staying."

"An issue?"

King nodded. The hammering at the Marshall place stopped and King turned his head sharply in that direction. "Break-in."

Megan felt her own pulse racing. This was good news for Dillon — who'd been home, under the watchful eye of Eloise.

"What happened?" Megan forced her voice to sound casual.

"I don't have time to go into detail now, but have you met Harriet Mantra?"

"Dr. Mantra? Yes."

"Someone stole papers from her room."

"What kind of papers?"

"Work documents."

Megan thought about the inn, about the old-fashioned locks for the rooms. "Someone *physically* broke the door lock?"

"That's just it. Mantra claims the papers are missing, but there were no signs of a break-in. No broken locks, no torn apart room. Just Dr. Mantra's word that her room was violated and work product was removed."

Megan considered the layout of the inn. "Mantra was in one of the apartments. Did anyone see anything?"

"No one has owned up to it."

The hammering next door resumed. Megan watched one of the construction crew as he stood on a platform, balanced precariously against the frame, his body attached to structure with ropes and a cantilever. "Are only BOLD employees staying at the inn?"

"There was another guest, but he checked out yesterday. We're looking into him too." King closed his eyes and rubbed his shadowed jaw with one paw-sized hand. "Look, I didn't come to talk through the break-in. I came to ask about your conversation with

213

Martine."

Surprised, Megan said, "What about it?"

"She told me that she went to you and Denver about her concerns related to her coworker, Jatin."

Megan nodded. "And you talked to her about it." Megan frowned. "Why are you asking about this again now?"

King stood in the driveway, his large frame turned toward the Marshall property, his gaze on the workers in the distance. He shuffled one foot and drew a line in the gravel.

"I have a house full of people accusing one another, Megan. Martine is pointing a finger at Jatin. Harriet is pointing a finger at Martine." He turned his attention to Megan. "And Xavier is intimating that we should be talking to Denver."

"Denver?" Megan's hands clenched. "Why Denver?"

"He's insinuating that Denver and Chase had bad blood between them. That perhaps there are things Denver isn't telling us."

"That's ridiculous."

"Denver doesn't have an alibi for the time of Chase's murder."

"He was kayaking."

"That's what he says."

"I found him there, Bobby. It's absurd

214

that you'd even consider this line of thought." Megan placed her hands on her hips. "Think about what you're saying. Denver has lived among us for years. He's saved animal and human lives. And now you think he'd throw it all away to . . . to what? To exact revenge for some unknown slight?" She nearly spit her words. "You're letting the stress get the best of you."

His face contorted into a scowl. "Maybe neither of us is in the best position to judge."

Megan knew he was questioning her ability to be objective because of her relationship with Denver, but she refused to acknowledge it. He was off his rocker with this one — period.

She'd try to appeal to his rational side. "Bobby, if someone broke into Dr. Mantra's room, don't you think that points to a business motive for the murder?"

"There is nothing definitive suggesting the murder and the break-in are connected. Assuming there even was a break-in."

"You don't believe her?"

"Everyone is under pressure. She could have misplaced documents and thought they'd been taken."

"Or she could be lying."

Bobby nodded slowly. "Or she could be lying."

"To cast doubt on Xavier?"

"Maybe." King turned toward his unmarked police car. "In the meantime, I have a few people to track down. Including Denver."

"Why did you come here, Bobby? Surely it wasn't to tell me you suspect Denver."

"No, it wasn't." The day was quickly warming, and a trickle of sweat ran down King's face. He wiped it away with the back of his hand. "When you spoke to Martine, did you get a sense that she was afraid of Jatin? Or angry at him?"

"I don't know. Neither, I guess. Why?"

"There was something about her demeanor, something I can't put my finger on, that has me wondering about her motive for disclosing the argument in the first place. It just seems odd. Like she was trying to tell me something without actually telling me anything. They were all coworkers. Why shine a spotlight on someone in your group unless . . . unless you really think they may have done something?"

Megan understood what he was getting at. "And then you would probably be afraid for your own life."

"Right. You were the first person we know of to whom she made this admission. Did she seem scared to you?"

Megan considered the question. She just didn't know Martine well enough to know what was "normal." "I'd say she seemed nervous more than scared, nervous about whether or not to tell. Denver is the one you want to ask. He knows her, not me."

King's nod was solemn.

"You don't really think Denver capable of murder." It was a statement, not a question.

"Of course I don't."

"You're worried about him nonetheless."

In the distance, Megan could see Porter's lanky form making his way down the hill, Gunther and Sadie in tow. When he saw Megan and King, he gave a friendly wave. Porter had made huge gains since she'd met him. He'd gone from alcoholic recluse to employed and recovering. The animals and the steady job helped, but so had Denver. He'd befriended Porter when Porter had no one.

The dogs perked up and ran full-speed to where they were standing.

"Good pups," King said. He patted Sadie on the head. Gunther nudged his hand away, and King dutifully petted the larger dog too.

"Bobby? Back to Denver? You're worried about him."

Still patting Gunther, King said, "Yeah,

I'm worried. As I said, I've got a group of supposed friends all pointing fingers at one another. I have a troubled kid with no apparent ties to anyone looking like the most likely suspect. And now I have a friend caught in the middle. But you know what the worst part is?"

Megan waited.

"Not having control. Now that we're fighting over jurisdiction, who knows what direction the investigation could take."

"Denver had nothing to do with any of this."

To the disappointment of the dogs, King stood straight and stopped petting them. "I know that, you know that. A wealthy scientist is dead, and the killer is unknown. This will become a witch hunt. If history has taught us anything, it's that witch hunts rarely result in justice being served."

SEVENTEEN

"I don't know what King was talking about." Denver placed a cloth bag of groceries on his counter. One by one, he pulled out bags of rice and beans and cans of soup, his back to Megan. "Chase and I never had an argument. I hadn't seen the guy in years."

"Since your divorce."

Denver took the last can out of the bag and pushed it along the concrete countertop. Megan watched the slight hunch of his broad shoulders, the clench of his jaw, the impatient way he pushed his unruly hair away from his face.

"Denver?"

Denver crammed the dog food cans into his pantry cabinet. "No. I've seen him since then."

Megan tensed. "When?"

Denver worked for a minute without speaking. Finally, he said, "About a year ago. He, Martine, and Xavier came up for a

219

weekend. I couldn't join them because I was working, but we met one night for drinks."

Megan heard the hitch in his voice. A year ago, Megan and Denver were already dating. Megan braced herself for more . . . the *more* being a night spent with the elegant Martine. She thought of the way Martine had stared at Denver during dinner, at his obvious reluctance to meet Martine's gaze. Megan's breath caught in her chest. She couldn't bring herself to speak.

Denver's kitchen, like the house itself, was a study in clean lines. Megan slid a stool out from beneath a Craftsmen-style island and sat down heavily. Denver continued to put away groceries, his body language under his t-shirt and jeans matching the rigidity of her own.

Denver's five dogs broke the silence. The doorbell rang and all five started to bark and howl. Denver glanced at Megan apologetically, and she saw tears in his eyes.

"Denver —"

"Megs, I need to get the door."

"Wait."

"It's King, I'm sure. He'll be wanting to ask his own set of questions."

He disappeared into the hallway. It wasn't Bobby King he returned with; it was Martine. Martine looked ashen and afraid. Her

220

slim frame was draped in a black silk wrap dress. She wore red wedge heels and a cream scarf was knotted around her stalk-like neck. Wide eyes fell on Denver.

"I didn't mean to interrupt." Her voice was barely a whisper.

"It's okay. I was just leaving." Megan stood and grabbed her purse, hating the waves of jealousy washing over her. Denver could talk to whomever he wanted. It didn't mean anything.

"Megs, don't leave." Denver's voice was a command.

"I —"

"Stay. Please."

Megan nodded. She sat back down on the stool. She felt frustrated and confused by Denver's behavior, but curiosity won out. She wanted to know why Martine was here.

Denver fixed Martine a glass of Sauvignon Blanc. He poured one for Megan as well and grabbed a beer for himself. "Let's go into the living room."

The women followed Denver into a cozy living space. Sparsely decorated, but warm and inviting, it smelled faintly of wood smoke and citrus cleaner. Megan sat on the couch across from the fireplace. All five dogs crowded around her, on the seats beside her, and by her feet. Megan felt a wall of canine protectiveness.

Again, she waited.

This time Denver broke the silence. "Martine, what do you want?" His tone was harsh, and Megan looked at him in surprise.

"Have you heard from Jatin?"

"No."

"Xavier?"

"I've heard from the police. Do you want to know why? Because apparently one of you told our Chief that I had a fallout with Chase and should also be considered a suspect." Denver's Scottish brogue had become more pronounced, and he was in full dialect now. "Do ye want to tell me about that, Martine?"

"I never said anything to the police about you."

"No? Then maybe it was that boyfriend of yours, Xavier?"

Martine flushed. "Xavier isn't my boyfriend."

"No? I can't keep up with who is shagging whom. You all are like your own small version of Peyton Place." Denver looked away, disgust marring his handsome features. "Just keep me and Megan out of the drama."

"I'm sorry . . . I didn't realize you were being pulled into any drama."

"It's always drama where you are involved." He turned away. "Or Chase, for that matter."

Megan again glanced at Denver in surprise. This bitterness was a side to the veterinarian she hadn't seen before.

Martine's voice was barely a whisper when she said, "Whatever Chase did in life, Daniel, he's dead. And someone murdered him. I don't think it was that boy. I think someone within BOLD wanted Chase dead. Something was going on in the weeks before we came here."

"How do you know that?"

Martine seemed to shrink back into her seat. "It's a gut feeling."

"You realize I've known these people for years? That all of them — including Jatin — are friends."

The implication Megan heard was that Martine was not his friend. Megan wondered what had happened between Martine and Denver . . . and between Denver and Chase . . . to cause so much hostility in her good-natured lover.

Martine looked down at her hands, which were twisted in her lap. "I know. This pains me, Daniel, but I don't know who else to talk to."

"How about Harriet?" Megan asked.

Martine's laugh came out as a snort. "Harriet hears only what Harriet wants to hear. Right now, she's all about damage control. For BOLD and for the school."

"I asked you before, what do you think Jatin and Chase were arguing about?" Denver's voice was cold. "You must have heard something that made you suspicious."

"I really didn't. It was the fact of their arguing. The shouting. Maybe I would expect it from Chase, but not Jatin."

Megan recalled King's question about Martine. "Are you afraid?" She asked now. "For your own safety?"

Martine's hands flitted to the scarf around her neck. She unraveled the knot slowly, revealing a neck covered in an angry pink rash, worse than the lacy rash Megan had seen on her neck at the Inn. "When I get stressed, I get rashes. Does this answer your question?"

"Stress is not the same as fear," Denver said quietly.

"Fear is a type of stress. And yes, I'm afraid." Martine put the scarf on a square coffee table and stood. She walked to the window, five pairs of canine eyes following her every movement. "Jatin hasn't come back today. Xavier is a raving madman. Harriet is preoccupied and not listening to anyone."

Denver asked, "And Barbara?"

Martine turned from the window, a small smile flirting with the bottom half of her face. "You know Barbara's feelings toward me. Even if we were the last two standing, she wouldn't give me more than the time of day."

Martine and Denver held a stare that seemed to last a beat too long. "Aye. She doesn't much fancy you."

"Isn't it your job to do damage control?" Megan asked. "As the public relations person, shouldn't Harriet be asking you for help?"

"Harriet is far too proud to ask anyone for help. She has me making statements and calling various media outlets, but I'm her gopher, not her go-to person."

"What do you need from me?" Denver asked. His voice had warmed marginally, but he still looked like a man who had swallowed nails.

"I want you to talk to Jatin. Find out what happened that night. Even if he's told the police what happened, they won't tell me. I want to know if I am making more of this than there is."

Denver regarded his guest with disdain.

225

He stood, walked into the kitchen, and returned with a fresh beer. He pulled the tab and took a long swallow.

When he was done, he said, "How do we know you're not the killer, Martine? Enough anger and those arms could bash in a man's head, no problem. And I suspect you had enough anger to handle the deed."

"Nonsense."

"Photographs, as they say, are much more telling than words."

The silence in the room grew heavy until it was nearly palpable. Megan didn't know what game Denver and Martine were playing, but she'd had enough. She stood.

"Denver, call me when you have this sorted out."

Denver shook his head. "It's Martine who is leaving."

Martine grabbed her scarf. Without putting it back on, she hurried toward the front door.

"I guess we're leaving together," Megan said. She gave Denver look of reproach. "Call me when you're ready to be honest."

Megan held back tears the entire way home. She trusted Denver. It wasn't that she thought for even a moment that he'd had something to do with Chase's death, but he did seem weird around Martine. The fact that he was hiding something from her — never mind the police — upped her angst. There was a strange wounded quality about Martine Pringle, and beneath Denver's Renaissance man exterior lived a chivalrous soul. He liked to help — people and animals. And Martine had the feminine quality of movie stars from yesteryear.

Even so, Megan believed Denver that there was nothing between them now. But then? And how long ago was *then*? Five years ago, when he divorced his wife? Or a year ago, when Martine was last in the area?

This line of thinking was doing her no good. Megan cranked the radio until it was loud enough to drown her anxieties. On impulse, she pulled over to the side of the road and dug out her phone. She ignored the four texts from Denver asking her to come back and instead pulled up the text Martine had sent her. She clicked the phone number. Martine picked up immediately.

"Megan?" she said. Her voice sounded hesitant, as though she was afraid she'd be reprimanded.

Megan asked if they could meet, there were some additional questions she'd like to ask her.

"It's late," Martine said.

"Please. Just a few minutes?"

"I'm tired. I think we've all had enough for one night."

Megan said she understood. She hung up, feeling discouraged and empty.

Megan was just pulling into the driveway when her phone rang.

"Do you still want to meet?" Martine asked.

Megan was home. She pictured her warm bed, the dogs. "Yes," she sighed. Sleep wouldn't come without resolution. "Same place as before?"

It felt like Groundhog Day. Megan pulled into the parking lot and swerved around to the back of the lot, in the shadows. Why, she couldn't say, but the anxiety she'd been feeling all night hadn't left her. No use being conspicuous.

Martine was one of four people in the Starbucks. All except one sat in front of a laptop, working away. Martine's laptop was a sleek Mac, and she was staring at the screen intently. When Megan came up beside her, she saw a series of photographs. All of people. None the polished kind you'd see on a corporate website.

Martine slammed down the screen.

"Megan. Sorry, you startled me."

"My apologies. Can I get you some coffee or tea?"

Martine pointed to a cup of hot tea. Megan ordered a decaf for herself before sliding onto the bench across from her. Next to them, a twenty-ish man in army fatigues was watching something on his phone while drinking something frothy and caloric-looking.

"I'm sorry about tonight," Martine said. "About barging in on you and Daniel that way. He seemed angry."

Megan weighed her next words. She didn't trust Martine. Denver had called her a liar, and her behavior seemed, at best, erratic. She'd left out the fact that she'd been there when Chase played back-up for the Stones. What else was she leaving out? But beggars couldn't be choosers, as the saying went, and right now, Megan didn't have much to go on.

"That's actually why I wanted to talk with you," Megan said finally. "To understand the relationship between Chase and the others. They all say they're friends, but they don't seem to like each other much."

Martine smiled. "You noticed?"

"Hard to miss."

"It makes working with them interesting."

Martine pushed her laptop forward. She drummed manicured fingers on its metallic top. "I guess you heard that someone broke into Dr. Mantra's room at the inn?"

"Any idea who it was?"

"No." Martine shrugged. "I doubt it was related to Chase. Someone upset about their bonus this year? Or a maid Dr. Mantra managed to piss off."

"I wonder what they were after."

Martine smiled. "Money. Trade secrets they could sell. Who knows?"

"Harriet — Dr. Mantra — seems like she could easily anger staff."

Martine laughed. "Any of them could."

"Rough crowd."

Martine blinked. "They're not so bad. Well, yes they are." She smiled. "Problem is, they have known each other for such a long time. What Daniel says is true: they are a bit like Peyton Place. Barbara's dated most of them. They've known each other's wives and husbands, been to one another's weddings. In some cases, they were the reason for divorce." A shadow crossed Martine's face. "Yet they work well together. The four of them have a quality that cannot be denied. They're visionaries. They're the reason BOLD came to be."

"I thought the visionary was Harriet Mantra."

"She and her husband financed much of the company's start-up. But Chase and Barbara had the idea for the drug that was the basis for the company. Jatin helped to get the financing, and Xavier was the force behind selling the concept. He still is."

"Yet Harriet is the boss?"

"Follow the money." Martine took a sip of her tea. "Great ideas are worth nothing without execution. Harriet's money made it all possible."

"How big is the company now?"

"A few dozen employees."

"Isn't all this —" Megan waved her hand around "— a bit much for such a small company?"

"We're small, but we have a big idea. Several big ideas, in fact. Once the FDA approves one of our drugs, we'll get bigger."

"When will that be?"

"Soon, I hope. We all hope."

"All?"

Martine met Megan's gaze with a contemplative one of her own. She seemed to be deciding how much to share. "BOLD is not a public company. Right now, we rely on private investors, a few grants, Harriet's husband's family money. A lot of pharma companies start out this way. The money comes when the product goes live. Until then, we work hard and hope. And that's where this team comes in. They're amazing. Maddening, but amazing. Now, without Chase . . . I'm not sure where the company will be. At first glance, he may not seem like a science whiz, but he had that rare mix of science smarts and business know-how."

Megan had a hard time matching the man she'd met to a scientific visionary. But she'd been wrong about people in the past. She tried not to repeat mistakes.

"Martine, I'm curious about Jatin. Your admission to Denver that he has you nervous. Has Jatin ever done anything in the past that's made you fearful? Anything to give you an indication that he could be violent?"

Martine hesitated. Only for a second, but Megan caught it. "No."

"Really?"

Martine looked down at her hands. She traced the edge of her paper cup with one red nail. "Okay, maybe once. He can be protective of Barbara. Barbara and I . . . well, as I mentioned, there's no love lost there. He thought I'd done something terrible and he confronted me. This was a while ago, not now." She rubbed her arms in short, hard strokes. "There's a lot of pent up passion beneath that calm exterior. He was more forceful in his confrontation than he needed to be."

"He hurt you?"

"He could have been gentler."

"What did he think you'd done?"

Martine didn't answer the question. Instead, she said, "Daniel's not immune to the bad blood in the group. Did he tell you what happened with him and Chase?"

"No, he didn't." A sore spot. Megan tried to shake her annoyance and concentrate on the conversation with Martine, but she couldn't get rid of the lump in her gut. Even as they sat here, she could feel her phone buzzing.

"It was my fault, I'm afraid. Or at least he blames me." Martine stirred her tea, thinking. "Daniel and I met in New York about five years ago. I knew he was married, but Chase told me the marriage between his friend and Lilian was basically over. I was single. Daniel was handsome, honest, educated. Kind." Martine gave Megan an apologetic smile. "All the things that are hard to come by in a single man, it seems. You're a very lucky woman."

Megan waited for more. This part she knew from what Denver had told her.

Martine sipped her tea, wiped her mouth with a neatly-folded napkin. "Daniel agreed to meet me for drinks or coffee — I can't remember which. Anyway, we went out, and I had a blast. He was so warm and attentive. I may have mistaken his kindness for genuine interest. Chase met up with us. I took some photos of Denver, Chase took photos of the two of us. It was all in good fun. Until Chase posted them on social media."

Understanding dawned on Megan. "Denver's wife, Lilian, saw them and thought he was cheating."

Martine nodded. "I called him after that, and his wife answered. I'm sure it made things worse. He refused to talk to me."

Megan understood the bitterness — toward Martine and even Chase. Chase the clown who didn't think through the consequences of his actions, or the impact on other people. Megan was starting to get a clearer picture of what Chase was about: Chase. And Martine the seductress, on the sidelines, looking for love. A cliché, perhaps. How to see beyond the cliché?

"Was that what happened between you and Barbara as well? She suspected a dalliance with her husband?"

"Oh, you say it so nicely, Megan." Martine's smile lacked warmth. "I'm glad to have someone to talk to during all of this. Someone nonjudgmental. Someone not at BOLD."

The unexpected compliment made Megan flush. She nodded. "It must be hard to deal with everything — and work on top of it."

"It is." Martine looked down at her laptop. "But you asked about Barbara, and I digress. In that instance, I wasn't at fault. Barbara's husband hit on me during our holiday party. He's a drunk and a gambler and I hate him. That night, he was drunk or stoned as usual, and I was by myself near the pool, in the shadows. He'd been leering at me for months, but the drugs made him bold enough to make a move. I told Barbara about it — a mistake — and certain assumptions about my role in the incident were made." Martine waved a hand, clearly uncomfortable. "We've all moved past it."

Megan frowned. *Or had they?*

Megan thanked Martine for her time. Before she left, she pointed to the laptop. "At the risk of sounding nosy, I saw the photos on your computer. They didn't look like corporate photos. They seemed . . . artistic."

Like that, Martine's face was transformed. She smiled broadly, a twinkle in her eyes.

"Did you think so?" She flipped open the computer and rebooted it. Immediately Megan got a better view of the array of photos she'd glimpsed before. Children. Elderly. Abandoned buildings. Empty streets. Street cats. Street children. Flowers. Happy faces, sad faces, loneliness so absolute it twisted Megan's heart.

"You have a gift," Megan whispered, awed. "So much . . . truth."

Martine sat back in her chair. "This is my passion. Photography. I discovered it late in life."

"It clearly gives you happiness."

"Happiness." Martine sat back. "I don't know if that's the right word, but it may be the closest thing I have to describe it. When I'm shooting, I feel complete. Like I'm doing what I was meant to do."

The man next to them got up with a huff and left the Starbucks. A woman in a burqa carrying a tall cup of something steaming took his place.

Megan glanced again at the photographs. Each so poignantly captured an emotion. "Have you considered turning this into a full-time career?"

Martine's glow faded. "Sometimes all a girl has are dreams."

EIGHTEEN

Megan stared at her cell phone. It was after ten and dark outside, but Denver had texted her six times. In the last text he said he was handling an emergency. Could she meet him at the farm afterwards?

Despite some misgivings, Megan agreed. After speaking with Martine, she was still upset that he hadn't told her the whole truth from the beginning, but clearly his feelings about Chase and Martine were wrapped up in his personal life from long ago, including his failed marriage. Sorting through that kind of emotional baggage could be hard for anyone. Denver, as gregarious as he was, was also a man of science who considered himself rational and above drama. He'd run from anything emotionally messy, and this was messiness personified.

Back at the farm, Megan was greeted outside by an ecstatic Sadie and Gunther. She petted the dogs and spoke to them as they followed her inside the house. She was surprised to find Bibi sitting in the kitchen with Denver.

"I didn't see the 4Runner," Megan said.

"Bobby dropped me off. The emergency was handled pretty quickly. He stopped by to ask me some questions, and then he drove me here."

"Which means he asked you questions at the station. Official-like."

Denver nodded. He looked tired, but his eyes shown with a fiery fervor.

"Denver was telling me about his friends," Bibi said. Her voice was carefully metered, which meant he'd also told her Megan was angry at him.

"They're quite a bunch." Megan pulled a seat and sat down at the kitchen table.

Bibi had poured lemonade for her and Denver, and she handed Megan a glass as well. "Life is complicated, Megan. You of all people should know that." She added a scone to the lemonade. "Eat something. If I know you, you haven't eaten all day."

Gratefully, Megan broke apart the orange scone. Her stomach growled. "You sound like Aunt Sarah, Bibi."

"It must be the end of days, then." Bibi smiled. "Seriously, we need to sit and talk through all of this. Like it or not, a person is dead and some people we care deeply about — Denver, Eloise, even Bobby — are involved. This isn't the first time we've been faced with something like this. We should be pros by now."

Megan laughed. She couldn't help it. Her grandmother was eighty-five now, and that tiny, stooped frame packed more punch than most people a quarter of her age. Megan felt a surge of love for Bibi. She was right, of course. King was in over his head, and people they loved had something at stake.

"I spoke with Martine again," Megan said. "She shared some interesting tidbits about Jatin." Megan repeated what Martine had said about Jatin's liberal use of force, and the issues between Martine, Barbara, and Barbara's husband. She left out the information about Chase's actions and the impact on Denver's marriage. Later.

Denver scowled. "When you have a chance, Megs, look up Barbara's husband. Self-made multi-millionaire and ass extraordinaire." Denver gave her his name.

"It doesn't sound like he recognizes boundaries."

"He has a strong personality. Believes himself above just about everything. Barbara met him after she and Jatin broke up. I think he was her rebound guy. He's older, handsome, and rich. I guess for Barbara he was what she needed at the time. Someone who took charge so she didn't need to."

"Do they have kids?" Bibi asked.

"No kids. Barbara miscarried a year into the marriage. She never spoke of babies again."

Megan took a few bites of scone, thinking about Barbara. Barbara seemed level-headed and good natured. She had trouble picturing her with someone like the man Denver was describing, and she said as much.

"He's a high-powered attorney and land developer in California. They had a bi-coastal marriage for a while. Barbara seems happy enough, but I can totally see him hit-ting on other women."

"Can you see Jatin reacting to Martine with violence?"

"No." Denver turned his cup around in his large hand. Megan saw Band-Aids on his thumb and forefinger and the rippled scarring of a recent wound on his palm. "I've told ye before, Megs, that Martine lies."

"Lies?" Bibi said.

"She's a compulsive liar." Denver took a deep breath. "I told you, Megan, that I met

Martine in New York City years ago, when my marriage was in trouble. Bonnie, do you remember Lilian?"

Bibi nodded. By the pinched look on her face, Megan didn't think she had particularly cared for the former Winsome resident.

"We were having some problems," Denver said, "and I needed to get away, so I went into the city to clear my mind and decide what to do. I knew things were bad, but I thought marriage counseling might help. I hadn't given up on our relationship. It's not in my nature."

Megan nodded. She placed a hand on his, careful of the wounds. He squeezed her hand gently.

"Anyway, Chase texted me and we realized we were both in the city. We met for drinks. Martine was with him. She was friendly and seemed down to earth. A good listener. The next day, Chase had business to attend to, so I said I'd show Martine around the city. We had coffee, went to the Strand bookstore, walked around. Nothing happened. I didn't even particularly care for her. My mind — my heart — were with Lilian."

He swallowed. Megan heard the ticking of the clock in the other room, the rattle of the loose boards on the porch. She glanced at

Bibi, who was studying Denver. Her grandmother was wearing pink plaid pajama bottoms and a white "Winsome is for lovers" t-shirt. Her white hair was pushed back from her face, and there was sadness in her eyes. Right now, Bibi looked like she'd taken on the weight of the world.

"How hard this must have been for you," Bibi said to Denver. "To be in New York while your marriage was collapsing."

"As fate would have it, the trip was the tipping point. Martine took some photos of me. Laughing. Smiling. Chase took a few of the two of us. He put them on social media, and Lilian saw them. She used them to justify sleeping with our contractor. And our accountant."

Megan closed her eyes. "Oh, Denver."

"Ta. It's okay. I understand now that our marriage was already over. Lilian had probably cheated before. This just made it easier for her to justify her actions. The worst part was that Martine called my house. Repeatedly. When Lilian asked who was calling, she said it was my girlfriend." He shook his head. "You can't believe anything she says. So when Martine accuses Jatin, I take it with a pound of salt."

"She remained friends with Chase?"

"She works with all of them, but if you

notice, she's more of an outsider."

Bibi poured more lemonade from a glass pitcher into Denver's cup. "People like that can be the most dangerous. Sometimes they make up in fantasy what they lack in reality."

"What do you mean, Bibi?" Megan asked.

"Maybe she was in love with Chase. Maybe she thought Chase was in love with her."

"Martine as the murderer?" Denver shook his head. "Liar, yes. Killer? I just don't see it."

Megan's mind flitted to other murders — and other murderers. "Stranger things have happened."

"Be right back." Bibi left the room, and Megan and Denver exchanged a glance.

"What about a year ago?" Megan asked. "You said you'd seen Chase and Martine then."

"Aye. Chase and I hadn't really spoken. I blamed him for contributing to my marriage issues. He wanted to make things better between us. They were here for BOLD. I agreed to see them."

"And you patched things up."

Denver shrugged. "We had drinks. Danced around the topic. Did the typical guy thing of sweeping it all under the rug. I guess part of me was still angry. Is still angry." Denver swallowed, looked away. "It wasn't so much what he did, it was the way he did it. No thought about me or my life. And afterwards? A big joke. But that was Chase."

"I'm sorry."

"*I'm* sorry," Denver said. "For not telling you all the sordid bits before. I guess I was still angry at Chase. I was afraid ye would think that meant I missed my ex-wife or the life we had together." He squeezed Megan's hand. "I don't. I never would have met you if we'd stayed together."

Megan smiled. "I'm sorry for everything you went through."

"Lilian was a confused woman. We met young. She wanted *me* — until she didn't. The life of a vet means late hours and unpredictable schedules." He smiled, and two dimples popped up on either side of his mouth. "And dog hair and a smelly car and a house that sounds like a zoo. Not her cup of coffee, I'm afraid."

Megan had only seen one photograph of Lilian. She was an attractive, slim Asian woman with long black hair and high cheekbones. In the photo, Lilian wore a white dress and high red heels. Her perfect skin had been shaded by a broad-brimmed black hat. More New York debutante than wife of

244

a country vet.

"I had nothing to do with Chase's death. My anger was more hurt. We should have talked about it, maybe, but you met Chase. Talking about feelings wasn't really his thing."

"It's okay," Megan said. "I understand."

Denver was about to say something else when Bibi returned with a giant wipe board. She propped it up on the counter, facing the table, and pulled five colored Erase markers from her pocket.

"I took this from the Bridge club. Who needs to be somewhere tonight?" Bibi asked.

Fighting a smile, Megan said, "Not me."

Denver shook his head. "Nor I — assuming no more emergencies."

Bibi gave a definitive nod. "Good. Megan, coffee. Denver, can you do a quick check on the animals?" Bibi pulled the black pen from the pile. "Then we can get started."

"It's late, Bibi."

Bibi smiled. "You two are too young to need that much rest. And the comfort of sleep is denied to me most nights, anyway. Might as well make some use of the witching hours."

Megan sat cross-legged on her kitchen chair. She'd changed into flannel pajama

245

bottoms and a tank top, and her shoulder-length dark hair was pushed back from her face with a barrette. The two cups of coffee she'd drunk had worked their magic, and she was feeling borderline manic. She watched as Bibi made notations on the board in her teacher-like script.

They'd created two categories of would-be connections: school student/associate and BOLD employee. Under each category, they listed possible suspects. They'd had "stranger" included, too, but realized there wasn't much they could do to track down a random murderer. They listed "stranger" in the corner, off by itself.

Under school student/associate they'd listed Dillon's name.

Under BOLD, they had Martine, Xavier, Jatin, and Barbara.

"Add Harriet Mantra too," Megan said.

Denver looked at her sharply. "Why? She wasn't even in town when Chase was killed."

"True, but this whole thing was her idea. As we very well know, you don't need to be present to be the mastermind behind murder."

Bibi added Harriet's name to the board in purple. "We'll omit you," she said to Denver. Megan couldn't tell if she was being cheeky.

"Is there anyone else you can think of who

246

should be on this list?" Megan asked.

"I mean, Chase has an ex-wife. Diana. It's possible she came into town and killed him. Possible, but doubtful."

"I remember you telling me about her," Megan said.

Bibi added Diana's name to the board.

Megan recalled the rest of that conversation with Denver. "Don't forget about the photos I found of Chase and Martine during his Rolling Stones days. They knew each other before BOLD. We should add a second line — maybe a dotted line — between Martine and Chase to indicate that connection."

"But all of them, other than Harriet, had a preexisting relationship with Chase."

"One that was obvious. The connection between Chase and Martine wasn't known. At least by us."

Denver nodded. "True."

Bibi added the dotted line to the board. "This is a good start. We have two avenues: the school and the company. Who wants to do what?"

Megan studied her grandmother. While Bibi was no stranger to action when she thought someone from Winsome needed her, she generally didn't seem so enthusiastic about getting involved.

"What's your angle here, Bibi?" Megan asked. "Why are you going all Nancy Drew on us?"

Denver laughed. He rubbed his chin with a calloused hand. "I rather think it suits you, Bonnie."

"You're both very funny." Bibi sat down on the chair she'd placed in front of the board. She rubbed her neck. "This one is a puzzle. Someone killed that man in an act of passion. Or at least that's what we're meant to believe. I hear the townspeople at Bridge. They all think the boy did it." She shook her head. "He is the obvious choice. But what's his motive?"

"Sometimes people don't need a motive," Denver said. "He could have snapped."

Bibi said, "He could have. But I don't think he did."

Megan walked over to the board. Bibi was right: Dillon was the obvious choice. She grabbed a pen and started a new graph at the bottom of the surface.

"We have connections at BOLD Pharmaceuticals, the school, and then personal connections like Diana and Denver." Megan drew a circle and put Chase's name in the center. She drew a box to the left and labeled it "BOLD" and a box to the right and labeled it "School." Under the school, she wrote Dillon's name, Harriet's daughter's name, and Dr. Star. She drew a line between Dillon and Chase. She repeated the exercise with BOLD, including Martine, Harriet, Xavier, and Jatin's name. She drew a line from each of them to Chase — denoting a direct connection. She also drew a line from Harriet to the school, Harriet to her daughter, and Harriet to Dr. Star. Beneath Chase's name, she wrote his wife's name and Denver's name and drew lines to each.

"Not because you're a suspect," she explained. "But because we're looking for connections."

With that in mind, Megan added her Aunt Sarah to the board and drew a line between her and Dr. Star. She explained the connection to Bibi and Denver.

"I think we have a place to start," Bibi said.

Megan nodded.

"Someone going to clue me in?" Denver said. "I'm not sure how this diagram helps us."

"Somewhere in here is the connection that got Chase killed," Megan explained. "If Dillon did it, then the connection will be simple. He snapped, or Chase did something to anger him. But if Dillon didn't do it —"

"In there somewhere is the real motive for murder. The company. The school."

"Or a personal vendetta," Megan said.

Denver stared at the board for a moment. "Or both."

"I'll look into Dillon," Bibi said. "I'm not as adept at the computer as you two are, but I can cook, and I can talk, and I can listen, so I'll have him and Eloise over for dinner. I'd rather like to meet him."

Megan nodded. "I can look into the company. Do some research, maybe contact my accountant to see what he can dig up. I'll also talk to Sarah again and see if I can't get in front of Dr. Star." Megan thought about her last discussion with the psychologist. She snapped her fingers. "Even better. When I was at the school last time, there was a reporter there. Donna something or other. I'll connect with her."

Denver looked from Megan to Bibi and back again. "Megs, I'm afraid I won't be much help."

"Oh, no, you don't," Bibi said. "We're a team. You can talk to your friends. See what they'll spill about one another."

Denver frowned. "That seems a bit . . . wrong."

Bibi pushed herself up from her chair. The look she gave Denver could have frozen

Niagara Falls. "*Murder* is wrong. Letting an innocent boy go to jail is wrong. Sorting through the who-did-whats-to-whom is justice."

The caffeine was wearing off and exhaustion lurked underneath. Despite the descending fog, Megan smiled. Leave it to Bibi to cut right to the heart of the matter.

If Denver was offended, he didn't show it. "I'm all for justice," he said to Bonnie. He gave her a kiss on the cheek. "I'll start with our missing Jatin and see just what had him so upset when he was talking with Chase."

"Be careful," Megan said. "Sorting through the who-did-whats-to-whoms can be the most dangerous job of all."

NINETEEN

Megan had promised Alvaro she'd help at the café the following day, so she packed up her laptop and headed for Winsome proper. The morning was dark and overcast. It had rained overnight, and Mother Nature left a muddy mess in the courtyard. The weather forecasters were calling for afternoon thunderstorms, but Megan wasn't so sure they would hold off until later in the day.

Canal Street was empty. Megan parked and climbed out of the truck. She walked into the café carrying her computer in a bag over her shoulder and a large bag of veggies from the farm: garlic scapes, peas, kale, and a variety of lettuces. The handwritten menu board at the café entrance said Alvaro was making a spring salad as an entrée. She hoped she'd remembered everything he'd asked for.

"Morning," her chef mumbled. He pointed to the large chopping block where a stack of carrots, celery, hot peppers, cilantro, parsley, and onions were sitting, washed and waiting. "Can you chop those?"

"I thought you were making salad?"

"It's for tonight. I'm serving a sofrito chicken stew over rice. Comfort food."

"Sounds amazing."

"I need a lot because I'm also . . ." He mumbled something Megan couldn't hear.

"What was that, Alvaro?"

The chef stopped what he was doing and turned around. His white hair was disheveled, his bushy eyebrows gave his stern expression an almost comical look. "I'm also making a vegan version with pozole. Okay?"

Megan laughed. "You don't need to get defensive. I like that you're doing more plant-based dishes."

Alvaro threw a towel down on the table. "Yeah, well, my mother, who taught me to cook, is rolling over in her grave. Vegan sofrito stew?" He shook his head. "What next? Vegan tamales?"

"You could stuff them with squash and sweet corn. I think that sounds pretty good."

Alvaro glared at her.

"You must really love Clover."

Alvaro's expression softened. "Ah, just

253

chop the vegetables. I need quiet when I work."

Megan set to dicing the vegetables and herbs, thinking all the while about family. Alvaro had been the chef at the commune where Clover and Clay grew up. He and his wife had been their quiet champions when they were children, and now they were their surrogate parents. People would go to great lengths for the people they loved.

Was that an angle she was missing in the case of Chase's murder? Was someone angry at Chase, not because of what he did to them, but because of what he had done to someone else?

It was mid-morning before Megan could disappear into the office with her laptop. By then, Emily had shown up to handle the late breakfast crowd, and Clover had taken over at the store's register. The whole place was perfumed by Alvaro's sofrito stew and the chicken roasting in the ovens. Alvaro, surly as ever, was putting the finishing touches on his spring salad ingredients, which included a choice of local chicken breast, Alaskan wild salmon, or barbequed tofu.

As she closed the door, Megan could hear Alvaro and Clover bickering about whether the honey he'd put into the barbeque sauce was vegan. No good deed, she thought. They'd work it out.

In the privacy of her office, Megan pulled up the article about the Pioneer Village School by Donna Lewis, the writer for *The Bucks County Times*. She skimmed the content, then went back and re-read it. It certainly wasn't a love note to the school. Lewis had done her research. The school had started out as an orphanage. Eventually the building was sold to an unknown benefactor who turned it into a school and hired Benjamin Star to run the admissions program and oversee the counseling services. Star had been there since inception.

Lewis acknowledged the school's lofty goals: to service an underserved population of at-risk, intellectually gifted students. She also underscored that the tuition was high and a majority of the kids who attended were from wealthy homes. Scholarships were few and far between.

Her parting shot had to do with Dillon. She blamed the school for covering up serious emotional and behavioral issues, issues that led to destruction in the community and even violence. She never came out and accused Dillon of Chase's death, but she insisted that the school didn't follow proper safety or security procedures. She gave no indication of what procedures they were failing to follow.

Megan scribbled down the little information she could find about Donna Lewis. Donna knew something about the school, that much was apparent. Maybe she knew more about the murder than she was letting on. Megan called the paper, which was headquartered in nearby New Hope, and left a message for the reporter. She also sent her an email at the address listed in her byline, providing her cell phone number too. She kept it simple, asking only for a few minutes of her time to discuss the school. After witnessing her dogged approach at the school, Megan suspected any mention of Dr. Star and his program would be enough. She'd hear back from Donna Lewis.

Megan sat back in her chair. Now she'd wait. Megan closed her eyes and rubbed her temples, trying to decide whether to make another visit to the school or whether to hit up Sarah for more information. Sarah could be stubbornly unhelpful when she wanted to be. She'd go straight to the school.

Megan was about to pull up BOLD's corporate page when her phone dinged. It was Donna Lewis already, agreeing to meet.

Megan texted back. *How about an hour from now? I'll treat you to coffee in New Hope.* She named a spot on the main road. She had an ulterior motive for wanting to meet in New Hope. Her accountant was there, and she thought maybe he could do some digging into BOLD's corporate structure and financial dealings.

Lewis agreed to her offer. Megan packed up her bag and tucked her briefcase in a desk drawer. She'd come back. To help Alvaro with the dinner rush, and to sample his vegan sofrito stew.

Coffee on Main was a quaint reminder that not all great coffee shops were chains. Tucked between an independent bookstore and a jewelry boutique, the café offered comfortable, upholstered chairs, plenty of table space, baked goods, and a rich array of fresh-roasted coffees. Megan ordered and then grabbed a pair of armchairs that sat across from each other in a cozy, sunny corner.

Within twenty minutes, Lewis arrived. Megan recognized her from the school. Today her silver hair was hidden under a teal beret. She wore a magenta shirt dress and a pair of thick-heeled, ivory sandals. The sour look on her face clashed with the cheeriness of her clothes.

"Megan Sawyer." Lewis placed her bag on the second armchair.

"Order whatever you want. They're running a tab for me," Megan said.

Donna Lewis came back ten minutes later carrying a toasted muffin, a large cup of coffee, and a croissant. "First meal of the day," she said as she sat. "And after all these carbs, I'll need a nap."

Megan smiled. She sipped at the coffee in her own mug and took a bite of her blueberry muffin. It was good, but she found she wasn't very hungry and put it aside.

"Your note said you want to talk about the Pioneer Village School." Lewis took a large bite out of her muffin and wiped her face with a crumpled napkin. "Right?"

"I read your article. I have a friend whose kid may go there. I was curious about what you said."

Megan waited while Lewis finished her muffin. She ate methodically, slowly, as though she was unaware that Megan was waiting for her to finish. Finally, she put the plate on a side table and sighed.

"You realize I'm a journalist, right?"

Megan nodded.

"Then you know part of my job is researching things and people? And I have access to all sorts of databases and information."

Megan nodded again.

"In that case, because we're now on the same page, do you want to start again?"

Megan studied her. "You're saying you know who I am."

"I know your boy toy is Dr. Daniel Finn, most eligible bachelor in Winsome and voted best looking veterinarian in a kilt. Didn't take me long to figure out that Finn was friends with the deceased Charles Mars. Or that his aunt is Eloise Kent, foster mother to the accused."

"He's not been formally accused."

"The investigation is still underway." Lewis picked up her cup and sloshed its contents. "Just a matter of time."

Megan didn't like the way Lewis was staring at her with a "gotcha" expression on her face. "You did your research well," Megan said. "But I've done some of my own. I know that you were once a reporter for *The New York Times*. That you were fired when they found out you'd fabricated sources for a piece you did on local law enforcement. I know since then you've pieced together a career with bit assignments for local news outlets. Dog bite stories. Robberies. The occasional wedding announcement." Megan matched stare for stare. "And I know you have a bug up your ass when it comes to the Pioneer Village School. I want to know why."

Lewis sat openmouthed. Eventually the edges of her mouth turned up into a smile, and she began clapping slowly. "Excellent. Your reputation as a local sleuth is well-deserved. You forgot, of course, to mention my messy divorce a year ago and the fact that I'm suing my chiropractor."

"I chose not to mention the former," Megan said. "And I had no idea about the latter."

"Because it's not true, and neither is the allegation about fabricating witnesses. They didn't like my witness, they couldn't take the heat, and so they fired me." Lewis put her cup on the table. She slapped her hands down on her ample thighs. "I like you. You have ovaries. What do you want, Megan Sawyer of Winsome? Dirt on the investigation? Information about Dillon Brown? The real story behind Dr. Benjamin Star's little fiefdom for smart, rich kids? Why did you want to see me today?"

"I wanted to hear about any and all of these topics, if you can deliver."

"What are you trying to do?"

"I just want an understanding of what's

going on." Megan decided to be honest. It was a risk — she didn't trust this woman — but what did she have to lose? "As you said, my boyfriend was friends with Chase Mars. Now his aunt's foster son is a suspect."

"He most likely did it —"

Megan held up a hand. "He's a suspect. And while everyone is focused on him, the real killer could be getting away, quite literally, with murder."

Lewis crossed her arms across her chest. "Why do you care?"

"Really? He's a kid."

Lewis openly studied her, her face inscrutable. "I'll make you a deal. I'll help you, but if you find out something that leads to an arrest, I get to use you as a source."

Megan considered the offer. She saw the kind of slam job Donna had done on the school. She didn't want to be on the other end of that typewriter.

"I will be your neutral source. You can use information I give you, but you must use it verbatim — as I give it. No twisting my words."

"Deal. So now that we're pals, what do you want to know?"

"In the article you wrote on the school, you accused them of not following certain safety or security standards. What did you mean?"

"For one, I've heard they don't follow internal safety standards. Schools like that use psychiatrists to monitor medications. Parents have complained that the structure is lax, and kids are able to get their hands on others' meds."

"That's not good. Were you able to verify that?"

"No," Lewis said, "which is why I didn't include it. But there's more. Those kids were out in public, on state lands, without the proper adult to student ratio."

"By law?"

"By common sense. There were four staff members there with twenty-six kids. Not enough when you're dealing with potentially dangerous youth."

"What about the mentors from BOLD?"

Lewis laughed so hard that spit sprayed from her mouth. "You have got to be kidding. Have you seen that bunch? Not one of them went through training — self-defense, CPR, safe restraint, nothing."

She had a point. "You said dangerous youth. I didn't think the kids at the Pioneer Village School were dangerous. Troubled, perhaps. Anxious. Mood or attention disorders. But not violent."

"You must have been talking to Dr. Star. Lies. Ask him about Cat Mantra. Or Ollie Olswager. Or Denise Byer-Helms. Or your boy, Dillon Brown. Theft. Destruction of property. Attempted rape. Fire setting. Murder. In that order."

Megan chose to ignore the mention of Dillon. "Those are kids, Donna. Confidentiality. How did you get their names?"

Lewis sat there smugly. "You didn't see their names in print. Next question."

Annoyed, Megan moved on. "What makes you so sure Dillon is guilty?"

"For the same reasons most people believe he's guilty. He was found with the murder weapon. We know Chase left to find him. No one else was present." She gave Megan a sly smile. "And there is one other small piece of information I got from a source."

"Which was?"

A pause. "You promised. Remember that. The police report indicated that the killer was most likely left-handed."

"And Dillon is left-handed."

Lewis nodded. "Smart girl."

Megan mulled this over. King hadn't mentioned a word about the killer being left-handed. But then, maybe the police were sitting on that piece of evidence and he couldn't share it.

"You have a source inside the Winsome police?"

Another sly smile. "You know I can't say." Lewis glanced at her watch. "I have to go soon, Megan. What else you got for me?"

"In the article you wrote about the school, you mentioned the history of the building and the fact that the school was started not that long ago by a wealthy benefactor. Do you know who the benefactor was?"

"It was actually a small group of benefactors, most of whom had children who needed somewhere to go. Self-interested bastards. I don't have names, but they could probably be found if you know where to search. County records and the like."

Megan nodded. She could see what she could find. "Why do you dislike the school — and Dr. Star — so much?"

Lewis seemed to sink into her chair. She made a fist with one hand and rubbed her knuckles into her thigh. "I don't dislike them. That implies personal interest, and this isn't personal. I don't think it's fair when rich people get away with things because they're rich. I really think it's unfair when rich kids get away with things because Mommy and Daddy have money."

"Like the things you mentioned. Destruction of property, etc."

"Like that." Lewis lowered her voice. "When I first moved to Philadelphia, I was asked to write about a kid from Strawberry Mansion. Been there?"

Megan shook her head.

"No surprise. Rough neighborhood. Kid born there is already a few football fields behind their peers in the game of life. Anyway, I was covering a young black man's journey to prison. He'd spent most of his life in juvie, and it all started when he stole a pack of gum from a local store. *Gum*. His first three offenses were all minor — shoplifting, loitering, graffiti."

Lewis shook her head. "Look, I'm not condoning theft or any other crime, but as I was writing that story, I was alerted to another story in Bucks County. Young girl arrested for vandalizing and torching a public area in the town of Blessings. The story isn't about her — she's underage and goes to a special school — it's about how bad things can turn good because the town got a new bird sanctuary out of it."

Cat Mantra. Megan listened, understanding Donna Lewis's outrage.

"My Strawberry Mansion kid gets beat up in juvie, joins a gang, goes down a path that leads him to prison. Mommy and Daddy didn't have the money or wherewithal to buy him out of trouble. Young woman runs away from hoity-toity school, causes thousands of dollars in property damage, and she gets away scot-free. Now she's running from homeless shelter to half-way house, a burden on the system."

"Life's not fair," Megan said. "I see that every day."

"It's not. But unless someone is willing to point it out, it won't get any better."

"And Dr. Star?"

"He's their puppet. Send Junior to Dr. Star. He'll arrange for some nice calming medication, a diet worthy of a four-star restaurant, and plenty of fresh air. And if Junior should try to rape or kill someone along the way?" Lewis shrugged. "Dr. Star can take care of that too."

Megan didn't doubt what Lewis was saying. Things weren't fair. Politicians and bankers avoided jail time for fraud, and poor people went to prison for possession of pot. Lewis's bitterness seemed disproportionate, however. She said it wasn't personal, but it sure felt personal.

Megan said, "They say they don't use medication, except when absolutely necessary."

"They lie." Donna adjusted her face from a frown to a sardonic smile. "They house sick kids, Megan. Some of them need medication. For some, it probably makes them easier to handle."

"Do you mean warehouse?"

"Your word." Donna Lewis stood. "Thank you for the coffee. I'm sorry I couldn't be of more help. You see, the answer is simple. Someone paid for Dillon to go to that school. After all Dillon had been through, he was a time bomb. He should have been in a psych unit, not out on a camping trip. It was just a matter of time before something like this happened."

Megan also stood. She towered over the diminutive reporter, and she used her size to stall Lewis's exit. "You said someone paid his tuition. I thought the school had a scholarship fund."

Donna laughed. "They did at one point, but look into the last time they had a scholarship student. It's been forever. I told you, these people are in it for themselves — not to help others."

Megan thanked her and watched her leave. Who had paid Dillon's tuition? Eloise? The boys' parents? But would their money even be available given the circumstances of his mother's death? She should be able to find that out easily enough — she just needed the courage to ask Eloise directly. If there was still a scholarship fund, she'd think a boy like Dillon would be a shoe-in. And again, she wondered about BOLD's funding for students who completed the mentoring program. If everyone was rich, no one needed that college money. What was the point? She could ask Martine about that.

Regardless of the answers, something seemed very odd about the whole arrangement.

TWENTY

Lou Tillery worked out of a three-floor walk-up in the center of New Hope. New Hope, a charming small Bucks County town along the New Jersey border, was home to an artsy crowd, as evidenced by the small boutiques, art galleries, and craft shops. But there was a practical side to New Hope, and Lou was a stalwart who'd been practicing in the hamlet since before it became trendy. His office was cramped and smelled faintly of pipe tobacco, the kind that wafted off a person who smoked a lot, and curry from the Indian restaurant downstairs.

Lou's elderly receptionist/tax preparer/handywoman greeted Megan at the door with a smile. "The boss is on a call, Megan. Is he expecting you?"

"No, Bernice. But I was in the neighborhood and thought maybe I'd catch him."

Bernice glanced backwards, toward Lou's closed door. "It's his husband. They could

269

be a while. The Samoyed got loose again, and Lou wants a fence around the yard."

Megan had been hearing from Lou year after year how he wanted to fence in their small-town lot, but his husband was against it — too many permits since theirs was an historical home.

Megan nodded. "I can wait."

She didn't need to wait long. Lou came storming out of his office a few minutes later. The scarlet of his face matched the scarlet on his bald scalp. He stopped short when he saw Megan and laughed.

"I was just about to start complaining to Bernie here, Megan. I think you saved her. Bernie, you should thank Megan."

Bernie smiled the smile of an eternally patient woman. "Thank you, Megan."

Lou gave a hearty laugh. "I think I won this time. He's already calling about the permits. He loves that dog more than he loves me." Lou opened his office door wider. "Come on in, Megan."

This is what Megan loved about Lou. He was always available — even when he wasn't.

"How can I help you?"

She sat in the familiar office, breathing in the ambience. Photos of Lou and his spouse hung next to paintings and photos from their world travels. The faces of Lou's two beautiful girls looked out at her from one wall. From the other, an array of dog portraits and memorabilia. The room was a homage to her accountant's eclectic and varied life. He was good at his job, his clients loved him, and he was well-connected.

She was banking on the latter now.

"BOLD Pharmaceuticals. Ever hear of it?"

"Only recently, in the news. That man who was killed. Wasn't he an employee?"

Megan nodded. "He was a friend of Denver's."

Lou held up a hand. "I'm not going to lecture you on the dangers of getting involved, Megan. Just tell me what you need. But don't give me more information than is necessary." He smiled. "Just kidding. Or not."

"BOLD is a private company, so I can't get much online. Articles of Incorporation, licenses, anything you can find that might show ownership structure."

Lou nodded. "Are you looking for something in particular?"

"I don't know what I'm looking for. Hopefully I'll know it when I see it."

Lou's eyes narrowed. "Shots in the dark?"

"When you don't have a light, it can be

271

the only way." Megan started to leave but thought of something else. "Are you familiar with the Pioneer Village School?"

"That's where the kid who was with the victim goes to school."

"Bingo. Can you see if you can find anything on that as well? Owners. Tax information."

Lou agreed. "You know, I have a neighbor whose son went to that school."

Megan perked up. "Really?"

"Alexander Raymond Giles Junior. Too many names for one kid, if you ask me." Lou frowned. "Parents are divorced now, but his mother would probably be happy to talk to you. She will discuss little Alex with anyone who listens, despite the fact that little Alex is a twenty-four-year-old grown man now."

"How can I reach her?"

"Give me a second."

Lou called his husband. After a quick exchange, he hung up. "Dee Dee Giles — that's her name, poor thing — is home. My husband will see if she'll speak to you. Give him a few minutes and then you can head over. I know Dee Dee, and I know my husband. It will be fine."

Twenty minutes later, Megan was pulling

272

into the Giles' home on Main Street. A sprawling Victorian, the house had more turrets and porches than Megan could count. The yard was small, but what it lacked in size it made up for in decorations. A bird bath sat to one side of the entrance, surrounded by flowers and a half dozen miniature gnomes. Across the walkway that led to the porch was another flower garden paved with mosaic stones and marked by randomly-placed sculptures, windchimes, and bird feeders. Even with the sullen sky, the combination was welcoming, if a bit overwhelming to the senses.

A woman sat on the porch. In her early fifties, she wore a flowered sundress and dark sunglasses. Her gray-streaked hair was pulled back into a ponytail. Her feet were bare, showing off toenails painted with tiny sunflowers. A pink bracelet on her wrist said "Survivor."

"I just love Lou!" the woman called out as a greeting. "A friend of his is a friend of mine." She met Megan on the steps and held out a hand. "Dolores Giles. Friends call me Dee Dee." She flashed another smile, one that spoke of an excellent orthodontist and many teeth-whitening sessions. "*You* can call me Dee Dee. Are you okay with the porch? It's such a lovely day. I made some tea. I hope you like tea. It's organic *and* free trade."

Megan sank into a white wicker chair cushioned with a cheerful green and white striped pillow. "Tea would be lovely. Thank you so much for agreeing to talk with me, Dee Dee. You have a beautiful house."

"Even more beautiful now that I don't have to share it with my cheating bastard of an ex-husband. He got syphilis, and I got the house."

Dee Dee said this with such airy cheerfulness that Megan almost choked on her tea.

"Well —"

"TMI. I know. Little Alex tells me that all of the time. *Too much information, Mom.* Yeah, yeah. Life is short. Unlike my cheating bastard of an ex-husband, I have nothing to hide."

Dee Dee was a lot to handle, but Megan felt an instant pull. She admired the woman's spunk.

After a few minutes of chit chat, Megan broached the subject of the school. "Pioneer Village School, Dee Dee. Lou told me your son went there."

"He did. Best decision we ever made."

"You were happy with it, then?"

"Understatement. Saved his life. Not our marriage, but that was unsalvageable, cheating bastard that my ex is." Dee Dee took a demure sip of her tea. "What do you want to know about the school?"

"How did the admission process go, what were your son's schoolmates like, that sort of thing."

"Well, let me start by saying that my Alex was a handful. Not a mean kid, but active. Crazy active. When he was young, he was always climbing on things or bothering the dog or taking my stuff apart. We found out later that he had ADHD really bad, and coupled with a crazy high IQ, he was just too much for us to handle."

"When did you find the school?"

"The school found us. When little Alex was sixteen, he was suspended from high school. He'd set off the school's fire alarm so he could steal chemicals from the chem lab. He got caught. It was his third offense. What could the school do? They had to set limits."

Dee Dee said all of this matter-of-factly, as though talking about a shoe sale or a favorite recipe.

"How did the Pioneer Village School come into play?"

"About a week after Alex was suspended, I got a call from Dr. Benjamin Star, the school's psychologist. He suggested a meeting. Thought little Alex might be a good fit for the program."

"How had he heard about Alex?"

"You know, I never asked. At the time, we were at wit's end and just so grateful to have another option."

Megan did the math. This would have been eight years ago, close to the school's inception and shortly before Cat attended the school.

"Did you like Dr. Star?"

Dee Dee's face lit up. "He's a brilliant man. Got Alex's dosage worked out, gave him some tools for dealing with his behavioral issues. Most of all, he challenged Alex. Alex loves to tinker. Dr. Star had him doing graduate-level math and engineering by the time he was a senior. Alex hated English and humanities, so he got to focus on the things he loved." She clapped. "Presto, Alex's weaknesses all turned into strengths."

Megan wasn't so sure it was that easy, but she had to admit that Dee Dee seemed to be a true fan.

"I know this is very personal, but did they offer your son a scholarship to attend?"

"Heavens, no!" Dee Dee waved at the giant house behind them. "My cheating bastard of an ex-husband was also cheap. Had they offered one, he would have taken it. We didn't need one, though, and it just never came up. I think some kids may have gotten them. I can't say for sure."

"And the admissions process?"

"Simple. A battery of aptitude tests, which my Alex passed with flying colors. Some psychological assessments. A conversation with his school counselor." She shrugged. "Took a week, tops. Painless."

Dee Dee was so forthcoming that Megan was afraid to push. The other woman seemed to enjoy the conversation, though, so Megan continued. "How about his schoolmates, Dee Dee? Were they similar to your son?"

Dee Dee appeared to give this some thought. "Now that you ask, not really. Alex never made many friends while he was there. Some of the kids had anger issues or severe social anxiety. Some were autistic. The school has both a residential component and a day treatment option. Alex was a day student. Some of the more severe cases lived at the school."

Like Cat.

"Did you hear of violent tendencies? Any outbursts, problems?"

Dee Dee took off her sunglasses and placed them on a square glass table. "Like the boy who was involved up in the park? I

277

heard he was a Pioneer student." Dee Dee didn't wait for an answer. "There were a few problems, but it's a school for smart kids with issues. Wouldn't you expect some things to happen here and there?"

Megan nodded. Her mind flitted back to the fact that the school had reached out to the Giles family.

"Had Alex gotten into any trouble outside of the school before he was admitted to Pioneer?"

"No." She shook her head. "Not really."

"Nothing that would have caused police involvement?"

"Just a few minor things — he spray-painted some nonsense words on a bridge, he and a friend were accused of vandalizing an abandoned outbuilding. And then the fire alarm. That was the worst. The fire department dispatched trucks. It was humiliating. The news people came out, we had to pay the town back." She shook her head at the memory.

"That must have been awful," Megan said, her suspicion confirmed. The school must have looked for potential students, kids who could afford the tuition. They would've learned about Alex in the media.

"Want to see a picture of my Alex?" Dee Dee asked, brightening.

"Of course."

Dee Dee disappeared inside the house. She returned carrying a photo album. On the cover was a photo of a rosy-cheeked infant with a shock of red hair. Dee Dee skimmed through the book and then held it out toward Megan.

"This is Alex at fifteen."

The picture she shared showed a short, slender young man with cherry-red hair.

"May I?"

Dee Dee handed Megan the album, and Megan started paging through it. It was in chronological order. Megan saw the cheating bastard ex-husband — also a wiry redhead, but with beady eyes — and the son at each stage of life. She paused when she got to the high school graduation pages.

"Little Alex just got a job with a defense firm. They're sending him to graduate school." Her expression darkened. "He still has his black days, but he's making something of himself. That's good, right?"

"He sounds like an amazing kid." Megan glanced down at the last few pages in the album. "This girl," she pointed to a pretty, tall, slender brunette standing near Alex in one of the graduation photos. Her resemblance to Harriet was uncanny. "Do you remember her?"

"How could I forget? Catherine. Kids called her 'Cat.' One of the troublemakers." Dee Dee distanced herself from the album. "A black spot on an otherwise bright sun. She used to make fun of Alex mercilessly."

"Did you report it?"

"Of course. Alex was already a lonely kid. He went there to make things better, not be tormented by some mean-spirited girl with a nose for trouble."

"Did the school address the issue?"

Dee Dee frowned. "Hardly. Her parents were founders. She was untouchable. After we told, she stalked him in the halls. Tortured him."

Megan let this sink in. It made sense. They had the money, and with a daughter facing juvenile prison, they had a reason. "As a parent, that must have been infuriating."

Dee Dee put her sunglasses back on so that Megan couldn't read her expression. "Sure, but ain't that life? Even in a school with kids who have much, some have more."

"Doesn't make it fair." Echoes of Donna Lewis, Megan thought.

Dee Dee was determined to put a good face on it. "Just the way life is. Some people meet Romeo, some get the cheating bastard of a husband who watches porn in the basement." She smiled and shrugged. "We were happy to have the school and grateful for Dr. Star." She poured herself more tea. "In the end, we didn't want to make waves."

Twenty-One

Megan arrived at the café just as the sky
opened up. Sheets of rain hit the pavement
and topped off an already roiling canal as
thunder boomed overhead. Megan searched
for an umbrella in her truck. Unsuccessful,
she pulled an old sweatshirt from behind
the seat and used it to run into Washington
Acres café.

Inside, she wiped the water from her eyes.
The chill from the air conditioner cooled
her wet skin, and she felt a shiver run
through her. She looked up to see the
restaurant was empty — except for a lone
patron sitting at the counter, reading a
book. She immediately recognized the
slender neck and narrow shoulders as
belonging to Martine Pringle.

Perfect.

Megan slipped behind the counter before
Martine saw her. She popped into her office
to dry off and deposit the sweatshirt. Taking

advantage of the relative privacy, she made a quick call to Denver to ask whether he'd spoken to any of his friends yet. He had not; he was on his way to the inn now.

"Martine is here. I'll ask her about Chase."

"Okay, Megs." His voice sounded hesitant.

"What's wrong? You don't want me to talk to her?"

"It's not that. I just . . . I got to thinking about our conversation last night. Your grandmother is right. Maybe Martine is someone worth watching. Maybe her efforts to point the police toward Jatin are a ruse."

"She's so tiny. Whoever did that packed a wallop."

"We already know she's a liar."

"There's a pretty big leap from liar to murderer." Megan heard Alvaro calling her from the kitchen. "I have to go. Call me tonight and let me know how things go?"

"Aye. I'd stop over but I think it's going to be a long night. The rain has the animals up in arms. Taylor farm has a cow revolt, and old Mrs. Nudy's dog is trying to mother a gaggle of ducklings."

Megan laughed at the image of Mrs. Nudy's dog and the ducks. "I should check on Camilla."

"Aye, you should. Maybe sit with her for a bit. Or if she likes the goats, let them be

283

together for the evening. This weather scares them."

As though on cue, thunder crashed.

"Love you," Denver said.

"I love you too."

Megan hung up, feeling uneasy.

Megan slipped a bowl of Alvaro's home-made berry crisp across the counter to Martine. "On the house. And it has berries, so you could consider it a fruit salad."

Martine smiled. "No, thanks." She touched her stomach. "I couldn't eat another bite. The spring chopped salad was amazing."

"Our chef has a gift."

"The farm fresh veggies didn't hurt."

Megan pointed to the book Martine was reading. It was a treatise on photography. "Good read?"

"Something to kill time." As though realizing what she'd just said, Martine covered her mouth. "I must sound so insensitive. You know what I mean. I'm afraid we're all on edge."

Megan busied herself by wiping down the counter. "How come you're here alone?"

"I needed some space."

"Understandable. Everyone else at the inn?"

"I have no idea. I left two hours ago. Thought I would work on some side projects and maybe get a bite to eat other than fast food."

"How are things going with your day job? Have you managed to quell the fervor?"

Martine closed the book. "Somewhat. There are still a lot of inquiries about Chase, but we've taken the focus off BOLD." Martine rubbed her hands together. "Although from an investor standpoint, the loss of Chase is a real problem."

"Is that part of what you do, deal with investors?"

"Technically, no. I put the good spin on BOLD so that current investors are happy and potential investors are interested. Xavier handles potential investors. Jatin handles current owners."

Megan put away her rag and poured herself a copy of coffee. "Would you like some?" she asked Martine.

"Yes, please." She eyed the crisp. "And maybe I'll have just a little of this. It looks delicious."

Megan set out the drinks. As she took a sip of the hot coffee, she watched as Martine took a tiny, dainty bite of the crisp.

"Mmm. My mother used to make this for me." She put the spoon down on the counter. "It's hard to put a good spin on a murder."

"I can only imagine."

"Would you like to join me?" Martine asked. "I could use some company."

"I need to help my chef get ready for the dinner crowd. If you stick around, you can try his sofrito stew. It's his mother's recipe."

"Sounds wonderful, but I really have eaten enough for two days. Besides, I need to get back to the inn to collect my belongings. I'm moving out. I've decided I'm going to rent a room here in Winsome." She looked down at her coffee. "The tension is too much."

"Harriet was okay with that?"

"She doesn't know. I've been avoiding her as much as possible."

Megan drank more of her coffee. Martine seemed even more off today. There was a melancholy aspect to her expression Megan hadn't seen before, and if it were possible, she seemed thinner, more pallid. "Are you okay?"

Martine smiled, surprised. "I'm fine. Thank you for asking."

Megan weighed whether to ask Martine more questions. Martine had been pretty open with her thus far, although Megan sensed that had more to do with her need for a confidante than any connection to Megan. She didn't have to weigh the decision long; it was Martine who brought up the school.

"My biggest issue is how to deal with inquiries about the school. Everyone wants to know how BOLD and the school are connected. They've tracked down Harriet and have even mentioned her daughter." Martine shook her head. "Harriet is livid, and I don't know how much to say."

Megan frowned. "I guess this is what you train for."

Martine smiled. "As a PR specialist, this is what you dread."

"Tell me, Martine, about the scholarships for college. The ones Harriet planned to give to anyone who completed the mentor program. How would that work?"

Martine tilted her head. "If the student had stayed with the mentor program and qualified for financial aid because of low income, we would step in and pay their college tuition. Within reason, of course. No Harvard tuition."

"Was there a pool of money set aside for this?"

"Not that I know of. Just a promise by the company."

Megan said, "Seems like a very generous offer."

"Harriet feels strongly about that school."

Megan nodded. "I see that." She chose not to mention the fact that Pioneer Village School educated rich kids — kids who were unlikely to need the scholarships. "I see what the students gain, but what about BOLD?"

"That good will I mentioned."

"How does that help reassure or attract investors? Aren't they more interested in the bottom line than a do-good project?"

"The type of investor we love to attract wants to combine investing with social activism. They get to make money, help find a cure for some terrible disease, *and* send kids to college. We let them feel good about making money."

Megan wasn't so sure the people who invested in BOLD were that worried about social justice. The door to the store opened, causing the bells to ring. "A win-win."

"Remember, what's good for the bottom line is good for everyone." Martine pulled a laptop from the bag on the chair next to her. "Want to see some more photos?"

Megan nodded. She watched as someone made their way back toward the café. The regal bearing and the dark tresses pegged the figure as Dr. Harriet Mantra.

"Good afternoon, Doctor," Megan said.

"Good afternoon. I was hoping to find Martine here." She took off her glasses and pinned her stare on Martine. "Where have you been hiding?"

Harriet was behind Martine, and very quickly Martine slammed her laptop lid down. She stood and spun around. "Dr. Mantra." Her eyes pleaded with Megan not to say a word.

"Berry crisp?" Megan asked Harriet.

The glance Harriet gave the bowl of berry crisp was full of contempt, as though the fruit had done her a grievous wrong. "Only if you can take away the crisp and leave the berries."

"Now what fun would that be?" Megan asked.

Harriet didn't crack a smile. "We're not here for fun. It would serve everyone, Martine, if we could all remember that."

Megan pulled into the farm's driveway and parked behind Eloise's Lexus. She wasn't surprised to find Eloise at the house, although she was surprised to see her so soon — and during such bad weather. Bibi had a way of making people feel at home, though, and maybe Eloise had gotten over her dislike for the Birch family long enough to consider Bibi's potential impact on Dillon. Long ago, Eloise and Megan's father Eddie had dated. Like many of Eddie's relationships, it hadn't ended well. Megan suspected Eloise held it against Bibi, Eddie's admittedly over-protective mother. It looked like Eloise had moved past any old hurts. Megan was glad; Bibi could be good for the teen. Bibi was the best kind of grandmother: fiercely protective, fiercely empowering, and fiercely nurturing. She was an equal opportunity grandmother too. Dillon could do worse.

The inside of the porch smelled of chicken soup and biscuits. Megan also smelled a hint of buttery chocolate in the air: cookies. Her stomach rumbled despite the plate of stew she'd eaten at the café.

"Hello?" she called when she opened the door to the kitchen, which was empty. "Anyone here?"

"Back here!" came Bibi's response.

Megan followed the sound into the parlor. She found Bibi and Dillon sitting side by side on the couch. A rerun of *The Office* was on television, and Bibi was laughing so hard tears were running down her face.

"Hello, Dillon. Bibi, since when do you like *The Office*?"

"Since Dillon introduced me to the show. It's hilarious!"

Megan noticed Sadie wedged between them on the couch. She had her head on Dillon's lap and her eyes on the television screen. Megan would have commented on it, but Bibi had a strict no dogs on the couch rule. Clearly, she was playing by a different rule book this evening, and even the dogs knew it.

Thunder roared overhead. Lightning immediately followed, filling the sky with brilliant white light. Megan saw Dillon wince.

"Where's Eloise?"

Bibi leaned toward the television. She was wearing a blue and white striped "Wacky Winsome" sweatshirt from the old store Megan's father once ran, and she used the sleeve to wipe her eyes.

"Dr. Kent had phone calls to make," Dillon said.

"I let her use the office," Bibi said. "I didn't think you'd mind."

Megan nodded. "Of course not."

"Dillon's hanging out with me. We had soup and biscuits. There's some left in the fridge if you want it."

"And cookies," Dillon said.

Bibi smiled. "And chocolate chip cookies Dillon helped me make."

Megan stood in the doorway for a few more seconds, watching the unlikely pair bond over reruns of *The Office.* Leave it to comedy, chocolate, and the power of one woman's love.

Megan finally excused herself, but the sound of her voice was drowned out by the thunder. "I'm going to check on the animals!" she yelled.

Neither answered. They were too busy seeming normal.

Camilla was running around her pen, eyes wide. Megan climbed over the enclosure and sat still on the ground until the young pig came toward her. When Camilla was close enough, Megan started to talk in a low voice. She'd brought a blanket and she spread it on the ground next to her. The pig finally calmed enough to sit by her. It was getting late, and the steady beat of the rain against the roof lulled Megan into a sense of peace. She sat next to Camilla for a long while, reassuring herself as much as the pig, until her eyes grew too heavy to stay open.

She woke up two hours later. Camilla was still next to her, cuddled against Megan's prone body. Three sets of eyes were staring down from above, their expressions a mix of amusement and relief.

"We thought you'd gone missing," Bibi said.

"We were worried about you," Eloise said.

Dillon's gaze was on the pig. He dropped down and put his arms around her. "She's scared."

"That's why I came out here. She's all alone."

Dillon looked ready to cry. Megan and Eloise exchanged a look, but it was Bibi who acted. She shimmied herself down on the floor by the boy and the pig.

"Storms should let up in the next hour. Eloise, I say Dillon and I do the next shift. That okay with you?"

Clearly Eloise didn't know what to say. She managed: "It's late, but I guess."

"Good." Bibi shifted so her back was against the enclosure. "That okay with you, Dillon?"

The boy didn't say anything. He simply stroked Camilla's head. The pig leaned into his touch.

To Megan, Bibi whispered, "Better bring a crane to hoist me out of here."

Megan smiled. She followed Eloise back to the house, her own frame aching from sleeping on the barn floor.

When they were inside the kitchen, Megan offered Eloise tea. She declined. Eloise wore pressed dark denim jeans and a red and white striped short-sleeve sweater. Despite her neat appearance, her eyes drooped and were bloodshot.

"You're not sleeping," Megan said.

"That obvious?"

"Has he given you any trouble?"

"None at all, which worries me more."

"You're waiting for the other shoe to fall."

Eloise's smile was wan. "Or the axe." She shook her head. "Okay, that wasn't funny."

"If you're that concerned, he shouldn't be staying with you."

"Where would he go?"

"He can stay here." Megan said the words before she could think them through.

Eloise sat down on a chair. She threw her head back. "The social services system doesn't work that way. There are background checks and hoops to jump through, and the only reason I got Dillon was because he was already staying with me. The truth is, that boy has been nothing but an angel. It's his calm. It's unnerving."

"He and Bibi were laughing away when I came in this evening." Megan walked to the window. She could see the glow of the light in the barn. The rain had slowed, and she hadn't heard thunder in a while. "He sure likes Camilla."

Eloise rubbed her eyes. "I wish they would put this mess to rest. Find who did this to Chase Mars."

Megan thought about the conversation she had with the reporter, Donna Lewis. "Eloise," she said, "is Dillon right-handed?"

"Left." She looked up. "You're asking because whoever killed Chase may have been a leftie, correct?"

Megan didn't need to respond. She could tell by Eloise's face that the woman already knew.

"I could tell by the questions they were asking. Yes, Dillon's a southpaw. So what? So are lots of people, including most of the people from BOLD. Anyway, we should go." Eloise stood. "Think your pig will be okay now?"

"I'll sit with her for a while if not."

Eloise touched Megan's shoulder. "Bonnie invited Dillon over again in a few days. Are you okay with your grandmother watching him? It does help me out. With school out for a few weeks of summer break, I only get time to myself when Dillon has therapy sessions."

"Anytime, Eloise." Megan thought about her conversation with the reporter, Donna Lewis. "Have you been happy with Pioneer Village and Dr. Star?"

"For the most part. Why?"

"Just curious. I read an article today that was very disparaging of the school."

Eloise smiled. "Ah. That must've been by Donna Lewis. She hates Star. Says the school is for spoiled rich kids."

"If you don't mind me asking, who is paying for Dillon to attend?"

"I don't mind, and he has a trust set up by the pro-wrestling foundation. They gave it to him when his father was incarcerated. He can use it for college too."

Another kid who didn't need the scholarship promise.

"Did the school contact you, or did you contact the school?"

Eloise looked surprised by the question. "Neither. It was arranged through the agency." She paused, her forehead bisected by a thinker's crease. "Come to think of it, his social worker mentioned that they approached the agency. Maybe they read about Dillon in the news."

Just like Dee Dee's son, Megan thought. The Pioneer Village School's recruitment program. Good thing Lewis hadn't gotten a hold of that tidbit.

Megan walked Eloise out. Dillon seemed reluctant to leave, but he followed his foster mother back to the car.

"Goodbye, Dillon," Bibi called.

Dillon's nod was barely perceptible, but even in the shadows, Megan saw the smile on his face.

TWENTY-TWO

Denver met them for breakfast at the farm. He showed up at six, just as Megan was making her list for tomorrow's farmers market. Bibi was still upstairs, and Megan had made coffee and heated bread in the oven. She put the bread on the table with butter and peach preserves. Denver piled a few slices on his plate after giving Megan a long kiss.

"Where's your first appointment?" Megan asked.

"Home," Denver said between bites. "I haven't slept yet."

Megan's eyes widened. "That bad last night?"

"Aye. I told you, the animal world went daft. How did Camilla fare?"

Megan related the tale of last night . . . her nap, the watch Bibi and Dillon shared, and the fact that Megan spent another two hours curled up with a pig.

"And that is why my marriage to Lilian didn't work," Denver said. "She would never spend her evening on the floor of a barn with a pig named Camilla."

Megan laughed. "Who knew I was such a catch."

"I did." Bibi walked into the kitchen with purpose. She wore jeans and an oversized, button down white shirt. A blue scarf was tied around her neck and she had sandals on her feet. "I'll be out most of today, so don't worry about me."

"You look nice, Bonnie. Where are you going?"

"To talk with Dillon's counselor. I think he's overmedicated."

Megan slapped a hand down on the table. "Bibi, you can't do that. There are rules . . . the psychologist — he's a psychologist, not a counselor — won't talk to you." Megan felt her head throbbing. When Bibi was on a mission, there was no stopping her. "You can't just barge into the school."

"Eloise agrees with me. She's taking me with her for support."

Megan sat back, stunned. "Well, that's a different story."

"He's so medicated that he can't emote. That was Eloise's word. He doesn't feel anything."

"Don't you think that may be a good thing right now?" Denver asked.

"No. I think it's a terrible thing to do to a child. He needs to work through what happened to him, not suppress it." Bibi waved a hand. "It will be up to the doctor. I'm going as moral support."

Megan wasn't sure when this conversation took place between Eloise and her grandmother, but she wasn't going to waste breath arguing. They had other issues. Megan filled them in briefly about her discussions with the reporter and Lou's neighbor, Dee Dee.

"I spoke with Martine later. One thing seems clear: the kids at the Pioneer Village School are from wealthy families. They don't need scholarship money."

"So what? It still looks good to offer it," Bibi said.

"Exactly."

"This really bothers you, Megs. Why? Why are you so focused on the event? It's no different than events done by companies all over the country."

"Yes and no. Making such a long-term commitment is unusual. But think about it, they set up this wonderful mentoring opportunity for troubled kids. A great photo op, right? We all know the public has short memories, and at the end of the day, why do they care about the altruism of some small private pharmaceutical company?"

"They don't," Denver said.

"Right. But what if you wanted to show the financial strength of your company?"

"Then making a long-term promise could underscore your company's confidence in its own future." Denver's eyes narrowed. "Where are ye going with this, Megs?"

"Martine told me that the company relies on investors — current and future — to keep the lights on until the FDA approves its drugs. I'm saying this whole thing was a ploy to lull investors into thinking the company is in great financial shape."

"Meanwhile, it's an empty promise because the kids who go there don't need scholarships." Bibi frowned. "Seems like a lot of trouble."

"Not if you're also a founder of the school. Now you get to make your company look good and do something for the school you help to finance. A PR win-win."

Denver and Bibi were silent. The sun had come out, bathing the kitchen in a golden glow. From outside, Megan could hear the din of the tractor. Soon the construction crew would be back out, working on the Marshall place barn. I need to stop thinking of it as the old Marshall place, Megan thought. *It's ours now.*

"I'm following ye, Megs, but I still come back to so what? What does this all mean in the context of Chase's death?"

"Everyone is focused on Dillon, but what if someone had a motive to kill Chase? And what better motive than financial gain."

Denver shook his head. "Still too many unconnected dots. Sorry."

Megan took a deep breath. Both Denver and Bibi looked confused but intrigued. "I've been thinking about this for a while. What if the company *is* doing poorly? What if investors are unhappy and Harriet is trying desperately to raise funds. What if Chase was part of that — and someone gains if the company goes under?"

Denver sat back. "Like a competitor?"

"Perhaps."

Bibi said, "Or what if the company is on the brink of something big?"

Denver asked, "What do ye mean, Bonnie?"

"What if Harriet is trying to raise funds not because the company is doing poorly, but because they have a great idea they're trying to bring to fruition?"

"Martine did say 'products,' not 'product,' " Megan said.

302

Bibi sat forward, excited. "Someone could have wanted Chase out of the way so they could either get credit or financial gain from whatever this new product is."

"One way or another, we need more information on BOLD," Denver said. He still didn't sound convinced.

"I asked Lou, our accountant, to do some digging. It's a private company, so there isn't a lot online. I'll poke around, see if this PR stunt is part of a pattern."

"What did you find out yesterday?" Bibi asked Denver. "When you stopped by the inn?"

"I didn't get over there."

"Why ever not?" Bibi scolded.

"As I told Megan, the animals were crazed during the storm. I had appointments steadily from early afternoon on."

Megan knew he was busy. She also knew he felt awkward questioning his friends.

"Do you want me to talk to them?" Megan asked. "We can even go together, and I can ask questions."

"I'll be fine. I'll go today."

"It might be easier this way. Lawyer background and all."

"True. You lawyers can be bulldogs." Denver looked relieved. "Would you?"

"Of course."

Denver pulled his cell from his pocket. "Let me text Jatin and tell him we're coming. From what Barbara told me yesterday, he leaves most days. She thinks he's having a hard time and is trying to avoid Harriet." He punched in a message.

Bibi began clearing the table. "It seems like we have two options: a personal vendetta against Chase. Or a business reason. And that could be any of them."

"Or Dillon," Denver said. To Megan, "Jatin can meet us at the Bucks County Inn at two. Will that work?"

"It will."

"What are you going to do in the meantime?"

"I have farm chores. I need to get ready for the farmers market. Clay can't go, so it will just be Porter and me. I may also make some calls to see what I can find out about BOLD."

"Focus there, Megan." Bibi pursed her mouth in the stubborn set Megan knew so well. "We have two options. Personal vendetta by an adult, or pure business greed."

It was after eleven when the construction crew manager, a stocky blond in his thirties, found Megan in the barn, washing and sorting vegetables.

"Have a few minutes? I'd like to show you something."

"Sure. Give me five."

Megan finished washing the rainbow Swiss chard. She'd set it aside to dry before packaging it into bundles. Reluctantly, she washed her hands and headed down to the adjoining property to meet with the construction foreman.

"We got some of the preliminary reports back from the structural engineer," the foreman said. "Doesn't look good."

Megan followed the foreman into the old house and down to the basement. The layout was a simple center hall with a dining room and kitchen on one side and a living room on the other. Upstairs were four bedrooms and two baths. In its glory, the house boasted deep sills and high ceilings — it was younger than its neighbor, which housed the farm. Now it was a mess of water damaged walls and scarred wood floors.

The foreman led Megan deeper into the basement. She ducked to get under the entryway without getting her hair caught in a series of cobwebs. The basement had been emptied of the years' worth of detritus it had contained when she bought the property. The clutter had hidden plenty of flaws, including a nasty black mold in one corner and a series of cracks in the foundation.

"Obviously you need mold remediation," he said. "But it looks like the house may need to be raised and the foundation fixed."

Megan listened to his technical explanations of what that would entail. Suddenly the money they'd set aside for the new barn — the teaching kitchen and classrooms — was shrinking by the second.

"I'm sorry," he said. "Do you want us to continue with the barn?"

The work on the house had to be completed before they could open the bed and breakfast, but the barn could operate independently. That said, she only had enough money to complete one of these projects this year.

"Keep going for now," she said finally. The smell in the basement was getting to her and her head was starting to throb. Next time, she'd wear a mask. "I'll have to think this over."

"You could tackle the house next spring," the foreman said. "That will give you time to save." He patted a concrete wall. "This baby has been standing for more than a century. I don't think a year will make a difference."

■ ■ ■ ■

Megan was still thinking about the new property and the foreman's news while she got ready to meet Denver. What had she been thinking? A new storefront and café had been hard enough to pull off. The farm and café were finally in the black and now she was going to create another money pit? But she'd gone this far . . . and she'd promised her father last year when he sent her that money. Plus, Mick would have told her to have faith.

Although, if Mick were still alive, she'd probably be back in Chicago, working long hours at the law firm and living in a modern condo downtown. Life had a funny way of diverting you from your original path.

Bibi still wasn't back from her trip to the school with Eloise, so Megan scribbled her a note. She traded her overalls for a knee-length black pencil skirt, a patterned blouse she'd found at a thrift shop in SoHo, and strappy black sandals. A touch of lipstick and mascara and she was ready to go.

She opened the porch door to leave and was greeted by Bobby King. He stood with his arm raised, ready to knock. A young female officer stood beside her. She carried a camera.

"Bobby," Megan said, closing the door. "I wasn't expecting you."

"I'm sorry to just swing by. Clover told me you were still here, and I figured I'd take a chance."

"What's up? Did something happen?"

"No, no, Megan. I just need to take a few photos of Camilla."

It took Megan a moment to realize he was talking about the pig. "Why?"

"We're still trying to find out who rented that storage unit. Camilla is evidence."

"You're not taking her, are you?"

"Just a few pictures, that's all."

"Any leads on who Saul Bones might be?" Megan asked.

King shook his head. "Afraid not."

Megan sent Denver a text to say she'd be a few minutes late, and she led King and the officer up to the barn. While the officer was shooting Camilla's good side, Megan asked King why he'd come.

"Seems overkill to send you out for a photo shoot," Megan said.

"I wanted an excuse to get out here. Anyway, the state folks are doing most of the murder investigation now. They're pulling rank."

Megan didn't like the sound of that. "Are

308

they still focused on Dillon?"

"They're doing their jobs, but he's the most prominent suspect."

When Megan didn't say anything, Bobby whispered, "I found out the press lady — Martine — and Chase were having an affair."

Megan's eyes widened. "Recently?"

"As in, they slept together the night before he died."

Megan looked up at him in surprise. "Really? Who told you that?"

"She did."

Megan's frown deepened. During all of their conversations, Martine never mentioned an affair with Chase. "Denver says she lies."

"Well, I only have her word since her sparring partner has met his maker. She says Chase and Jatin fought, Chase came to her all upset, and they had sex."

"Funny she never told me that."

King gave her a quizzical look. "Why would she have?"

"Because I've had four talks with her now and she failed to mention her relationship each time." Megan filled King in on the photos she discovered — Chase and Martine as groupies twenty years ago. "She never mentioned that either."

"Hmm. I take it you think that means something?"

King's officer had returned. "Cute pig," she said. "I think she was posing."

Megan smiled. "We've all become attached. Maybe too attached, given that she's not ours yet."

King's face said he was still thinking about Martine. "Lying to the police is serious business."

Megan held up her purse. "I have to leave, Bobby, but I will say this before I go. Martine should stay on the 'maybe' list. In fact, I'd move her up to the 'highly possible' category. She lied about Denver years ago, and that pattern hasn't seemed to have changed. She doesn't seem to do well with the other women in the group, and she seems to obsess about men. I may be drawing too many conclusions from too few data points, but that's all I have. Martine and the truth are not friends." Megan clutched her bag to her side. "She may very well be the key to the mystery of who killed Chase Mars."

"If not the killer?"

"Don't let a pretty face fool you."

TWENTY-THREE

Megan found Denver and Jatin sitting outside in the courtyard under a teak umbrella table. Jatin was sitting in the shade, his legs stretched out before him, a glass of something amber-colored in his hand. He wore khaki shorts and a pink Polo shirt tucked in. His hair was neatly combed, but he'd grown a beard in the days since Megan had last seen him. The beard accentuated his eyes, and Megan noticed he had deep amber eyes and long, dark lashes. Those eyes were his best feature.

Denver was still in his work clothes: jeans and a t-shirt. He smiled when he saw Megan and pointed to the other seat under the umbrella. He'd taken the sunny spot and sweat was running down his face.

"Jatin thought we'd have more privacy out here."

"You're going to give yourself heatstroke." She kissed Denver, shook Jatin's hand, and sat down. "Good to see you again, Jatin."

"Likewise."

"Jatin was just filling me in on the investigation."

Jatin placed his empty glass on the table. "I was saying that it should be wrapped up soon. Hopefully we can leave in the next day or so."

Megan glanced at Denver. "They're ready to make an arrest?"

"From what I understand." Jatin pulled a pack of cigarettes from his pants' pocket. "Want one?" he asked Megan. "Nasty habit. I thought I'd given it up, but it seems my mind had other ideas."

When no one wanted one, Jatin lit the cigarette and took a deep inhalation. He watched as the smoke left his mouth. "I will only have one. I promise." He glanced around. "Harriet is out, or I wouldn't have this one." He waved the cigarette with slender fingers. The fingers of his left hand. "Between her and the innkeeper, I'm lucky I'm allowed to talk. It's like a damn mausoleum in here."

Megan asked, "Have the police been questioning you?"

"Again and again and again. I tell them the same story every time. Yes, I was in the camping area. No, I didn't see Chase leave.

No, I wasn't with anyone. Yes, I arrived late, but that doesn't make me a murderer."

"Where were you?" Denver asked.

"Looking for a spot for our tent."

"Alone?" Megan asked.

"Yes, alone. The kid was off doing something, and I was looking for a spot for the tent."

Denver said, "If you were late, who knew you'd arrived?"

Jatin pushed himself away from the table. He walked to the garden and stubbed the cigarette out in the dirt. "Are you the police now too?"

Denver's voice was quiet. "I'm your friend. And we're trying to help."

Jatin took a moment to respond. "Chase knew I was there." He sat back down, hand now clenched by his side. "I was late. I ran the length of the hike until I caught up and saw Chase. I explained what had happened. We spent a few minutes talking and admiring the view. He told me I had to find a spot to camp." Jatin looked toward the inn. "That was the last time I spoke to him."

"Were you fighting with one another?" Megan asked.

"No. Why do you ask that?"

"Someone said they heard you the night before, arguing," Denver said.

"Would that someone be Martine?" Jatin scowled. "You of all people should know she's full of shit most of the time. Chase and I bickered, but only because he was drunk. You don't get drunk the night before you're dealing with kids."

Megan agreed. Despite his neat appearance, Jatin was clearly on edge. She decided to take a different tact. "You must be anxious to return to work. Have you been able to do much here?"

"Spotty internet, nosy colleagues, and constant police attention seem to have disrupted my flow."

"You're welcome at the farm anytime." Megan smiled. "You can set up in one of the spare rooms if you need to get away."

The offer seemed to have disarmed Jatin. He unclenched his hand and nodded. "That's extremely kind. Thank you."

"I told you before, Jatin. You can stay with me too. I have a spare room."

"Thank you. Thank you, both." The innkeeper had opened the door to the courtyard and was walking toward them. He glanced at her and said. "She is attentive. That's been nice."

"Would any of you like a drink?" The innkeeper glanced at Denver sweating in the sun. Alarmed, she said, "Oh, my, Dr. Finn.

314

It's hot out here. Why don't you come inside where it's air conditioned?"

"I'm fine." Denver thanked her for the offer.

"He's a vet," Jatin said. "He's used to being outside."

"Nevertheless! Let me get you a nice cold beverage. For you too, dear." She looked at Megan. "Megan, right? From the café in Winsome."

The older woman went back inside, and Jatin took the opportunity to smoke another cigarette. "I need to stay here," he said. "But I do need to work."

"How has business been?" Denver asked casually.

"Despite all of this, fine. Lots of interest in our drug. It's quite unique. Once the FDA approves it, we'll be off and running."

"And until then?"

"We keep scraping by." He gave his first real grin. "But that's the fun of this job. We know we have a great product. Every day is a challenge trying to get it to market."

Megan asked, "And what if the FDA doesn't approve it?"

Jatin nodded. "That's a real risk. I see no reason why the FDA wouldn't approve it. Then bam! No more issues getting investors."

"Do you have issues now?" Megan asked. "Based on the mentoring outing BOLD sponsored, I'd think the company was doing quite well."

Jatin met her gaze. "Let's be clear. There is never enough money."

"Xavier brings in the new investors?" Megan asked.

Jatin nodded. "We work together with a few other people. We have an in-house attorney, a bunch of external counsel, and a few MBA types. But Xavier leads the way with new money."

He turned toward Denver. "Had you not gone into animal medicine, you could have joined us. Used your science background to cure disease. Better hours, more perks."

Denver smirked. "Is that so? Seems like you're all doing just fine, but I don't think the Rockefellers have anything to worry about just yet."

Jatin pointed the cigarette at Denver with his left hand. "Just you wait until the FDA approvals come in. That's when it will all change."

Denver said, "You'll go public?"

Jatin shrugged. "Go public. Get bought out by Merck or Johnson & Johnson or one of the other biggies. Doesn't matter. I win either way."

"How so?" Denver raised an eyebrow. "You seem pretty sure."

"It's in my contract," Jatin said. "Harriet couldn't pay me what I was worth, so she added options and restricted stock and a big fat change in control bonus." He stubbed the cigarette out on the grass beside his foot. "As long as BOLD wins, I win."

Denver pulled his hand through his thick hair. "The others too?"

"Those of us who started with Harriet." Jatin grinned. "See? Don't you wish you'd chosen the lab over the pasture?"

"Does sound like a sweet deal." Denver took Megan's hand and squeezed it. "But my animals repay me in ways that can't be quantified."

"Ha!" Jatin grinned. The innkeeper came with the drinks, and Jatin grabbed a fresh glass. "Try and deposit that in the bank, my friend. Gratitude is great, money is better."

Megan left at four p.m. She thought about tracking Martine down at her new hotel but decided against it. Denver could handle his friends; she'd had enough for one day. Anyway, Xavier wasn't answering his texts, and Barbara was shopping. Denver accepted Jatin's offer of dinner, and Megan headed back to the farm to check on Bibi and talk to Clay about the Marshall property.

Jatin was right about one thing: gratitude was nice, but money paid the bills.

Bibi was in the barn, sitting with Camilla, when Megan arrived. She'd taken off her jeans and pressed blouse and now wore a "Winsome Wins" casino night t-shirt and a pair of gray velour sweatpants. She was handing the pig slices of apple, one by one, and ignoring the pleading looks of Gunther and Sadie.

"I see who ranks in this house," Megan said. "How quickly you're replaced, dogs. I think Bibi would let Camilla stay in the house over you two."

"Not true." Bibi tossed each dog an apple slice. She pet the pig on the head and fed her another. "This pig is smarter than the two dogs put together."

"I don't think so."

Bibi grunted. "I told Alvaro to take bacon off the menu."

"Did he agree?"

"He mumbled something about me and Clover having lost our marbles and stormed off." She smiled. "The day he agrees will be the day we bury him."

"True."

Megan perched on the enclosure beside

318

her grandmother. "How'd it go with Dillon?"

"Not well." Bibi put a hand in the air. "Here, help me up. And tell Clay to get a chair in this barn. I can't keep sitting on the damp ground."

Megan gently pulled her grandmother up. "You okay?"

"Just a little tired." She gave the pig a last pat and walked toward the barn exit. "Some tea will perk me up."

Megan knew that meant her special tea — tea with brandy. "Whatever works, Bibi."

Bibi was silent for the walk to the house. The weather had remained warm and sunny, no signs of the storms, and Megan could hear Clay and Porter taking advantage of the long period of daylight. Clay was still preparing goods for the farmers market, and Porter was getting two large beds ready for a fresh planting of baby lettuces. The baby lettuces were a good seller with local restaurants. As long as they were carefully tended and picked before they bolted, it was a crop they could continue all season long.

Inside, Bibi started to disappear down the hallway toward the stairs.

"Dillon?" Megan reminded her.

"Can we talk tomorrow?" Bibi asked. "I'm pretty tired and my stomach is off. I'm going to bed."

"Bibi, it's not even dinner time. Are you sure you're alright?"

Bibi turned and smiled. "I'm fine, Megan. Just not young anymore." She put a hand on her stomach. "And I think maybe what I ate at the café didn't agree with me."

Megan nodded. She watched her grandmother make her way up the stairs, one slow step at a time.

"These are the greens." Clay patted a large pile of individually portioned Swiss chard, kale, bok choy, and mustards. "Three dollars a bunch. And here are the garlic scapes, the spring onions, and the radishes." He pointed to three boxes in the corner of the CoolBot. "We have four varieties of radish, but the French breakfast radishes are my favorite." He handed Megan a stack of recipe cards. "Sautéed French breakfast radishes. People don't realize you can cook radishes. They're actually quite delicious with herbs and butter."

Megan took the cards, glancing down at the Washington Acres logo and beautifully printed radish recipe ideas. Not for the first time, she was overwhelmed with gratitude that Clay still worked here. He never ceased to amaze her with his creativity and work ethic. She knew he went home at night to study for his engineering degree and still somehow found time to make recipe cards. She dreaded the day he moved on to greener pastures.

"I adore you."

Clay grinned. "Do you have what you need?"

"Yes, Clay. You're like a worried new parent. I have done the farmers market before."

"Not in a while. And this is a new one." Clay push his long hair away from his face. He reached into the pocket of his jeans and pulled out a hairband. Tying his hair in a ponytail, he laughed. "I do sound like a helicopter parent."

"It's okay. I will be fine, though. You and Emily enjoy yourselves."

Ever since Emily's father went missing almost two years prior, she and her daughter had become close family friends. Megan observed from the sidelines as a friendship developed between Clay and Emily. They were quiet about it, but she'd watched as that friendship blossomed into more. This was the first time they were going away together, and it would be just Porter and Megan for the Saturday farmers market.

"If we've covered this, I have one more thing to talk with you about." They left the cool interior of the CoolBot and stood in the barn. Megan shared the conversation she'd had with the construction foreman earlier that day. "We need to decide what to do first — house or barn."

Clay's mouth pressed into a frown. "That's too bad. What do you want to do?"

"I was thinking we go forward with the barn and save the house for next year. I don't have the funds for both right now, and I think we could use the barn for winter projects."

Clay looked thoughtful. "What's your hesitation?"

"I guess I was just excited to tackle both. I can't wait to see the house restored. What if we don't address these issues this year, and the house falls apart in the meantime?"

Clay gave her a reassuring smile. "The house has stood for over a hundred years. Another year won't spell disaster."

"That's what the foreman said."

"I think you have your answer."

Megan gave Clay's arm a quick squeeze. "I'll go check with Bibi. If she's fine with it, that's what we'll do."

The house was quiet inside. Sadie followed Megan inside. The dog ran down the hall, and Megan placed the recipe cards and pricing paper on the kitchen table so she'd be ready in the morning. She needed to get the bags and cash to make change. Otherwise, she should be set.

It was ten minutes after six, and Megan was hungry. She decided she'd make sandwiches and a small salad for her and Bibi. Her grandmother needed to eat. She was in the process of slicing cheese for grilled cheese when she heard Sadie whining. She ignored it at first — the dog was probably locked out of Bibi's room — but when Sadie's whines turned into yippy barks, Megan grew concerned. She tossed the knife on the counter and raced down the hall, taking the steps two at a time.

Bibi's door was open, and Megan could make out Sadie standing by the bed. The dog barked when she saw Megan. Megan ran to the bed where she saw her grandmother lying, skin red and dry to the touch. She was breathing — barely. Her eyes opened. They moved back in forth with terror.

"Meg . . . mm . . . meg . . ." Bibi's voice slurred. She closed her eyes.

"Bibi? Bibi!"

Megan pulled her phone out and dialed 911. She kept her voice steady while she gave the address, but once she hung up, the tears wouldn't stop.

Twenty-Four

"Sadie may have saved Bibi's life. They're not sure, but they think she may have had a stroke. There are some mild neurological symptoms." Megan sank into the couch in the family waiting room, next to Denver. He wrapped his arms around her, and she molded herself against him. "This was all too much for her. I should have known better."

"Your grandmother is a force, Megs. Ye couldn't have foreseen this."

"She seemed so happy. Driven to help Dillon." Megan buried her face in Denver's chest. "I brought Camilla home, then I brought this tragedy home. Bibi's eighty-five."

Denver took hold of Megan's shoulders and gently pushed her back so she was facing him. The room was empty except for an older man asleep on a chair across the room. Megan felt the tears coming again, and she choked them back, willing herself to be strong.

She gave voice to her biggest fear. "What if she doesn't make it?"

"Megs?" Denver placed two fingers under Megan's chin and tilted her head up so they were eye to eye. "There's a saying in my country: *Whit's fur ye'll no go past ye.* Simply put, we can't control the future. Your grandmother is a strong woman. She's got more grit than a dozen people. If anyone can get through this, she can."

Megan nodded. Clay and Porter had come into the waiting room, their faces as long as her own. Denver was right — Bibi had grit. And she'd expect her granddaughter to exhibit the same now.

"How is she?" Clay asked.

"It's a waiting game," Denver said.

Megan stood.

"Where are ye going, Megs?"

"To sit with Bibi. Once the doctors are done examining her, they said I could stay by her side." She kissed Denver. He'd left his friends to run over to the hospital as soon as Megan called. "Will you handle the townspeople? I've already gotten a dozen calls."

Denver agreed.

"And don't worry about tomorrow," Porter said. "I can handle the farmers market solo."

"Oh, we're not leaving," Clay said. "Not until we know Bonnie's okay."

Megan looked from one to the other, her bruised heart full of gratitude. She may not have any siblings, but she had the best adopted family she could have asked for.

Megan felt her hand being squeezed. She sat up with a jolt, remembering where she was and what had happened in a burst of despair. The room was dimly lit with artificial light, and a series of beeps told her Bibi was still alive.

Another squeeze. Megan wiped the drool from her mouth and sat up. Her head was on the bed and one arm was draped across Bibi's body, holding her grandmother's hand. She felt it again and finally realized it was Bibi squeezing her fingers.

She stood, excited. Her grandmother's eyes were closed. They fluttered open, she smiled.

"Bibi, I'm here. It's going to be okay."

Megan felt the squeeze again. She reached over and pressed the call button. The nurses were there immediately.

"She squeezed my hand and opened her eyes."

The nurses ushered her out. Megan wandered back to the family room where she found a half dozen Winsome residents and Denver. Some were talking quietly, Denver was dozing. She crawled on the couch next to him and waited.

"You couldn't pay me to eat that." Clover eyed Denver's chicken sandwich with disdain. "Hospital food is bad enough, but use enough breadcrumbs and deep fry something and you can hide anything."

"When you're hungry enough, you *can* eat anything. And I'm famished." Denver took a large bite. "Mmmm."

Clover clucked her disgust and turned her attention to Megan. "Bibi is doing well?"

"Still a little out of it, but she wants to come home."

"Do they know what happened?"

"It wasn't a stroke. She may have had a seizure."

Both Clover and Denver looked at her. "A seizure?" Denver said.

Megan nodded. "They said she's progressing well. She'll be fine — eventually."

Clover studied her. "You don't seem great for someone who got great news. What are you not telling us? Do you know what caused the seizure?"

"Not yet." Megan poked at the flaccid salad in front of her. She knew what the doctors were thinking, but she couldn't speak about it. Not here.

She felt Denver's hand on her knee. He gave her a reassuring squeeze. "Your Aunt Sarah and your mother were here while you were in with the doctors. They didn't want to bother you. They'll be back to visit Bibi."

Megan gave a weak smile. A year ago, the sight of Megan's mother would have set Bibi's blood pressure soaring, but now that they'd reached a truce, her grandmother would probably enjoy a visit.

When Clover had finished her peanut butter and jelly sandwich and Denver his chicken, Clover cleared the table. While she was gone, Megan asked Denver if they could talk. Alone.

"Of course, Megs. Is everything okay?"

"No, it's not. I know what happened to Bibi, and I think we may need to speak with Eloise. The sooner the better."

They drove along Canal Street in silence. It wasn't until they'd reached Eloise's street that Denver said, "I just can't believe it."

"I know. I don't know what to think. I really don't know what to do with this." She peered at Denver across the truck's center console. "Eloise may not take this well."

"I know."

"Maybe we should wait until Bobby arrives. It took everything I had to convince him to let us do this. Maybe he was right."

Denver shook his head. "We should tell her. I owe her that, at least. The question is whether she can be objective."

"We have to trust that she can."

Denver agreed, but Megan could tell by the expression in his eyes that the trust wasn't in him.

"Did Bibi say anything? Hint at anything out of the ordinary?"

"No. But I didn't want to press her." Megan looked at Denver and wiped the tears from her eyes. "The damage could have been permanent. What you said about her having grit? Yeah, that's what saved her."

Megan turned into Eloise's property and parked the truck. It was Sunday afternoon and the cheerful weather had continued. Eighties and sunny. Weather that demanded light-hearted fun — not introspection and suspicion. Eloise was outside waiting for them, and she had jogged to the truck before Megan even killed the ignition.

"Dillon's watching a movie. We have fifteen minutes before it's over. How about the barn? We should have some privacy there." Eloise looked like a shell of the woman they knew. Her jeans were stained, her shirt untucked, and dark circles shadowed her eyes. Denver had called to say they needed to discuss something with her, and looking at her now, Megan could tell she'd immediately figured the worse.

Denver climbed out of the truck. He gave his aunt a hug, whispered something in her ear, and started for the barn. Megan stood by the truck for a few seconds, staring at the house. She swore she saw a curtain on the ground floor move, but she wasn't sure. Could have been a trick of the sun.

"Bibi was poisoned." Megan spoke softly, controlling her voice to hide the panic she felt rising up in her gut.

"I don't understand." Eloise moved a rake and sat down on a hay bale. Her face was pale, her hands shaking. "Poisoned?"

"The EMTs thought at first she'd had a stroke, but the tests didn't back that up. After a lot of educated guesswork, they realized she'd overdosed on lithium." Megan closed her eyes. "They thought she'd done it herself accidentally."

"Does your grandmother even take lithium?" Eloise asked.

"No. That's just it, she doesn't. My grandmother takes brandy in her tea and the occasional pain reliever. Other than that, she refuses all medication, even vitamins."

Eloise was silent for a moment. "Lithium is dangerous stuff. Even people who have a prescription have to be carefully monitored. There's a fine line between therapeutic dose and toxic amount, and it can cause thyroid and other complications."

Megan nodded. "I know. I've had a crash course."

Eloise said, "Acute lithium poisoning . . . will Bonnie . . . will Bonnie be okay?"

Denver said, "She should be fine. Megan talked to the doctors today. The tremors and slurred speech are gone. There was some concern that the neurological effects could be long-lasting or even permanent, but that won't be the case." Denver's eyes were moist, and he turned his head away toward the rear of the barn. "In fact, her age may have contributed to her symptoms. Someone may not have *meant* to cause lasting harm or really hurt her, but because of her age, they could have killed her."

"Playing with lithium is like pharmaceutical Russian roulette." Eloise glanced from Megan to Denver. "I assume the fact you're here means you think Dillon may be the culprit."

331

Megan didn't wait for Denver to speak. "Not necessarily. The police will be here soon, and they can tell you more. But we were worried about you, and Denver wanted to get here as quickly as possible. Just in case. To give you time to digest the news."

Denver interrupted, "And to give you time to decide if you want Dillon moved."

Eloise shook her head. "He couldn't have gotten it here."

"Is Dillon on lithium?"

"A very low dose. They put him on it after his mother was killed. He'd always had bipolar disorder, but they were worried about suicide and wanted to curb the manic episodes. I keep it locked in a cabinet with his other medications. I saw it just this morning, though. Nothing appeared to be missing." Eloise put her hand to her mouth. "Unless . . . unless he's palming the medication. I never thought to check his mouth."

That's what Megan had been wondering: if Dillon was spitting the pills out when Eloise wasn't looking.

"Surely his blood is tested regularly," Megan said. "Wouldn't it show up in his levels?"

"Not if he just started doing it," Denver said.

Eloise agreed. "He gets tested every three

332

months, and his last test was almost two months ago. Even a week's worth of palmed medication may have been enough to hurt Bonnie." She shook her head. "Why would he hurt Bonnie of all people? She was kind to him. He seemed to adore her."

"Maybe Dillon slipped and told her something incriminating," Denver said. "Something he regretted later."

Eloise rocked back and forth on the hay bale. "I don't know. It just doesn't sound like him."

Denver took his aunt's hand. "Look, Bobby King will be here soon. We wanted to tell you ahead of time, but Megan promised Bobby we wouldn't say anything to Dillon until he got here. Can you think of *anything* that happened Friday that could have led to this? Is it possible Bonnie somehow took this medication by accident?"

Eloise stood. As she talked, she paced around the room. "I met Bonnie at the café at ten. She was already there, and I found her talking to a group of people, including Merry Chance."

"Was the café crowded?" Denver asked.

Megan held up a hand. Her phone was beeping with a text from King. "Bobby will be here in five minutes." She looked at Eloise. "Don't say anything else until he arrives. It may be important and should be fresh."

Eloise nodded. "Dillon's movie is almost over."

"Why don't I go in and check on him," Denver said. "I'll watch a new movie with him. This way you two can talk to King without distraction."

Eloise thanked him.

"Don't say a word about Bibi," Megan warned.

Denver kissed her forehead. "I want to get to the bottom of this mess as badly as you do, Megs. Mum is the word. I'll go bond with him and wait to be called."

TWENTY-FIVE

"Tell me again, Dr. Kent. Everything you remember about Friday."

Eloise, Megan, Bobby King, and an officer were sitting in the barn. Megan and Denver had fetched folding chairs from the house before Denver returned to watching a movie with Dillon. The interior of the barn was cool, and Megan found the earthy smells of hay and horses comforting. She sat back in the chair, listening intently to Eloise's recounting of Friday's events.

Eloise cleared her throat. "I was to meet Bonnie at the café at ten in the morning. She was already —"

"Did anyone know you were going to meet her?"

Eloise looked surprised by the question. "It wasn't a secret, if that's what you mean, but nor did I broadcast it. Dillon knew because he requested it."

King's eyes widened. "He requested it?"

"Yes. Bonnie spent a lot of time with Dillon last week. She showed him great kindness."

Which makes this all the more horrible, Megan thought.

"Megan, did Bonnie tell many people?"

"I have no idea," Megan said. "But I doubt it. She didn't tell me about it until that morning. She was — is — fond of the boy, and she would have respected his privacy."

King nodded to Eloise. "Go on, please."

"When we arrived, Bonnie was already talking with a group of people. Merry Chance was one of them. Bonnie saw us and grabbed her bag and we left."

"Who else was at the café? Do you recall?" King asked.

"A few people I didn't recognize. A young woman in her twenties. An older man and what appeared to be his wife. Alvaro and Clover. And several people from BOLD."

King perked up. "Do you remember who?"

Eloise shook her head. "I really wasn't paying attention. I was thinking about what to say to Dr. Star."

King made a motion and the officer wrote something in his book. "Was Bonnie eating or drinking anything when you arrived?"

Eloise closed her eyes. "I recall a cup in front of her. I don't know if it was hers. After that, we left, and Bonnie drove with me to the school."

"Did she sit near Dillon?"

"She sat in the front, he sat in the back. Before you asked, she had possession of her purse the whole time in the car. She never placed it in the back seat or anywhere near Dillon."

The officer was taking notes, and he scribbled as Eloise spoke.

"Okay, now tell us about the visit with Dr. Star."

"It wasn't great. His receptionist alerted Benjamin — Dr. Star. He brought us to his office. I explained who Bonnie was. We discussed taking Dillon off some of his medications, especially the lithium. Dr. Star suggested we wait until this whole mess —" Eloise's voice broke, but she quickly regained her composure. "Well, until this mess is over. He thought Dillon needed the extra time to adjust. I argued, he refused to budge. Threatened to get Dillon's agency involved."

"Did Dr. Star seem agitated or surprised to see Bonnie?" King asked.

"Come to think of it, no. Dillon may have mentioned something earlier in the week.

Dr. Star is his therapist."

King glanced at the officer. "How long were you there, Dr. Kent?"

"The meeting took about thirty minutes. We waited for ten minutes before then. Dillon wanted to give Bonnie a tour, and Benjamin agreed. We walked around for about an hour."

"Did Bonnie eat or drink anything while you were there?"

"Not that I recall."

"Did she seem ill at all?"

Again, Eloise closed her eyes. "Not really. At one point, she fell behind us on the tour, but when I looked back, she was watching out a window." Eloise's eyes snapped open. "She didn't say she felt poorly, but she might have seemed a little less energetic than normal."

"You got back to the café around what time?" King asked.

Eloise thought for a moment. "We arrived at the school at ten thirty. We were there until about twelve fifteen or twelve thirty. I think we were back in Winsome around one o'clock." She glanced at Megan. "We went to the café afterwards. Dillon, Bonnie, and I had lunch, and then we left but Bonnie stayed."

King, whose expression had been unreadable during the whole process, sighed. "Eloise, think. Was Dillon alone with Bonnie at any point during lunch?"

"I used the bathroom. We'd ordered drinks, which had come by then, but not the food."

"Then it is possible that Dillon could have put something in Bonnie's beverage?"

Eloise looked like the next words cost her. "Yes, Bobby. It is possible."

King sat back against the seat and placed his ankle over his knee. He was wearing khaki pants, a striped short-sleeved shirt, and a pair of brown leather loafers. He was too big for the chair and gave the impression of an adult in an elementary school seat.

"I'm almost done, Dr. Kent. I know this is unpleasant, but we need to figure out if somebody intentionally gave Bonnie lithium, or if she somehow ingested it by accident."

"This was no accident," Megan said. "Bibi doesn't take medications."

King held up a hand. "I just need to be thorough, Megan. You know that." To Eloise, he said, "Who else was at the café when you returned?"

"It was the end of the lunch rush, and the café was crowded. I only recognized a handful of people. Clover and Emily. Alvaro, of course. A few townspeople." She gave King their names. "Merry Chance."

"Again?" the officer asked.

Eloise nodded. "It's a testament to Alvaro's cooking, but a lot of people go for multiple meals a day."

Megan nodded. "We see Merry a lot."

"Some of the BOLD people were there too. I don't know them by name, but they were together." Eloise sat up straighter. She slapped her hand against her thigh. "That reminds me, Bobby. There was someone from BOLD at the school. I know because I overheard that receptionist complaining about it."

"Did you hear a name?" King asked.

"No, just the company."

"Did you see anyone?" Megan asked. She knew it must have been Harriet, but she didn't want to lead Eloise in any way.

"I'm afraid I have no idea. I'm sure Dr. Star can tell you."

King told the officer to make a note of that. "I think this will do for now, Dr. Kent. Thank you for your time. I'd like to speak to Megan in private for a few moments. After that, I thought you and I could break the news to Dillon. See how he takes it."

Eloise nodded.

"We may need to search your house. I can get a warrant, but it may be less upsetting if you give us permission."

Eloise nodded again. "Whatever you need to do."

Megan looked at Eloise, her heart aching because of the foster mom's dilemma. "Do you think Dillon should stay here? I know Denver isn't comfortable with it."

"Dillon didn't do this," Eloise said. "I may have had concerns before, but they're gone now."

"Why is that?" King asked, sounding surprised.

"I really think Dillon likes Bonnie. He asked that she come on Friday. He wanted to show her around the school. He hasn't shown me around the school, nor has he asked me to do anything. Unless Dillon is truly a sick child, he didn't hurt Bonnie. And if he didn't hurt Bonnie, someone else did."

"Someone who may be trying to cover up another murder," Megan said.

Eloise nodded. "Search away, Bobby. I don't think you'll find a thing."

"Eloise is right," King said when they were alone in the barn. "There is a much bigger picture here."

Megan was closing the chairs, and King was petting one of Eloise's cats who had wandered in.

King stood. He placed a hand on the chair Megan was closing. "Stop for a second, okay? This is important. We have the break-in at the inn, and now this with Bonnie. We know the boy didn't break in to Dr. Mantra's room, and although he could have done this, if he didn't, someone else is out there — and dangerous."

"I know, Bobby. We've been saying that all along."

"My people are looking into each of the BOLD employees, including Harriet Mantra. We know that Harriet is a founding benefactor of the school, so my guess is that she's the one who was at the school on Friday. We can confirm that."

"Do you think she could have poisoned Bibi?" It sounded unlikely, but Megan felt like all possibilities had to be considered at this point.

"We'll talk to her. I really don't know."

"Isn't lithium a controlled substance? Shouldn't you be able to track it?"

"Not that easy. It's not a controlled substance, Megan, and I already have officers talking to the local pharmacies, but many people take psychiatric meds these

342

days. Whoever did this could have gotten it from anywhere, including the school."

Megan thought about Harriet at the school. The fact that she'd shown up after Chase's murder made it impossible for her to have wielded the knife that killed Chase, but that didn't mean she wasn't somehow behind his murder. "Are you also looking into BOLD Pharmaceuticals?"

"We are, but are you wondering about a certain angle?"

"The FDA approval process. I'm curious, Bobby, did the papers Dr. Mantra claimed were missing have to do with the FDA results?"

"You know I can't tell you that."

Megan smiled. "You could deny it if they weren't."

No response. That was enough for Megan. "Martine told me that they're waiting on the approvals for one of their drugs. Jatin seemed pretty certain that it was coming through, and if so, they would all soon be very rich. You and I both know greed is a strong incentive for murder. There could be a motive buried somewhere in there, Bobby."

King gave a curt nod. "We'll see what we have on that, but I really wanted to talk to you about safety: yours and Bonnie's."

King's face was a mask of concern. "I'm going to talk to Denver about staying with his aunt."

"Eloise won't agree."

"Maybe not, but I'll try. We'll search the house. We don't need a warrant if she consents, and if we come up empty and Eloise wants Dillon to stay, he can. It would be best if she wasn't alone with him."

"Understood. I'll talk to Denver too."

King moved a step closer. "Bonnie, though, may be in trouble. I have no idea why someone targeted her, but they did. I'm going to have a patrolman stay at the hospital, and when you return, I'll have someone ride by the house regularly."

"Appreciated, Bobby."

As he turned to leave, Megan touched his arm.

"Yes?"

"What if the lithium wasn't meant for Bibi?" she asked. "What if it was meant for Dillon? Or Eloise? Or even someone at BOLD? It feels like we've broadened the possibilities, not narrowed them."

King met her gaze. He nodded again, and without another word, headed to the house.

TWENTY-SIX

Megan waited for Denver in the truck. She was thinking about what Eloise had said about who was at the café. Eloise didn't remember — why would she — but Clover, someone, *should* remember which BOLD employees were there. She called Clover, got voicemail, and left a message. The café was still open, so she could just stop by.

She thought too, about Harriet at the school. She couldn't very well ask Harriet Mantra about it directly, but maybe Martine would know something. As head of PR, Martine would be involved with efforts to help the school, and she likely had Harriet's itinerary. Megan sent Martine a text, asking if she could meet with her.

The truck's windows were down, and Megan heard voices. She looked up in time to see Denver leaving Eloise's house. She put her phone away while he got in the truck.

"How did things go?" Megan asked.

"Not well."

"What do you mean?"

"The kid did what he did after Chase was killed. He retreated inward. Just stopped talking."

"Did he look upset? Say anything?"

"Aunt Eloise told him. He stared at her, his eyes wide as dinner plates. When she finished, he just sat there. She asked him some questions and he didn't — wouldn't — respond. Not even to King."

Megan put her head down on the steering wheel. When she sat up, she said, "This is too much for him, Denver. Think about it. He effectively lost both parents less than a year ago. Now he's witnessed an atrocious act, and he's just learned that a favorite adult has been victimized. Any kid would be traumatized. What are they going to do?"

"Eloise called Dr. Star. He's going to see him."

Dr. Star. The school. Lithium.

"Do you think that's a good idea?"

"I doubt Dr. Star is in on this, whatever 'this' is. Plus, it's that or he goes back to the hospital. Aunt Eloise is afraid that will make things worse. The police will be searching the premises. We'll know more after that."

He buckled his seatbelt and nodded toward

the steering column. "I want to talk to Martine."

"One step ahead of you. I already texted her. She said she's busy and she'll get back to me."

"Just go to the inn."

"She's not there." Megan told Denver how Martine moved to a room in Winsome.

"Winsome?" Denver frowned. "What hotel is in Winsome?"

"Until Washington Acres bed and breakfast is up and running, the boarding house is the only palatable option in town."

"Let's go there, then."

"Martine will agree to talk with us — she likes me, and she wants you to like her. In the meantime, let's head to the café to see if Alvaro or Clover remembers who was in on Friday. That way, we know which of the BOLD people to talk to."

"That's fine, Megs," Denver said, "but I want to talk with Martine. She claims she was dating Chase. He never said anything, and she never mentioned it before. I'm waiting to hear back from Chase's ex-wife. If anyone would know, Diana would." He shrugged. "I can't help but wonder what Martine is up to. She has a history of lying, but she seems to make some new revelation at every pass."

"We'll talk with her, Denver." Megan started the truck. "I have some questions of my own."

Denver's phone rang. He glanced at the caller ID. "Unknown caller. It's Diana. Why don't you pull over? You can listen in."

They were still a few miles from Canal Street. Megan pulled into the parking lot of the local dry cleaners. She kept the motor running and the air conditioner on so they wouldn't have to roll down the windows.

"Diana? Good to hear from you. I'm so sorry about Chase."

"It was a blow, Denver. I still can't believe he's gone." The voice on the other end was high-pitched and smooth, with an unexpected British accent. "Do they have a clue yet as to who killed him? Was it that poor boy?"

"I don't think the police know, but that's part of why I'm calling."

"I've already talked to the police, Denver. I told them what I know, which is very little."

"I know, and I'm sorry to bother ye, Diana. It's just that there is a lot going on here and now my girlfriend's grandmother was harmed. I was hoping maybe Chase told ye something that would prove useful."

"What do you want to know?"

"Was Chase seeing anyone?"

Diana laughed. "Do you mean was he shagging someone, because you and I both know he was not the commitment sort."

"Fine," Denver looked at Megan and shrugged. "Was he sleeping with anyone?"

"No one he told me about. I know he was interested in seeing someone while he was in Pennsylvania. I told the police that."

Denver looked uncomfortable when he said, "Was her name Martine?"

"His coworker?" Diana paused. "He didn't mention her. Why?"

"She claims they were seeing one another."

"They knew each other back in the day when Chase had stars in his eyes and empty pockets. I guess it's possible something kindled between them, but I doubt it."

"Why?"

"He never really liked her in that way. Even back then he said she was a bit mental, if you know what I mean."

"Oh, I think I do." Denver moved the phone to his other hand. "Too well."

There was a pause. "You know, Chase was a leader in his own way. He attracted followers. I know he could be insensitive and obnoxious, but he had a good side. Martine was one of those people who was attracted to his spark. I really don't think he reciprocated."

"Do ye remember who he was going to see while he was here, Diana?"

"I only remember a first name, and only because he mentioned it in passing before he left. I don't think he meant to, and he caught himself right off. Said he could kill two birds with one stone and visit Moira while he was there."

"Moira?" Denver's eyes asked Megan if the name seemed familiar. She shook her head no. "I don't know a Moira."

"Nor do I, which is why I figure it's a new fling. Maybe someone he met online?" Diana laughed. "The beauty of being exes *and* friends was that I didn't have to be bothered by his extracurriculars anymore."

"Extracurricular" seemed such a sterilized word for something as hurtful as cheating. Denver seemed to think the same thing because he said, "Chase hurt you, Diana."

Diana sighed into the phone. "I know, Daniel. I wanted him to be faithful to the vision of who we were. Diana and Charles, artist and scientist, together forever. He wasn't wired that way. Wanted the next young, attractive adventure." Diana's voice became softer. "And how are you, Denver?

350

Chase told me you have a new love in your life."

Denver glanced at Megan. "Aye, I do. She's pretty remarkable."

"A lawyer-turned-farmer. Well, with everything you went through with that bloody wench Lilian, I hope you find happiness. You deserve it."

"Thanks, Diana. If ye think of anything else, call me. Like Moira's last name. That would be a help."

"Right after I call the police, I'll ring you. But he never mentioned a last name, so unless I trip over it somehow, I'm afraid that won't happen."

Denver hung up, and Megan started the truck. "What did you make of that?" she asked him.

"We have a name, at least. Moira."

Megan said, "And it seems unlikely Martine was sleeping with Chase."

Denver didn't respond right away. When he did, she heard the bitterness back in his voice. "Why say it if it wasn't true? Because you want to mislead the police?"

Megan had another idea. "Maybe she was in love with Chase. Maybe she'd been in love with him for a while."

"So she just made things up?"

Megan turned onto Fledgling Avenue. She

351

remembered what Martine had said about a girl living on dreams. "She built a fantasy world, like she did back when she called herself your girlfriend to Lilian. She wished it to be true." Megan glanced at Denver. "We all create fantasies in our head, Denver. Most of us know what's real and what's not. Perhaps Martine prefers her fantasies to the pain of real life."

TWENTY-SEVEN

It was between lunch and dinner, so the crowd at the café was thin. Clover was handling a few orders at the register in the store portion of the business, and Alvaro and Emily were in the kitchen. Clay and Emily had postponed their trip over worries about Bibi, and Megan was thankful for the extra help. Sunday afternoons were often Bibi's favorite time to cook. She liked to see the townspeople after church services, and though she'd never admit it, she enjoyed hearing the local gossip. Her absence was felt, and Alvaro immediately gave Megan an uncharacteristic arm squeeze.

"Sit. I have something for you to try."

Megan and Denver took a seat at the counter. The only other patron in the café was a thirty-ish woman on her laptop. She was sipping a coffee, a half-eaten slice of strawberry rhubarb pie in front of her.

"Don't try to take that pie," Emily said.

"She griped at me twice."

Megan smiled. "How's Grace?" Grace was Emily's toddler, and another of Bibi's favorite people.

"She's great. I was going to bring her to see your grandmother. Think that's okay?"

"I think Bonnie will love seeing Grace but will scold you for bringing a child to a hospital," Denver said. "Germs and all. I'd wait until she's home."

Megan agreed. "And then I'd plan to stay the whole day, because she will not want that child to leave."

Alvaro returned with two steaming plates of food and a small bowl of honey. Megan saw tamales and rice and pinto beans and a small salad, plus a warm sopapilla. The food looked and smelled heavenly.

"Mexican comfort food. I know this is a hard time. I know you're upset . . . well, you eat. There's a surprise in there."

Alvaro returned to the kitchen and Megan raised her eyebrows at Emily. "I think that was almost a proclamation of love."

"Best you're going to get. He's been snapping at me all day because I don't chop like Bonnie or grate like Bonnie or roll dough like Bonnie. Clearly he misses your grandmother." Her eyes darkened. "How is she?"

"She's better, thank you." Megan willed

herself to convey something other than the dread she was feeling. "I have a feeling she'll be home by Tuesday. Maybe earlier if she continues to drive the staff crazy."

Emily smiled. "Enjoy your meal."

"When you're done with that customer," Megan nodded her head toward the pie lady, "Can we talk to you? We have a few questions about the day Bibi got sick."

"Of course, but I thought she'd had a mini-stroke. At least that's what the folks around here are saying. Was it something else?"

Megan and Denver exchanged a glance. "You'll have to trust us on this one," Megan said. "Just a few questions."

With a knife and fork, Megan moved the corn husks surrounding the tamale and cut into the dish's soft center. She took a bite. Immediately, she tasted the creamy sweetness of corn, the bite of poblano peppers, and the earthiness of zucchini.

Megan smiled, her first real smile of the day. "Alvaro made vegan tamales. I challenged him to do it, and he did it. And they are phenomenal."

Denver was dipping his sopapilla into the honey. "These are amazing too."

When Alvaro returned, Megan complimented the chef. "I have a plate of food for

355

Bonnie," he said, ignoring the praise. "Tell her Emily is even worse in the kitchen than she is. I would welcome her so-so skills back here anytime."

Denver laughed. "We'll tell her."

"Alvaro, the day Bibi got sick, she was here twice, in the morning to meet Eloise Kent and in the afternoon when they stayed for a late lunch. Do you remember?"

Alvaro nodded. "It was a crowded day. All those people from that company. Tourists. And the Winsome people who never cook for themselves."

"Do you recall seeing anything out of the ordinary? Anyone who made you suspicious?"

"Besides Merry Chance and her constant need for eggs? She must have the highest cholesterol in all of the world." He shook his head. "Just crowded that day, that's all I remember."

When Emily returned, they asked her the same question. "I waited on Bonnie and Dr. Kent. Bonnie ordered soup, and Dr. Kent had the salad special. The boy, he asked for a plain sandwich, and Alvaro made him grilled cheese. I remember that. It was a normal day, nothing weird or out of the ordinary. My tips were good that day, better than usual."

356

"Who was here from BOLD?" Denver asked. "Do you remember?"

Emily gave an apologetic smile. "I'm afraid I don't know them by name, so I couldn't say."

"What if I showed you their pictures? Would that help?"

"Maybe."

Denver pulled out his phone and started sorting through photographs. He showed Emily a photo from dinner the night before the hike began, when Megan first met his college friends. Clover had joined them by now, and she looked over Denver's shoulder at the photo.

"That person was here for lunch." Emily pointed to Xavier. "He was sitting with her," she pointed to Barbara, "and her." She pointed to Martine. "I remember because the skinny one left before lunch was finished."

Denver glanced up at her. "You mean Martine?"

"Yes. They seemed to be in deep discussion much of the lunch. She had spreadsheets and files out on the table. The man was pointing and doing most of the talking. Every once in a while, I'd hear his voice above the fray."

"Did they interact with Bibi or her table at all?"

"I saw them throw a few nasty glances toward Dillon. But to be honest, they all were."

"When you say 'they,' who do you mean?"

"All of them, I guess. Especially the woman."

"Her?" he pointed to Martine.

"The other one."

"Barbara." Denver glanced at Megan. "Makes sense. She was not only Chase's friend but his boss." To Emily, he said, "What about the man, Xavier? Did he seem bothered by Dillon?"

"Not that I witnessed."

It was Clover who spoke up: "I heard him say some pretty harsh things. He asked why the kid was still free and suggested that he be in a mental hospital for life."

"But again," Emily said, "it seemed liked everyone was reacting to Dillon's presence. Most were just less overt about it."

"How about the morning shift? Bibi got there before ten to meet Eloise and Dillon. Did you see her with anyone then?"

"I wasn't here," Emily said.

"I was, but I don't remember seeing Bibi with anyone." Clover leaned closer to the photo.

"Did you see this man there earlier in the day?" Denver pointed to Jatin.

Jatin's face was obscured by the table center piece. "I can't really see his features," Clover said. "I remember seeing her." She pointed to Martine. "And her." She pointed to Barbara.

"Let me see if I can find a better picture." Denver flipped through photos on his phone. He paused at one point, flipped forward and backward. "Hmm," he said. "Look at this, Megs."

Megan took the phone from him. On the screen was a shot of Chase. He was standing by the pond at Lyle State Park. He wore khaki cargo shorts and a red "STAFF" t-shirt. A red hat sat on his head, shielding his eyes. He was grinning and making a peace sign to the camera. It was a selfie, but Chase must have extended his arm to capture his whole upper torso.

"That was sent to you the day Chase was killed, right?" Megan leaned closer. "He sent this to you while you were kayaking."

"He did, and I must have downloaded it to my phone. Look closer, Megs."

She studied the photo. It only took her a second to see what he meant. A shadow was visible behind Chase. Megan could make out an arm and something else.

Something like a knife?

"Have you shown that to Bobby?"

"No. I forgot I even had it."

"Look." Megan pointed to the arm. "Chase seems oblivious to their presence."

"Oblivious," Clover said. "Or relaxed about it."

"He doesn't seem stressed, that's for sure." Denver looked up. "Are you saying this is or isn't the killer, Megs? Because frankly you can't see much about the person from this slice of shadow."

"I'm saying that either the killer snuck up on him with the knife in hand, which implies forethought and malice — not impulsive anger — or the killer was standing with him beforehand. Someone Chase knew. Someone he wasn't the least bit worried would use that knife."

"Not like a troubled teen," Emily said. "Even a fool would know better than to give a group of troubled teens knives."

Denver wasn't so quick to concede. "I see a happy Chase standing by the water. I see what looks like a shadow of a person standing behind him. I see what could be a knife in that person's hand. But that's a lot of 'coulds,' Megs. It could just as easily be a trick of the light. Or a teenage boy standing behind him, ready to swing."

Megan said, "That would suggest premeditated murder."

Their eyes met. "And poisoning a woman with lithium would suggest the same."

"I just got a chill," Clover said. "And not the good kind."

"One thing's for sure," Megan said. "We need to get this photo to Bobby. The police have more puzzle pieces than we do. Maybe it will mean something to them."

King took the photo and Denver's statement about how it came into his possession. They were at the Winsome police station, in a small, dank room at the end of a small, dank hallway. Night was quickly closing in, and the police chief looked tired and sounded cross. He seemed less excited about the photo's importance than Megan had, but he conceded that it could mean that an angry outburst in the course of an argument with Dillon was less likely.

"How did the search go?" Megan asked.

"Nada. Nothing. Zilch. The kid is still there." King glanced at Denver, who was staring once again at Chase's picture. "You heading over to your aunt's?"

"I'll stop by and check on them, but she doesn't want me sleeping there. Says it will be disruptive to the boy."

King huffed out a sigh. "I can't talk people into having common sense. Sorry, I know she's your aunt."

"No offense taken."

Megan and Denver were getting ready to leave when King stopped them in the hallway. "Megan, I forgot to mention that we got a lead on Camilla. It looks like someone may have been living in the storage unit next door. We found a desk and a sleeping cot and blankets. A whole set-up."

"How did you figure that out?" Denver asked.

"One of the customers reported seeing the same car there every day. An older model BMW four series. She followed the person to the unit and reported the number to management. When they saw it was the unit next to Camilla's, they grew suspicious. The units were rented under two different names, but we suspect the pig may belong to whoever was in that unit."

"Do the plates match a Saul Bones?"

King shook his head. "Plates are stolen. Both units are rented out to men, so we're still investigating, but I thought you'd want to know. Camilla may have been someone's pet — nothing more nefarious than that."

"She still lived in a five-by-five, hot space."

362

King nodded. "As did the person who had her."

Megan thanked him. As they made their way to the truck, Megan thought about what Bobby had told her. What would drive someone to live in a warehouse? At least this one was climate controlled, but the person would still have to deal with mice and heat and cold. Desperation, she decided. Mental illness. The vagaries of life. She was grateful Camilla was with them.

"Stop by the boarding house?" Denver said.

Megan looked at her phone. It was almost nine already. "It's late. I need to swing by the hospital and then get home and feed the animals."

"Want me to join you?"

Megan shook her head. "I'll drop you off at your car. Check on Eloise, I'll check on Bibi. Between the two of us, we have this covered."

Denver's kiss was long and hard and full of need. "I'll come to your house afterwards," he said. "With my dogs."

Megan smiled. "That's fine. We'll be like the Brady Bunch of the canine world."

"Someday, Megs," Denver said. "Someday."

TWENTY-EIGHT

Bibi was asleep when Megan arrived, and she was still asleep when she was ready to leave, an hour and a half later.

"She's had a lot of visitors," the night nurse said. "She's fine, just tuckered out."

"I brought her some food."

The nurse looked at the bag in Megan's hand, which was stocked with three covered dishes, bread, and even Bibi's favorite fruit-flavored soda water.

"That might be pushing it," the nurse said. "It's a lot of food."

And it was all from Alvaro. "Could you just give it to her? She won't eat it, but it will mean a lot to her."

"Okay," the nurse said eventually. "She *is* doing well. I think we can accommodate it."

Indeed, Bibi looked fine. Her coloring was back to normal, and she slept without the horrible twitches and ticks Megan had seen Friday night. Megan said a prayer of thanks, kissed Bibi on the head, said goodbye to the officer stationed outside her room, and went home.

Clay was still at the farm. He said he was tending to evening chores, but Megan knew full well he didn't want her to come home to an empty house. She offered to heat him up some soup, but he declined. Within fifteen minutes, Megan was in the kitchen with Gunther and Sadie, her laptop open.

Again, she focused on BOLD Pharmaceuticals. Again, she came up empty handed. Lots of good PR — much of it from Martine, she imagined. Nothing that gave Megan a clue about the company's financials.

Next she turned her attention to Harriet Mantra. Harriet's presumed presence at the school made her curious. Was she there to talk about Dillon? About the failed charity event? About donations to the school?

Presumably she'd given money to found that school so her daughter had somewhere to go. But why continue her involvement after her daughter graduated?

Harriet had no meaningful social media presence. A general search turned up lots of scholarly papers, a few patents, and an article or two about her husband, a wealthy investor. Megan plugged "Catherine" and

"Cat" into social media outlets and was immediately rewarded with too many hits.

One thing seemed certain: Cat Mantra may have graduated, but unlike Dee Dee's son, the graduate student, Cat hadn't gotten too far. Megan switched to an images view. She was rewarded with snapshots of Cat Mantra in lingerie. Getting into a police van. With a bruised face. There was even a mug shot. Cat Mantra was no success story, at least based on this. Megan switched back and perused the articles. There was a police report from two years ago — shoplifting. Another from nine months previous — stalking a celebrity.

Or was this old news and Cat had turned her life around more recently?

Megan jotted down a few notes before turning to her last search for the night — the singularly named "Moira." She searched Chase's friend circles for the name but came up empty-handed. Ditto for LinkedIn. She looked at Martine's social media pages but had similar luck.

On impulse, she sent a friend request to Martine. If Denver wouldn't, she would. The woman hadn't texted her back, but what did she have to lose?

Moira . . . Chase was going to see a woman named Moira.

Megan was at a loss. Unless the police found something in his phone or computer, Moira would remain a mystery.

Megan's phone beeped. It was a text from her accountant, Lou. *Check your email,* was all it said. He knew her so well. She hated email — always had.

Sure enough, there was a new one from Lou:

Megan, I looked into BOLD Pharm with no real luck. The Articles of Incorp show Harriet Mantra and her husband to be the founders. Not much on their financials. They do seem active with charities, most notably the school you mentioned, Pioneer Village School. One oddity: the husband sold his interest in the company to Harriet about three months ago. She's now the sole owner. Doesn't mean anything except that the money had to come from somewhere. BTW, Dee Dee says hello. She enjoyed talking with you. Warmest, Lou.

Megan re-read the note. Harriet bought out her husband three months ago. Because she knew the FDA approvals were coming and the company would be worth way more? They were married, though, and nothing she saw indicated their marriage was in trouble. If that was the case, why not keep it as it was? What if the FDA approvals weren't going through? Then Harriet might have reason to want sole ownership of the business. If it was going down, she wanted to be the only captain to drown along with it. Her husband's money — family money — would be out, safely invested elsewhere.

Intriguing. And it went along with the empty promise to the school. Scholarships for rich kids. Empty gestures.

Megan was about to put her laptop away when she had another thought. What if the FDA approvals were going to be denied, and *Chase* knew it? Would he stay at BOLD? Maybe Moira wasn't a person after all.

Megan searched pharmaceutical companies within one hundred miles of Winsome. She found a number of start-ups, but none named Moira. She made a list of the start-ups. She could plug them into LinkedIn, one by one, and search for a Moira who worked at one of them. She could get lucky and "Moira" could be a human resource associate at one of the firms.

This could take all night.

Megan was searching under the third company name when she heard the door to the kitchen opening. Denver stood there, but he was alone. No dogs. The expression on his face said he was bearing bad news.

"Just tell me," Megan said. "Nothing will

surprise me at this point."

"Dillon ran away."

Megan placed a hand on her throat. "Oh, no."

Denver nodded. "Aunt Eloise isn't coping well, and of course the police are on high alert." Denver rubbed his eyes, which were red and irritated. "I'm afraid for the kid. He's big and clumsy and medicated and on the top of the police's suspect list. If someone decides vigilante justice is warranted . . ."

"Don't even think it." Megan wrapped her arms around Denver's torso. "Did he say anything to Eloise?"

"Not a word. She said good night, closed his light, and when I stopped by to check on them he was gone. His window was open. Best we can guess, he climbed out the window and down the trellis on the back of the house. The bottom of the trellis was broken."

"I'm so sorry," Megan whispered. She thought of Bibi, alone in that hospital room. "I know the police are there, but —"

"Go, Megs. I'm going to stay with Eloise, whether she likes it or not."

Megan nodded. She'd pack a bag and sleep on the chair in Bibi's room. Denver waited for her and walked her to her truck.

"Call me in the morning," he said. "Before you come back here. I'll meet you at your house."

"No need. Clay gets here by six. I'll warn him to be on the lookout for Dillon."

Denver gave her another hug. "I'd still like to come. Just call me. Promise."

Megan promised. She prided herself on her independence, but in the world where no one seemed to be who they pretended to be, she would be grateful for the company.

Bibi slept soundly that night; Megan did not. Whether it was the uncomfortable angle of her neck on the chair or the knowledge that Dillon was out in the world, either alone and scared or alone and angry, Megan wasn't sure. Probably a mixture of both.

She still believed, deep down, that he was innocent. Running away would make a certain sense, especially if Dillon was once again witnessing someone he cared about getting hurt. He wouldn't understand that he wasn't in trouble at this point, and neither was Eloise. Leaving home would seem like a solution to everyone's problems.

Bibi whispered Megan's name at 5:12.

Megan smiled. "Well, hello there."

"Why are you here?"

"I was worried about you."

Bibi frowned. She looked tiny in the hospital bed, connected to wires and tubes and swathed in cotton. "Nonsense. I feel great."

Megan decided to be honest with her grandmother. The doctors had told her about the lithium — it was the only way to question whether she'd overdosed herself. She didn't know about Dillon, though.

"Dillon ran away, Bibi. The police searched his home yesterday and he left later that night. There was some concern that he'd come here."

"That would be fine if he came here. Wouldn't it be a good thing?" Bibi looked genuinely confused.

"The police are concerned he's the one who fed you lithium."

Bibi put her head back on the pillow. She blinked, then closed her eyes. For a moment Megan was afraid she'd sunk back into unconsciousness, but her eyes snapped back open and this time she looked angry.

"Do you know what he told me, Megan? That he loved his mother. She was the only person in the world who truly cared about him. He said his father was a tyrant who degraded him every chance he got, but it was okay because he had his mother." Bibi met Megan's gaze with a fiery one of her own. "He said he wanted to better himself at the school so he could become a doctor one day and help kids like himself, kids who have trouble socially. Does that sound like a murderer to you?"

"It's not me who has to be convinced."

Bibi shook her head. Megan could see the numbers on the monitors creeping up, Bibi's anger needed to run its course.

"I couldn't tell you these things because of the lithium. He didn't do that. I don't know who did, but it wasn't Dillon."

"Bibi, I need you to be objective for a moment. *Please.* Dillon admitted to you that his father was a tyrant. He must be very, very angry with his father for what he did. In the time you spent with Dillon, did he at any point talk about Chase? Is it possible Chase was merely a surrogate for his dad?"

Bibi's gaze never wavered. "I did ask him at one point. We were sitting in the parlor watching that office show. I asked him how he was dealing with everything that happened at the park. He said he tries not to think about it, but he's scared that the real killer will come after him."

Megan hadn't considered that angle. Not until the lithium incident, anyway.

"I didn't ask him straight away if he'd killed a man. He didn't. I know people,

Megan. He's a large, anxious, brilliant, awkward young man who needs someone to believe in him." A tear snaked its way down her face. "And now the only person who truly believes in him is locked in here."

Megan stared at Bibi, open-mouthed. Was *that* the motive? Was Bibi getting too close, and someone was afraid she'd cause the case to swing another way? But who would have known that Bibi and Dillon were friends?

His therapist, Dr. Benjamin Star.

Megan couldn't think of a reason for Star to kill Chase, but Dr. Star surely owed a debt to Harriet Mantra. And Harriet had been at the school the day Bibi was poisoned.

If Harriet was behind this, that meant she was colluding with someone else because she didn't come into town until after the murder. Or had she? Megan shot a text off to King. Hopefully the police checked that out. Even if she had been in California while Chase was being murdered, Jatin was not.

When Megan and Denver talked to him, Jatin had been nearly salivating at the thought of the money the FDA approval would bring in. What if Chase had somehow threatened that approval? And what if he and Harriet decided they'd be better off without Chase. For all Megan knew, the company had a life insurance policy out on Chase, money that could see them through if they lost their best scientist. Not unheard of in the corporate world. She sent another text off to King.

"Megan, are you listening to me?"

Bibi's voice cut through the chatter in her head. "I'm sorry, Bibi. I was thinking about who else could have committed the murder."

"That's what I was trying to tell you."

One of Bibi's monitors began beeping. "Now listen before these nurses come in and start fussing over me. Dillon told me something important. He saw someone fleeing the scene of the crime. He didn't know who it was, and at the time he didn't know Chase was dead, so he didn't think too much of it."

"Did he have a description of the person who fled? Anything to go on?"

One of the nurses came barreling into the room. She raced to the offending monitor. "I think your grandmother needs some rest. You should probably step out for a bit."

"Bibi?" Megan asked over the din. "Anything that could help."

Bibi strained her neck to see around the nurse. "It was a woman. That's all he could remember. He wasn't sure if she was the killer or just a witness."

"And why didn't he tell the police?"

The nurse took Bibi's arm and began doing a blood pressure test. "Your granddaughter needs to leave."

"She's right here. You can talk to her yourself." Bibi frowned. "Dillon says he did, but no one took him seriously."

"That could be important. I'll speak to King." And Martine, Megan thought. Perhaps all of her drama over Jatin is because she witnessed something she's afraid to tell.

"Tell King Dillon is a good boy," Bibi said. "Tell him for me."

Another nurse came into the room and ushered Megan into the hall. "I will," she called over her shoulder. "I'll be back later."

When Megan and the second nurse were by the nurse's station, the woman said, "Next time, please bring something quiet for your grandmother to do. Maybe some knitting or a crossword puzzle."

Megan smiled. "You don't know Bonnie Birch very well."

But she did, and her grandmother wouldn't rest until Dillon was found and his name cleared.

Twenty-Nine

True to his word, Denver was at the farm when Megan arrived. He and Clay were sitting in the kitchen drinking coffee and eating donuts Denver had brought with him. The day was cloudy and humid, and a thick fog shrouded the house and muted the sunlight coming into the windows.

"Have some donuts," Denver said. He fixed her a cup of coffee and put it in front of her. "No word from Dillon. Aunt Eloise is a basket case."

Megan chose a sour cream donut and ate it in four bites. She shared her conversation with Bibi. "A woman fled the scene. Dillon wasn't sure if she'd witnessed something or was the killer."

"And he told King this?" Clay asked.

"He told the police. That could have been the state cops or even the state park folks."

Denver seemed quiet this morning. His face was shadowed by several days' worth of beard, and his hair was brushed back, off his face.

"I think I have to face the fact that one of my friends is a murderer," he said finally.

"It could be Harriet," Megan said. "I asked King if he was able to confirm her whereabouts the Saturday Chase was killed. I haven't heard back."

"Small consolation." Denver poured himself more coffee. "I got a call from Diana, Chase's ex-wife. She said she'd been thinking about her conversation with Chase. She assumed he said 'Moira' because she expected he'd see a woman while here. She said he could have said More-a or something similar."

Megan told Denver about her research into pharmaceutical start-ups. "I was wondering if it was a job offer he was entertaining. If he was their chief scientist and the visionary behind their main drug, someone may not have wanted him to go."

Denver stared into his coffee mug. "Someone like Jatin."

Megan hadn't wanted to say it out loud, but yes — someone like Jatin. "He did seem preoccupied with the financial gain."

"He did." Denver pushed the cup aside. "Anyway, I did my own research. Called some of my contacts at the pharma companies I use. Still waiting to hear back, but I had the same thought that Chase was leaving BOLD."

Clay finished his meal and was rinsing out his coffee mug. "Porter and I are fine here today, Megan, if you need to help Alvaro at the café in Bonnie's absence."

"Thanks. I'm hoping they discharge her today, but we'll see. In the meantime, I'll shoot over to the café, but first I have a stop to make."

"Where are you going?" Denver asked, concern in his tone.

"I'm going to talk with Martine. I think she's been holding out on us. If my hunch is right, she's the person Dillon saw running from the scene."

"I have rounds this morning. Can it wait until after that and I'll go with you?"

"Let me call her again this morning. If I can wait, I will."

Denver didn't look pleased with the answer. "I'll let you know what I hear from my pharma contacts."

Megan watched him leave. She'd head to the barn to tend to the animals, and then she'd be off as well.

Megan checked her phone at 8:06 a.m. Martine had accepted her friend request but still hadn't returned her call or her text. That seemed odd, but then the woman seemed odd, so who knew.

Megan was tidying up the goats' pen, warding off Dimples' play head butts and attempts to chew the hem of her jeans, when Clay and Porter joined her.

Clay held up a granola bar wrapper. "I don't suppose this belongs to you?"

Megan shook her head. "Maybe it was Bi-bi's. Why?"

"Found it stuffed in the barn near Camilla's enclosure." Porter's lean, handsome face darkened. "Doubt this belongs to Bonnie." He held up a comic book.

"Nope," Megan said. "Before we get too ahead of ourselves, Dillon was here before. Could be he left it then."

"Don't think so," Clay said. "I'm in there daily. No wrappers, no comics."

"Well then," Porter said, "either the kid came back to finish his job or he wanted to be with your grandmother."

"I'm betting on the latter." Megan grabbed her cell phone from her jeans pocket. "Calling Eloise, Denver, and King to let them know."

By 9:22, Megan was tired of trying to reach Martine. She looked up the boarding house on her phone and entered the address into her phone. She swung by the café first to see if Martine was there. No luck, but Megan did find Xavier and Barbara sitting at a corner table, eating oatmeal and fruit.

"Good morning," Megan said. "The café treating you alright?"

Xavier nodded. "Can't say the same for your boyfriend. Any idea where he is?"

"Out on rounds. I think he'll be by later today."

Barbara moved over a seat. "Want to join us? Is that allowed?"

Megan smiled. "One good thing about being your own boss is that almost anything's allowed." She glanced around. "Speaking of bosses, where's Dr. Mantra today?"

"Dealing with her daughter's craziness, no doubt," Xavier said. Barbara glared at him and he looked down. "Well, it's true. The queen bee has her own problems to deal with on top of this mess."

"I thought the school really turned her around?"

"If you mean they made her into a drug addict instead of a criminal, okay, sure."

Another withering look from Barbara.

Barbara said, "Harriet's daughter takes up a lot of her energy these days. She and her mother don't get along, part of the reason the school worked. Distance. Now that she's an adult, she has more freedom but very little responsibility. She wanders, and Harriet has trouble keeping track of her."

"She's crazy," Xavier said. "They both are."

Barbara sighed. "Nothing like airing our dirty laundry."

"We all have it." Megan started to rise. "Have either of you seen Martine? We're supposed to get together," Megan lied, "and she doesn't seem to be answering her phone."

"Speaking of dirty laundry," Xavier said. Xavier snickered, Barbara's lip curled into a mean smile.

Annoyed, Megan said, "Okay, well, if I see Denver, I'll tell him where you are."

"Please. I think we'll be leaving tomorrow or day after next, so it would be great to say goodbye." Barbara touched Megan's hand. "I hate to leave like this. It's been a rather awful trip."

Megan nodded. "I think Denver would like that." Another lie. She understood now why Denver was so bad at this.

THIRTY

The boarding house was a testament to
yesteryear. The owner, an older woman
from Winsome, catered to couples and small
families traveling through the area but also
to lone business travelers who just wanted a
hot meal, a comfortable bed, and a clean
environment. The owner had inherited one
of the largest homes in Winsome when her
father died. Unsure how to keep up with
the upkeep and the taxes, she converted it
into a four room and one cottage property.
These days it would be considered a bed
and breakfast.

"Martine Pringle? I don't know this one,"
the owner said to Megan. She wore a black
velour sweat suit and colorful beaded brace-
lets. Her hair, once a tawny color, was now
a harsh whitish-yellow that she wore swept
away from her face in a bob. They were
standing in the center hall of the large but
worn Victorian. A vase of sunflowers sat in

the middle of a round table atop a faded Oriental rug. Despite the overcast day, light streamed in from floor-to-ceiling windows, highlighting dust swirling in mini cyclones around the room.

"Martine said she was staying at a boarding house. This is the only one in town." Megan pulled out her phone, looked Martine up on social media, and showed the woman the picture. "Look familiar?"

"Ah, that girl. Yes. She asked for a room, but we were full." The woman wore false teeth. She either didn't have them in today or they weren't fitting correctly, because she covered her mouth when she spoke. "I suggested she go to New Hope or Doylestown. She said no, she wanted to stay close to her work people — but not too close. Strange bird. Very nervous."

"Any idea where she may have gone?"

"The only other gig in town is the Motor Way Suites. Hardly what I'd call suites, but plenty of motor way. I know the manager. Want me to call for you?"

"That would be great."

Megan sat in one of the overstuffed Queen Anne chairs while the woman made her call. She busied herself checking out Martine's social media pages. The trail started with professional pages showcasing professional photos of Martine and listings of all her professional credentials. Her Instagram page had a suggested link to "Photos By M," which seemed to be Martine's hobby page. There, Megan found dozens of photos. One in particular caught her eye: Chase, sitting on a rock in a park by the ocean. He had a genuinely happy smile on his face. His body looked braced for flight, his hair was flying behind him, his hands were spread wide. It was a look of anticipation, excitement . . . even joy.

It was also Martine's most recent work. The setting looked to be California, so it had to have been more than a week old, at least. Maybe the two were an item. This only increased Megan's desire to talk with Martine.

The owner came back out of her office in a rush. "She's there. Checked in a few nights ago. Manager thinks she's there now, matter of fact." She handed Megan a piece of paper with a room number and a cell phone on it. "He's kind of a lazy ass, but he owes me. If you need him, call. He'll answer."

"This is fantastic. What can I do to repay you?"

The corners of the woman's smile were just visible behind her hand. "Next time I come to the café, you have Alvaro make his famous huevos rancheros? They're not on the menu most days. I ask, he tells me no. He'll listen to you."

Megan wasn't so sure about that, but she happily agreed. "On the house."

"Even better."

Motor Way Suites was a dump. The boarding house owner obviously thought it odd that a woman with Martine's credentials and money would want to stay there, and Megan shared her surprise. No more than twenty "suites," it was housed on a dirty strip of lawn next to busy Route 611. The building was single story with parking spaces outside each unit in a central, crumbling lot. A kidney-shaped pool had long been neglected and now sat forgotten next to the main building, its top covered with a moldy green tarp puddled with brown water. A neon sign next to the office read "ACANCY," the lights in the "V" coming on sporadically.

Megan found Martine's room and knocked. A quick glance showed Martine's car parked in the lot, on the far side under the trees. Megan knocked again. She dialed Martine's number and called.

No answer, and Megan didn't hear the

phone through the door.

She debated whether to leave or ask the manager for help. She decided on the latter and dialed the number on the paper that'd been given to her.

"You the woman looking for one of my guests?" a gruff male voice asked. "That Martine girl?"

"That's me." Megan explained that she was worried about Martine. "No one has seen her in days."

"Knock on her door."

"I tried that."

"Look, lady, I work nights. I'd have to get dressed and come down in person. Not happening." He hung up.

Damn. Megan stood in front of Martine's motel room and tried Martine one more time in case the other woman was simply napping or taking a bath. Still no answer. She called Denver next. When he didn't answer, she left him a voicemail telling him where she was.

She took a deep breath and tried the door. It was locked.

Two large windows flanked the door. Both had blinds that were drawn most of the way, but the blinds on one window had snagged. Megan glanced around the empty parking lot before kneeling down in front of the window. It was no use; she couldn't make out anything on the other side.

Bracing herself, biting back a persistent wave of anxiety-induced nausea, Megan tried the old credit card in the door. That didn't work either. Face it, she thought, you're no criminal-in-the-making. She was about to call the manager again when she noticed the edge of one window was cracked. The crack extended to the metal frame, and part of the exterior sill was rotted and crumbling. Megan tugged on the window. She felt it give a little — enough to encourage her to continue. She kept at it, glancing around as she did so.

With a rush of frigid air, she felt the ancient window give way and slide open.

The first thing she noticed was the cold. The air conditioner must have been maxed because the air coming from inside the room was icy. And laced with a sickeningly sweet smell.

Megan called out. No answer. She could make out Martine's purse on a cheap side table, the scarf she'd worn during one of their meetings on the bed. A suitcase lay open on a dresser, two pairs of pumps nearby on the floor.

No Martine.

A chill ran down her spine. The nausea

grew worse. She toyed with calling the manager again and asking him to join her. If something had happened, she didn't want to mess with evidence. But Martine could be injured or trapped, and waiting for him would waste time. She got another whiff of the putrid smell. This was an emergency. She climbed through the window, keys out, meager protection against whatever was inside.

Megan reached the bathroom. The door was closed, and using her shirt as a glove, she opened it slowly. The bathroom light was off. Hand covered, Megan flipped the light on, and it took a moment for her eyes to adjust. She saw a cheap gold-colored sink, a matching toilet, and blood.

Martine was in the tub. From the look of her body — and the smell — she'd been dead for days. Blood splashed the interior of the room, soaking the floor and staining the tiles. Another stabbing.

Oh, Martine. Megan stared at the body, fighting back tears and holding back the bile that threatened to rise. While they'd been talking about the woman as a suspect, she'd been victimized herself. She'd been alone — and vulnerable. And now this.

Megan hit 911 as she fled the room. She ran the length of the parking lot and into the office. A young receptionist was there, chewing gum and staring at her computer.

She explained what happened in a jumbled mass of words.

The woman stared at her, confusion plastered on her face.

"Dead. I called 911. I think you'd better come."

When she didn't move, Megan called the manager. He listened calmly before saying, "Oh, shit."

Clearly, he wasn't going to be much help. Megan jogged back to Martine's room. It was only minutes before she heard the sirens wailing in the near-distance.

She called King, then Denver. Poor Martine. She may have obscured the truth, but she'd been honest about one thing: something bad was afoot at BOLD.

THIRTY-ONE

King took Megan's statement at the scene before letting her go. He seemed frustrated that she couldn't tell him more.

"I've been trying to reach her for days. I think someone else has her phone." Megan explained her attempts to talk with Martine, the texts that were answered with short responses, and the accepted Facebook friend request. "Whoever has it did enough to make Martine seem alive — without giving anything away. Find her phone, find her killer."

King stared off in the distance at the ambulance and firetrucks that had appeared. "I got your text, about the kid seeing someone flee the scene. I've been following up on that."

"And?"

He nodded toward the motel. "I thought it was Martine. We were all convinced she was hiding something. Seems like we were right."

"Now we may never know what."

King studied Megan in a measured way that made her uncomfortable. "Remember the other day when I told you I couldn't say what was stolen from Harriet's room?"

"How could I forget?"

"It was about the FDA approval process notes. Harriet refused to say whether the drug was accepted or not, but either way, the information is powerful. I suspected Martine was the person who stole it."

Megan tried to hide her surprise. "Martine? Why?"

"Gut. Her reaction when I questioned her. She seemed squirrely." His gaze trailed off to the motel again. "I really thought she'd killed Chase. Perhaps out of anger that he didn't return her feelings."

Megan looked at King with renewed appreciation. She told him about the photos Martine had taken of Chase. "I think there had been something between the two of them, which may explain her odd behavior. Perhaps she'd initially been hiding the affair from the others."

King nodded. "Perhaps."

"Some things are coming together, Bobby. I have another piece or two I need to check out, but I think someone in their circle killed Chase, hurt Bibi, and now this."

"That's yet to be established."

Megan did everything she could not to roll her eyes. "The phone."

"The phone." King's voice trailed off. He watched in the distance as the body was removed in a bag and placed in the ambulance. "Why go after Martine?"

"She clearly knew too much."

"But with a trail of bodies, whoever did this is bound to get caught. It's hard to pin this one on Dillon. He's still missing."

Megan said, "Did you get my message? We think he slept in our barn last night."

"I did. Not good." Another officer jogged over, and King excused himself. "No more sleuthing around, Megan. This one is too dangerous."

He didn't wait for an answer, so Megan didn't have to make a promise she couldn't keep.

Megan drove to the Bucks County Inn in the hopes that the innkeeper could help her track down Harriet Mantra. She wasn't at the front desk. Instead, Megan was met by an older gentleman with a ring of gray hair and a salty demeanor. He wore a blue bow tie and argyle socks and seemed intent on not answering any of Megan's questions.

"Is Dr. Mantra in?"

"I couldn't say."

Megan gave him the rest of the BOLD employees' names. Same response. She didn't see their cars in the lot; it was possible they'd already been called in to the police station.

Megan left feeling frustrated. She needed to collect her thoughts. The last thing she wanted to do was tip off the killer, and if she acted impulsively, she just might do that.

She decided to head to the hospital. She didn't want to excite her grandmother, but she could check on her progress with the doctors and find out when she could come home. The drive would give her time to think things through.

Megan chose a spot toward the back of the visitors' lot. She sat in silence, considering recent events. Bibi had been poisoned. The words still caused a stabbing pain in her chest, which made the urgency to find the culprit overwhelming. She forced herself to be calm, to think, only the image of Martine's mutilated body plagued her. She rested her head against the seat. Had Bibi been chosen because she was too close to Dillon? If so, the only one who knew that was Dr. Star.

All things seemed to lead back to the school. Dr. Star was an enigma. Lou's neighbor Dee Dee loved him, Eloise had nothing bad to say about the man. Yet Megan suspected he'd told Harriet Mantra that Dillon had a confidante in Bibi. Dillon had seen a woman flee the scene of the crime, important information the police should have considered. What if that woman had been Harriet? What if she'd been in Pennsylvania all along, only pretending to arrive after Chase's murder?

Then there was Martine's death. From the first time Megan met her, Martine seemed like the outsider in the group. She didn't have the college roots to bind her to the others. Even Denver, who saw the good in just about everyone, didn't like her. Had Martine been murdered because she knew too much? She'd overheard the fight with Jatin. She claimed she was sleeping with Chase. She may have had information she was afraid to share.

Megan returned to Martine's Instagram page. Her photography really was amazing. Megan again studied the photo of Chase at the beach. Martine had captured a Chase Megan would not have imagined existed. A Chase poised to take on the world.

Because he was leaving BOLD for a new

life? Or something more?

Chase Mars had a reputation for being impulsive, for seeking adventure. The Rolling Stones. The jump into science and business. The pharma start-up. If the FDA was turning down their star drug and Chase knew it, he didn't seem like the type to sit around and mope. He would move on, a new venture and a new idea. If he had left, where would that have left the company?

Lou's research showed that Harriet had bought her husband out of the business. Hardly a show of faith in a private company. Then there was the empty promise to send Pioneer Village kids to college. Megan was pretty sure BOLD wasn't performing well. Harriet had a lot to lose. They all had a lot to lose. Options. Change in control agreements.

Megan's phone rang, startling her. It was Lou.

"Did you get the information I sent you?" her accountant asked.

"Yes, thank you."

"There was an article on BOLD this morning in the *LA Times*. I thought of you. Did you happen to see it?"

Megan admitted she hadn't. Outside, it started to drizzle, and she couldn't see out of the truck's window. She watched the droplets cloud the glass, listening to Lou's description of the piece.

Lou said, "Bottom line, the FDA turned down their drug ahead of the date their decision was due. Inconsistencies in the trial results. A huge problem for the company."

Megan wasn't surprised. "All the options and agreements those executives have in place. What will they mean now?"

"That depends. If the company has another drug in their back pocket, or if the current drug is salvageable, they could still make good on their promises. May take a while, but those options could be worth a hell of a lot of money. And every change in control agreement probably allows for a giant payout if the company goes public or is purchased."

Which is what Jatin had said. "And if that doesn't happen?"

"They're worthless."

"Which means Harriet Mantra would still own the assets of the company, but those who started with her, like Jatin, Barbara, Xavier, and Chase, would get nothing."

"Right. They win if the company wins."

Also how Jatin had put it. "Thanks, Lou. I owe you."

"Nah. Well, maybe some tomatoes when they're in."

"I can do that." She owed a lot of people.

After hanging up, Megan continued staring at the water streaming down the windshield. The grayness echoed her own mood. Whoever had killed Chase had either been angry or was trying to prevent him from doing something. Megan originally thought it was the latter. Now she was convinced it was the former. If the FDA denied the company's drug approval, BOLD would need Chase. If he was threatening to leave, someone with a lot to lose could be very angry.

Jatin. Xavier. Barbara.

Megan unlocked the truck. As she was about to climb out, her phone rang. Clover.

"I have news, Megan. Brace yourself. That woman, Dr. Mantra? She's here now. I overheard her talking to the man, Jatin something or other." Dramatic pause. "Martine Pringle was murdered."

"I know," Megan said, feeling suddenly drained. "I'm the one who found her."

"Oh, Megan! I'm so sorry." Clover paused again. Megan could hear the clatter of dishes and the steady hum of conversation. Such normal sounds. "She also said something else you might find interesting. When Harriet and that other woman were at the Pioneer Village School, they saw your grandmother with Dillon and Eloise."

The skin on the back of Megan's neck prickled. "Wait a minute, Harriet and *that other woman*? Who was the other woman?"

"The other woman from BOLD — not Martine."

"Barbara?"

"Yes. She was at the school with Harriet that day."

"I have to go, Clover. Please call Denver and ask him to meet me at the hospital as soon as possible."

"Megan, are you okay?"

"Just ask him." Megan hung up. "Thank you!"

Barbara. With a sudden blast of insight, Megan realized Dr. Star hadn't had to break confidentiality. If someone saw Bibi with Dillon at the school last Friday, they would have witnessed the special bond developing between the two. Barbara was there. She was at the café later. What would it have taken to drop a few lithium tablets in Bibi's tea? Clover and Emily had admitted the café had been crowded.

Barbara. The woman whose husband was a cheat — and, if Martine was to be believed, a gambler. The woman who hated Martine and knew Chase very well — well enough to read the restlessness and excitement on his face. The woman who stood to lose a lot of money if Chase left the company — he was the visionary, he was the one who could pull off another drug, another chance. The woman high enough up in the company to know things weren't looking good with the FDA. A woman willing to pin murder on a teenage boy. A woman sociopathic enough to risk killing an eighty-five-year-old woman if it meant getting away with murder.

Martine had suspected her. That's why she broke into Harriet's office to steal the FDA papers. She wanted proof that things with the company were not good. Martine had been sleeping with Chase. She knew he was leaving — or she suspected it based on his demeanor.

She thought Jatin was the killer, but she realized soon enough it wasn't him. He wanted the money, sure, but Barbara *needed* the money.

Megan climbed out of the vehicle and into the rain. She reached back into the truck and felt for her umbrella. That's when she felt cold metal against her forehead.

"Get back in the truck," Xavier said. "And maybe you'll live."

THIRTY-TWO

Megan slid into the truck. She had no choice. He had a gun and she had nothing. Her phone was still in her hand. She pressed the home button and tried without seeing the screen to activate the emergency call. It didn't work — she needed to get past security.

"Keys."

Megan handed Xavier the keys. He took them with a gentleness that surprised her.

"Lock your door." Xavier didn't bother with his seat belt. He started the truck and backed out of the spot.

"Where are we going?"

"Back to where it all began."

Xavier glanced at her. Megan saw darkly shadowed eyes and pale skin. His normal insouciance seemed to be replaced with a malicious sense of resignation. She felt like he didn't want to be here, but he was, and he was too far gone to turn back.

Megan tried to manipulate her phone, which was in her right hand under the umbrella she'd been holding. "I thought for sure it was Barbara."

"Yeah, well, you thought right."

Surprised, Megan said, "She killed Chase?"

"And Martine." He stared straight ahead, hands gripping the steering wheel with white-knuckled fervor. "And now maybe you."

"Why are you helping her?"

It was Xavier's turn to look surprised. "She's my friend."

Megan joked with Denver about having the kind of friend who would help you hide the bodies. She never meant it. Apparently, this group did.

"Seems above and beyond the call of friendship."

"It was my fault to begin with."

"How so?" Megan had used the thumb pad to get into her phone. She pictured the icons on the screen and tapped where she hoped the phone icon would be. She kept tapping, hoping like hell she was calling 911 or Denver or Clover — any of the useful numbers she'd called in the last twenty-four hours. The motel manager, for instance, would be useless.

"I tipped Chase off to the opportunity with Morey."

"Morey?"

"Moreyville Pharma Corp. The pharmaceutical company he was supposed to meet with to pitch his new idea. The idea no one knew he had. Except Barbara and Martine."

Megan considered this new information. "An idea for a new drug?"

"Right. Our agreements with BOLD prevent us from using anything we learn at BOLD elsewhere. Standard noncompete. They don't prevent us from leaving and developing a brand new drug elsewhere." Xavier put on the turn signal and made a left. "Pain management. That was Chase's newest passion. Something to relieve things like arthritis pain without the side effects other drugs have had. Had he stayed and developed the drug at BOLD, it could have salvaged the company."

"And your stock options." Megan shifted in her seat, moving her hand under the umbrella. "Had Chase not shared his new idea with anyone, he could have left and no one had been the wiser."

Xavier nodded. "I told him Morey was recruiting, thinking we could go as a team if the FDA bailed on our latest drug. I didn't know about this new project. In a moment of weakness, he shared his idea with Barbara. Neither of us realized just how bad things were for her. We're her friends. We should have known."

Xavier pulled along Mulberry Street, which led to Lyle Lake State Park.

Back to where it all started.

Xavier was talking with the relief of someone who'd been keeping things in for a long time. Megan wanted to glance down at her phone, but she couldn't risk tipping him off. She hoped like hell she had called someone. She needed to keep him talking. Once they were deep into the park, she'd have no recourse, and maybe no cell reception.

Megan said, "Barbara killed Chase to prevent him from leaving."

Xavier's look was sharp and full of reproach. "Barbara tried to reason with him. He wouldn't listen. Things got out of hand. She didn't mean to hurt him."

"She let a young boy take the blame."

"She let the chips fall where they may. This has been hell for her. Chase was her friend."

Megan didn't argue. His moral reasoning seemed so flawed, but she was afraid to incite him further.

"Where are we going?"

Xavier didn't answer. He pulled into the park entrance, past the self-service kiosk, and down a wooded drive. The rain had given way to a steady, steely drizzle.

Megan thought about the truck. What tools were inside? A flashlight. The umbrella she was still holding. There was a utility knife in the glove compartment. A dog leash. She knew this park better than they did. If she could get out and run, she might be okay.

After what felt like miles, Xavier pulled into a small clearing along the drive. He shoved the truck into four-wheel drive and drove over the grass, onto an old logging path. He stopped when the truck was hidden in the trees.

"Get out."

Megan pretended to fumble while climbing out of the truck. She managed to stick her phone in the pocket of her jeans. Frantically she searched for something, anything, she could grab, but Xavier was pulling on her arm.

"Now."

Megan obeyed. Xavier pulled her another fifty feet, until they reached a small tent in the woods. It was a basic camping style tent, probably the one they had purchased for the Pioneer Village outing.

Xavier pushed Megan from behind. "Get in." Megan refused, but Xavier placed the gun barrel against her back. "Now."

Megan crawled inside the tent. Her heart was racing, her breathing came in ragged spurts. As scared as she was, she felt an odd sense of calm. These were Denver's friends. Or had been. Perhaps in their twisted world that meant something.

It hadn't meant anything for Chase. Or Martine. But it was an angle she could try.

The inside of the tent was dark. It took Megan a moment to realize they were alone. "Where's Barbara?"

"She's not here."

"I don't understand."

"She's coming. With a surprise. I thought between you and me, we could fix this." He zippered up the tent.

"How exactly would we do that?"

"I'd like to count on your cooperation. For example, if someone close to the Winsome Chief of Police called and said she thought the boy was guilty, she could sway his thinking. And then if the police happened to search her barn, where perhaps the boy was hiding out, and found a bloody remnant from Martine's house, that could also sway the police."

With dawning horror, Megan said, "You

were the ones in my barn! You planted the wrapper and the comic book so we'd think Dillon had been there."

Xavier's smile was one of sadness rather than triumph. "What a god-awful mess this has become. I think we all just want it to be over." He clapped one hand against his thigh while holding the gun toward Megan. "We just need the police to believe the boy did it. He'll be admitted to a psychiatric hospital for life, somewhere he should probably be anyway." His eyes took on a menacing quality. "And if you should ever come forward . . . Denver, your grandmother . . . I think we've proven ourselves capable of extreme measures."

Megan heard the distant sounds of an engine. She hoped it was the police and that somehow her phone had connected to help. Her hopes were dashed when Xavier smiled, head cocked toward the sound.

"There she is now."

"You're supposed to be Denver's friend." Megan nearly spat out the words. "What kind of friend does this?"

"Denver left us years ago. He had the chance to go in with us. He chose a different path."

There was a commotion outside the tent. With one eye on her and the gun still cocked, Xavier unzipped the opening. Barbara crawled through, but she wasn't alone.

THIRTY-THREE

"You were kidnapped," Megan said, awed at her own lack of vision. "You didn't run away."

"She's a smart one." Barbara wore hiking pants and a sleeveless shirt. Her slender, muscular arms bulged as she pulled Dillon into the tent with her. She carried a small pistol down by her side. "What a pain in the ass this kid is."

Dillon's face was completely blank. He plodded along, his large frame bulky in the small tent. Megan studied him. He had a fresh break-out on his face, and his hands were shaking. Other than that he seemed to be okay. He'd been gone for more than twenty-four hours. That was twenty-four hours without his meds. She hoped he could cope.

She hoped they could both cope.

"Xavier says you want me to play along with your charade and blame Dillon. Why should I?"

Barbara knelt on the ground, her pistol aimed at Dillon. "Because you don't want to die."

"Why not just leave me out of it? Plant your evidence and frame Dillon. I would have been none the wiser."

Xavier said, "That would have been great except for Martine. You kept texting her, meeting with her. We didn't know how much you knew." He cocked a shoulder toward Dillon. "And then your grandmother and this kid. What was that about?"

"You were afraid they'd gotten too close. That Dillon shared things with her that would lead authorities to you. So you poisoned her." With dawning horror, Megan realized the dose was meant to permanently harm or kill Bibi. Barbara was a scientist. She could have gotten the medicine from the school if their med procedures really were lax, or she could have gotten it through her own pharmaceutical connections. One way or another, she would have been aware of the overdose's effects on the nervous system — and the risks the drug presented to an elderly woman.

Megan felt rage rush through her veins, swell her chest. These people could have killed Bibi as carelessly as they'd swat a fly or step on an anthill.

"You could have killed my grandmother," Megan said.

Barbara nodded. "We could have, but she's still alive." Her ponytail swung with her head, forming an arc. "So now your only choice is to become one of us."

The threat hung there, as potent as if she'd said it aloud.

Megan said, "And Dillon?"

Barbara was silent, but in that flash of a second, Megan saw regret in her eyes. Regret because they planned to kill him too. Maybe both of them.

Plant evidence connecting him to two murders. Have him die while killing a third person — murder suicide, perhaps. No more evidence. Smart.

"I'm assuming you have Martine's phone? That you're going to plant that with Dillon as well?"

Barbara pulled a phone out of her pocket. "See, you are smart." She glanced around the tent. "We don't have a lot of time. Here's what we're going to do since I no longer trust you to cooperate. Dillon, you're going to drag Megan out by the lake. You need to make it look real. You can try to drown her or hit her with a stone . . . something believable. Megan, you're going to play along."

Megan knew once they got out there and staged a struggle, it would be bye-bye for both of them.

"Get up." Xavier pulled her to her feet. "Let's go."

Barbara was pushing Dillon back out of the tent. Megan tried to catch his eye, but the boy was staring down at the ground. His gaze flicked toward her, but only for a second, before aiming at the ground again.

That's when Megan saw it. The rock they must have used to hammer in the tent spikes. It was holding back part of the tent rain hood now. Dillon's eyes flicked toward it, and Megan realized he'd seen it too.

Barbara shoved Dillon onto the ground outside of the tent. She was a wiry woman, but athletic and strong. Xavier was behind Megan, urging her out. The rain had begun again in earnest this time. As Megan bent down to go through the tent opening, her phone started to ring. Her initial feeling was disappointment — her attempts to call someone had been unsuccessful — but the sound seemed to catch Xavier off guard.

After that, everything happened quickly.

Megan saw Dillon reach for Barbara's ponytail. He yanked hard and she yelled, causing Xavier to turn and lose his balance.

Megan grabbed the stone and flew on top of Xavier, pounding him in the head. He held on to the gun, but his arm was pinned under Megan. She sat on it, bending his arm backward. He moaned and dropped the gun.

"Stop." Barbara's voice was an angry whisper. "Get off of him or I kill this kid."

Barbara had Dillon in a headlock, pistol aimed at his head. Dillon's eyes were dancing back and forth widely. At first Megan thought it was terror, only he seemed to be motioning toward the trees on either side of the tent.

Trying to alert her to something or someone.

Or asking her to pretend.

Megan stared beyond Barbara, into the trees. She opened her mouth slightly, feigning relief and surprise. Dillon's eyes stopped moving.

Barbara turned slightly in the direction of Megan's stare. Xavier was bleeding profusely from his head and neck where Megan had attacked him with the stone. He'd dropped the gun, and Megan snatched it. She was still sitting on him. She dug her butt into Xavier, incapacitating him as much as possible, and raised the gun toward Barbara's head just as Dillon kicked Barbara behind the knees. Barbara fell and he grabbed her hand, trying to wrestle the gun free.

Megan shot at the tree in the distance. The shot reverberated up her arm, throwing her off balance, but the sound was enough to startle Barbara. She was tall and strong, but Dillon was taller and stronger. He pulled the gun from her grasp and forced Barbara onto the ground. Megan motioned for him to come to her.

He handed Megan the pistol.

"There's rope in her bag," he said, pointing to a knapsack under the tent's small rainfly. "She was going to use that to . . ."

"It's okay, Dillon. Get it out and let's tie them up."

Dillon worked quickly. He secured Barbara to a tree and tied Xavier's legs and arms together. Megan was relieved to see they had reception. She called King and 911. Denver had been the one trying to reach her, and she called him as well.

"Let Eloise know Dillon is safe."

"I will. Megs, I'll get there as soon as I can. Are you sure you're okay?"

"We'll be fine."

Megan didn't want to waste battery, so she sat quietly by Dillon while they waited, his hand in hers, each holding a gun on the miscreants.

Eventually, Megan said, "I know two ladies who are going to be so happy to see you."

Dillon gave her a tentative smile. "I heard about Mrs. Birch. Is she okay?"

"She'll be better knowing you're safe."

Sirens wailed in the distance. After a few moments, he said hesitantly, "Think I can stay over some time? I can help with the animals, earn my keep."

"Of course." Megan squeezed his hand. "You're welcome any time."

THIRTY-FOUR

Camilla snuggled in the hay next to Heidi. Her pink snout snuffled around the ground for more apples, but Bibi's basket was empty. The pig settled for a belly rub from Dillon, resting her head against this thigh.

"You know," Megan said, looking at Dillon, "Camilla was bred to be a pet, not a farm animal. She'd much rather be indoors, sleeping on a bed with her person."

"I know," Dillon said. "She's so cute." He glanced up at Megan. "I think she's happy."

"You're really good with her. I think she's happiest with you."

Dillon beamed.

"Would you like to have her?"

Dillon didn't say anything for a moment. They'd learned that he would become quiet with any sort of emotional turbulence, positive or negative. Megan glanced back at Eloise, who was standing by the gate of the enclosure looking in. They'd discussed this

415

beforehand, and Eloise had agreed that Camilla would be good for Dillon. The ordeal with Barbara and Xavier had set him back, but now that it was a few weeks behind them, he had some stability in his life, and he was making rapid gains.

"I sure would love to have her," Dillon said, staring down at the pig. "If you really mean it."

Megan smiled. "Of course, we really mean it."

Bibi put his hand on her shoulder. "How about if you and I hang out here with Camilla and the goats and let your foster mom and Megan work out the details."

Bobby King and Denver were waiting for them in the kitchen. King said, "How'd he take it?"

"Over the moon." Megan smiled. She hugged the Chief, who was wearing shorts and a t-shirt today. He was heading to a basketball game, not a murder scene, and for the first time in weeks he looked well-rested.

Megan poured four glasses of Bibi's sun tea and asked them to have a seat.

"I can only stay for a few minutes," King said. With a sheepish grin, "Bibi have anything sweet?"

Megan pulled a container of chocolate chip cookies out of the cabinet and handed them to King. Ever since Dillon had entered their life, Bibi was baking daily — and not out of stress.

After wolfing two down, he offered the container to Eloise, who declined.

"We're all set with Camilla?" Eloise said.

"Yes. Damnest thing, aye?" King was referring to Cat Mantra. "The person living in the storage unit had been Harriet's daughter. She'd heard about the BOLD-Pioneer Village event and wanted to see for herself. The pig had been hers. She'd shown up at the school the day Barbara and Harriet were there, finally exposing her whereabouts to her mom."

"Crazy," Denver muttered, grabbing a cookie. "She returned to the only home she'd had — the school in Pennsylvania."

"I guess you could say that." King continued. "The storage unit was all Cat could afford, especially with a pet. It let her fly under the radar, given that she was hiding from her parents. Plus, the storage folks don't ask questions or do credit or background checks. Cat paid a month's cheap rent upfront and that was the end of it. She was in no position to take the pig — she's back in treatment — and Harriet felt like that was the least she could do for Dillon given what all her company's employees had put him through."

Megan said, "Saul Bones, huh?"

King smiled. "The woman had a twisted sense of humor."

"They can't take Camilla back?" Megan wanted to be sure everything in Dillon's life was stable — as stable as it could be — from here on in. That meant Camilla too.

"He's yours and Dillon's. If Dillon can't take care of him, he goes back to the farm."

"How about BOLD?" Eloise asked. "Closing its doors for good?"

"No," Denver said. "Jatin and Harriet are regrouping, finding some new funding. Maybe renaming. Jatin says they believe in their product and plan to continue pursuing it."

"So he never had anything to do with any of the this?" Eloise asked.

Denver frowned. "Bobby can verify, but Jatin says he was grilled by the police over and over, and he claims he knew nothing about Chase's plans to leave or Barbara and Xavier's actions. Same for Harriet."

King nodded. "His fight with Chase the night before Chase's death really was about Chase's drinking. At least that's what we believe." King shrugged. "Neither Xavier or

Barbara have pointed a finger at Jatin, so for now we think he's clean."

"Clean but broken," Denver said. "It's hard to recover from a betrayal like that.

Megan agreed — only she was pretty sure Denver was talking about himself as much as about Jatin. They had a special bond now, one that would deepen and serve their friendship. Despite that small upside, Denver had been quiet since the events took place, waffling between anger and remorse that his so-called friends put Megan and her family through so much. He'd also been talking in his sleep, and it was through his night-time ramblings that she understood the depth of his wounds. She stayed with him most nights, holding him close, as though she alone could be a barrier against the dark.

King interrupted her thoughts. "Loved the article you were quoted in. The one by Donna Lewis. The best news is for the school. Dillon's ordeal brought attention to its mission. Donations have poured in, donations for real scholarship funds so that kids from all kinds of families can attend." King grabbed another cookie. "I didn't want to stress him by going out there, but it seems like he's doing pretty well. Maybe the school isn't such a bad place."

Megan looked toward the window at the barn beyond. "He's found two new friends, Bibi and Camilla." She looked at Eloise. "How's he doing at home?"

"Better. He sleeps through the night. The nightmares have lessened. In a weird way I think surviving that, being instrumental in both of your survival, helped him to deal with what happened to his mom." She glanced at Denver. "And having you around has helped as well." Eloise smiled. "He looks up to you."

Eloise's smile broadened. "He even brought me flowers yesterday. He'd cut them from my perennial beds, but I could forgive that." She laughed. "Benjamin Star said he's opening up more in therapy."

King took two more cookies and stood. "For the road." Before leaving, he asked Megan about her grandmother. "Going through that must have been a punch."

Megan pictured Bibi in the hospital bed, eyes ablaze despite the tubes and wires protruding from her body. "I think she felt it ended well. She never stopped believing in Dillon. It may sound silly, but I think Dillon embodied faith in her mind. He was vindicated, and her faith was justified. The lithium was just a trial, one she endured."

Eloise laughed again. "I think that's a

fancy way of saying Bibi is a tough lady."

"Ah, it goes beyond that," King said. "I see stuff every day. You have to have faith that there is good in the world. And every once in a while, that faith is rewarded."

"I suppose," Eloise said. "I prefer to be a pragmatist. Expect the worst and you don't get disappointed."

"I don't believe you for a second," King said. "You would have never taken in that boy if that was your core belief."

Eloise didn't respond. She reached into the cookie container, grabbed one for herself, and tossed one to King and one to Denver.

"Go," Megan said. "Before you miss your game." She put the cookies in the cabinet and turned to face Eloise. "Ready to claim your new family member?"

Eloise smiled. "Let's do this."

ABOUT THE AUTHOR

Wendy Tyson's background in law and psychology has provided inspiration for her mysteries and thrillers. Originally from the Philadelphia area, Wendy has returned to her roots and lives there again on a micro-farm with her husband, three sons and three dogs. Wendy's short fiction has appeared in literary journals, and she's a contributing editor and columnist for *The Big Thrill* and *The Thrill Begins,* International Thriller Writers' online magazines. Wendy is the author of the Allison Campbell Mystery Series and the Greenhouse Mystery Series.

The employees of Thorndike Press hope you have enjoyed this Large Print book. All our Thorndike, Wheeler, and Kennebec Large Print titles are designed for easy reading, and all our books are made to last. Other Thorndike Press Large Print books are available at your library, through selected bookstores, or directly from us.

For information about titles, please call:
  (800) 223-1244

or visit our website at:
  gale.com/thorndike

To share your comments, please write:
  Publisher
  Thorndike Press
  10 Water St., Suite 310
  Waterville, ME 04901